Matthew Arnold

Essays in Criticism by Matthew Arnold

Matthew Arnold

Essays in Criticism by Matthew Arnold

ISBN/EAN: 9783742809544

Manufactured in Europe, USA, Canada, Australia, Japa

Cover: Foto ©Andreas Hilbeck / pixelio.de

Manufactured and distributed by brebook publishing software
(www.brebook.com)

Matthew Arnold

Essays in Criticism by Matthew Arnold

CONTENTS.

PREFACE.

SEVERAL of the Essays which are here collected and reprinted have had the good or the bad fortune to be much criticised at the time of their first appearance. I am not now going to inflict upon the reader a reply to those criticisms; for one or two explanations which are desirable I shall elsewhere, perhaps, be able some day to find an opportunity; but, indeed, it is not in my nature,—some of my critics would rather say, not in my power,—to dispute on behalf of any opinion, even my own, very obstinately. To try and approach Truth on one side after another, not to strive or cry, not to persist in pressing forward, on any one side, with violence and self-will,—it is only thus, it seems to me, that mortals may hope to gain any vision of the mysterious Goddess, whom we shall never see except in outline, but only thus even in outline. He who will do nothing but fight impetuously towards her on his own, one, favourite, particular line, is inevitably destined to run his head into the folds of the black robe in which she is wrapped.

I am very sensible that this way of thinking leaves me under great disadvantages in addressing a public composed from a people "the most logical," says the

Saturday Review, "in the whole world." But the truth is, I have never been able to hit it off happily with the logicians, and it would be mere affectation in me to give myself the airs of doing so. They imagine truth something to be proved, I something to be seen; they something to be manufactured, I as something to be found. I have a profound respect for intuitions, and a very lukewarm respect for the elaborate machine-work of my friends the logicians. I have always thought that all which was worth much in this elaborate machine-work of theirs came from an intuition, to which they gave a grand name of their own. How did they come by this intuition? Ah! if they could tell us that. But no; they set their machine in motion, and build up a fine showy edifice, glittering and unsubstantial like a pyramid of eggs; and then they say: "Come and look at our pyramid." And what does one find it? Of all that heap of eggs, the one poor little fresh egg, the original intuition, has got hidden away far out of sight and forgotten. And all the other eggs are addled.

So it is not to build rival pyramids against my logical enemies that I write this preface, but to prevent a misunderstanding, of which certain phrases that some of them use make me apprehensive. Mr. Wright, one of the many translators of Homer, has just published a Letter to the Dean of Canterbury, complaining of some remarks of mine, uttered now a long while ago, on his version of the Iliad. One cannot be always studying one's own

works, and I was really under the impression, till I saw
Mr. Wright's complaint, that I had spoken of him with
all respect. The reader may judge of my astonishment,
therefore, at finding, from Mr. Wright's pamphlet, that
I had "declared with much solemnity that there is not
any proper reason for his existing." That I never said ;
but, on looking back at my Lectures on translating Homer,
I find that I did say, not that Mr. Wright, but that Mr.
Wright's version of the Iliad, repeating in the main the
merits and defects of Cowper's version, as Mr. Sotheby's
repeated those of Pope's version, had, if I might be
pardoned for saying so, no proper reason for existing.
Elsewhere I expressly spoke of the merit of his version;
but I confess that the phrase, qualified as I have shown,
about its want of a proper reason for existing, I used.
Well, the phrase had, perhaps, too much vivacity : alas !
vivacity is one of those faults which advancing years will
only too certainly cure ; that, however, is no real excuse ;
we have all of us a right to exist, we and our works ; an
unpopular author should be the last person to call in
question this right. So I gladly withdraw the offending
phrase, and I am sorry for having used it ; Mr. Wright,
however, will allow me to observe that he has taken an
ample revenge. He has held me up before the public
as " condemned by my own umpire ;" as " rebutted," and
" with an extinguisher put upon me " by Mr. Tennyson's
remarkable pentameter,

"When did a frog coarser croak upon our Helicon?"

(till I read Mr. Wright I had no notion, I protest, that this exquisite stroke of pleasantry was aimed at me); he has exhibited me as "condemned by myself, refuted by myself," and, finally, my hexameters having been rejected by all the world, "somewhat crest-fallen." And he has himself made game of me, in this forlorn condition, by parodying those unlucky hexameters. So that now, I should think, he must be quite happy.

Partly, no doubt, from being crest-fallen, but partly, too, from sincere contrition for that fault of over-vivacity which I have acknowledged, I will not raise a finger in self-defence against Mr. Wright's blows. I will not even ask him,—what it almost irresistibly rises to my lips to ask him when I see he writes from Mapperly,—if he can tell me what has become of that poor girl, Wragg? She has been tried, I suppose: I know how merciful a view judges and juries are apt to take of these cases, so I cannot but hope she has got off. But what I should so like to ask is, whether the impression the poor thing made was, in general, satisfactory: did she come up to the right standard as a member of "the best breed in the whole world?" were her life-experiences an edifying testimony to "our unrivalled happiness?" did she find Mr. Roebuck's speech a comfort to her in her prison? But I must stop; or my kind monitor, the *Guardian*, whose own gravity is so profound that the frivolous are sometimes apt to give it a heavier name, will be putting a harsh construction upon my innocent thirst for knowledge, and again taxing me with the unpardonable crime of being amusing.

Amusing—good heavens! we shall none of us be amusing much longer. Mr. Wright would perhaps be more indulgent to my vivacity if he considered this. It is but the last sparkle of flame before we are all in the dark; the last glimpse of colour before we all go into drab. Who that reads the *Examiner* does not know that representative man, that Ajax of liberalism, one of our modern leaders of thought, who signs himself " Presbyter Anglicanus ?" For my part, I have good cause to know him; terribly severe he was with me two years ago, when he thought I had spoken with levity of that favourite pontiff of the Philistines, the Bishop of Natal. But his masterpiece was the other day. Mr. Disraeli, in the course of his lively speech at Oxford, talked of " nebulous professors, who, if they could only succeed in obtaining a perpetual study of their writings, would go far to realise that eternity of punishment which they object to." Presbyter Anglicanus says " it would be childish to affect ignorance " that this was aimed at Mr. Maurice. If it was, who can doubt that Mr. Maurice himself, full of culture and urbanity as he is, would be the first to pronounce it a very smart saying, and to laugh at it good-humouredly? But only listen to Mr. Maurice's champion :—

" This passage must fill all sober-minded men with astonishment and dismay; they will regard it as one of the most ominous signs of the time. This contemptible joke, which betrays a spirit of ribald profanity not easily surpassed, excited from the Bishop, the clergy, and laity present, not an indignant rebuke, but 'continued laughter.' Such was the assembly of Englishmen and Christians, who could listen in uproarious merriment to a Parliamentary leader while he asserted that the vilest iniquity would be well compensated by a forced perusal of the writings of Frederick Denison Maurice!"

And, for fear this trumpet-blast should not be carried far enough by the *Examiner*, its author, if I am not greatly mistaken, blew it also, under a different name, in half a dozen of the daily newspapers. As Wordsworth asks :—

> " . . . . the happiest mood
> Of that man's mind, what can it be ? . . ."

was he really born of human parents, or of Hyrcanian tigers? if the former, surely to some of his remote ancestors, at any rate,—in far distant ages, I mean, long before the birth of Puritanism,—some conception of a joke must, at one moment or other of their lives, have been conveyed. But there is the coming east wind! there is the tone of the future!—I hope it is grave enough for even the *Guardian* ;—the earnest, prosaic, practical, austerely literal future! Yes, the world will soon be the Philistines'; and then, with every voice, not of thunder, silenced, and the whole earth filled and ennobled every morning by the magnificent roaring of the young lions of the *Daily Telegraph*, we shall all yawn in one another's faces with the dismallest, the most unimpeachable gravity. No more vivacity then I my hexameters, and dogmatism, and scoffs at the Divorce Court, will all have been put down ; I shall be quite crest-fallen. But does Mr. Wright imagine that there will be any more place, in that world, for his heroic blank verse Homer than for my paradoxes? If he does, he deceives himself, and knows little of the Palatine Library of the future. A plain edifice, like the British College of Health enlarged : inside, a light, bleak room, with a few statues ; Dagon in the centre, with our English Caabah, or Palladium of enlightenment, the hare's stomach ; around, a few leading friends of humanity or fathers of British philosophy ;—Goliath, the great Bentham, Presbyter Anglicanus, our intellectual deliverer Mr. James Clay, and . . . yes! with the embarrassed air of a late convert, the editor of the *Saturday Review*. Many a shrewd nip has he in old days given to the Philistines, this editor ; many a bad half-hour has he made them pass ; but in his old age he has mended his courses, and declares that his heart has always been in the right place, and that he is at bottom, however appearances may have been against him, staunch for Goliath and " the most logical nation in the whole world." Then, for the book-shelves. There will be found on them a monograph by Mr. Lowe on the literature of the ancient Scythians, to revenge them for the iniquitous neglect

with which the Greeks treated them; there will be
Demosthenes, because he was like Mr. Spurgeon: but,
else, from all the lumber of antiquity they will be free.
Everything they contain will be modern, intelligible, im-
proving; *Joyce's Scientific Dialogues, Old Humphrey,
Bentham's Deontology, Little Dorrit, Mangnall's Questions, The Wide Wide World, D'Iffanger's Speeches,
Beecher's Sermons;*—a library, in short, the fruit of a
happy marriage between the profound philosophic reflection of Mr. Clay, and the healthy natural taste of
Inspector Tanner.

But I return to my design in writing this Preface.
That design was, after apologising to Mr. Wright for my
vivacity of five years ago, to beg him and others to let
me bear my own burdens, without saddling the great and
famous University, to which I have the honour to belong,
with any portion of them. What I mean to deprecate
is such phrases as, " his professional assault," " his
assertions issued *ex cathedrâ*," " the sanction of his name
as the representative of poetry," and so on. Proud as
I am of my connection with the University of Oxford, I
can truly say, that, knowing how unpopular a task one is
undertaking when one tries to pull out a few more stops
in that powerful, but at present somewhat narrow-toned
organ, the modern Englishman, I have always sought to
stand by myself, and to compromise others as little as
possible. Besides this, my native modesty is such, that I
have always been shy of assuming the honourable style

of Professor, because this is a title I share with so many distinguished men,—Professor Pepper, Professor Anderson, Professor Frickel, and others,—who adorn it, I feel, much more than I do. These eminent men, however, belonging to a hierarchy of which Urania, the Goddess of Science herself, is the sole head, cannot well by any vivacity or unpopularity of theirs compromise themselves with their superiors; because with their Goddess they are not likely, until they are translated to the stars, to come into contact. I, on the other hand, have my humble place in a hierarchy whose seat is on earth; and I serve under an illustrious Chancellor who translates Homer, and calls his Professor's leaning towards hexameters " a pestilent heresy." Nevertheless, that cannot keep me from admiring the performance of my severe chief; I admire its freshness, its manliness, its simplicity; although, perhaps, if one looks for the charm of Homer, for his play of a divine light . . . . . . Professor Pepper must go on, I cannot.

My position is, therefore, one of great delicacy; but it is not from any selfish motives that I prefer to stand alone, and to concentrate on myself, as a plain citizen of the republic of letters, and not as an office-bearer in a hierarchy, the whole responsibility for all I write; it is much more out of genuine devotion to the University of Oxford, for which I feel, and always must feel, the fondest, the most reverential attachment. In an epoch of dissolution and transformation, such as that on

which we are now entered, habits, ties, and associations
are inevitably broken up, the action of individuals
becomes more distinct, the short-comings, errors, heats,
disputes, which necessarily attend individual action, are
brought into greater prominence. Who would not gladly
keep clear, from all these passing clouds, an august institution which was there before they arose, and which will
be there when they have blown over?

It is true, the *Saturday Review* maintains that our epoch
of transformation is finished ; that we have found our philosophy ; that the British nation has searched all anchor-
ages for the spirit, and has finally anchored itself, in the
fulness of perfected knowledge, to Benthamism. This
idea at first made a great impression on me; not only
because it is so consoling in itself, but also because it
explained a phenomenon which in the summer of last
year had, I confess, a good deal troubled me. At that
time my avocations led me to travel almost daily on one
of the Great Eastern lines,—the Woodford Branch.
Every one knows that Müller perpetrated his detestable
act on the North London Railway, close by. The English
middle class, of which I am myself a feeble unit, travel
on the Woodford Branch in large numbers. Well, the
demoralisation of our class,—which (the newspapers
are constantly saying it, so I may repeat it without
vanity) has done all the great things which have ever
been done in England,—the demoralisation, I say, of
our class, caused by the Bow tragedy, was something

bewildering. Myself a transcendentalist (as the *Saturday Review* knows), I escaped the infection ; and, day after day, I used to ply my agitated fellow-travellers with all the consolations which my transcendentalism, and my turn for the French, would naturally suggest to me. I reminded them how Cæsar refused to take precautions against assassination, because life was not worth having at the price of an ignoble solicitude for it. I reminded them what insignificant atoms we all are in the life of the world. " Suppose the worst to happen," I said, addressing a portly jeweller from Cheapside ; " suppose even yourself to be the victim ; *il n'y a pas d'homme nécessaire.* We should miss you for a day or two upon the Woodford Branch ; but the great mundane movement would still go on ; the gravel walks of your villa would still be rolled ; dividends would still be paid at the Bank ; omnibuses would still run ; there would still be the old crush a the corner of Fenchurch Street." All was of no avail. Nothing could moderate, in the bosom of the great English middle class, their passionate, absorbing, almost blood-thirsty clinging to life. At the moment I thought this over-concern a little unworthy; but the *Saturday Review* suggests a touching explanation of it. What I took for the ignoble clinging to life of a comfortable worldling, was, perhaps, only the ardent longing of a faithful Benthamite, traversing an age still dimmed by the last mists of transcendentalism, to be spared long enough to see his religion in the full and final blaze of its triumph

This respectable man,—whom I imagined to be going up to London to buy shares, or to attend an Exeter Hall meeting, or to hear Mr. D'Iffanger speak, or to see Mr. Spurgeon, with his well-known reverence for every authentic *Thus saith the Lord*, turn his other cheek to the amiable Dean of Ripon,—was, perhaps, in real truth on a pious pilgrimage, to obtain, from Mr. Bentham's executors, a sacred bone of his great, dissected Master.

And yet, after all, I cannot but think that the *Saturday Review* has here, for once, fallen a victim to an idea,—a beautiful but deluding idea,—and that the British nation has not yet, so entirely as the reviewer seems to imagine, found the last word of its philosophy.   No ; we are all seekers still : seekers often make mistakes, and I wish mine to redound to my own discredit only, and not to touch Oxford.   Beautiful city ! so venerable, so lovely, so unravaged by the fierce intellectual life of our century, so serene !

> " There are our young barbarians, all at play."

And yet, steeped in sentiment as she lies, spreading her gardens to the moonlight, and whispering from her towers the last enchantments of the Middle Age, who will deny that Oxford, by her ineffable charm, keeps ever calling us near to the true goal of all of us, to the ideal, to perfection,—to beauty, in a word, which is only truth seen from another side ?—nearer, perhaps, than all the science of Tübingen.   Adorable dreamer, whose heart has been so romantic! who hast given thyself so prodigally, given thyself to sides and to heroes not mine, only never to the Philistines! home of lost causes, and forsaken beliefs, and unpopular names, and impossible loyalties! what example could ever so inspire us to keep down the Philistine in ourselves, what teacher could ever so save us from that bondage to which we are all prone, that bondage which Goethe, in those incomparable lines on the death of Schiller, makes it his friend's highest praise (and nobly did Schiller deserve the praise) to have left miles out of sight behind him;—the bondage of *was uns alle bändigt, DAS GEMEINE!* She will forgive me, even if I have unwittingly drawn upon her a shot or two aimed at her unworthy son; for she is generous, and the cause in which I fight is, after all, hers. Apparitions of a day, what is our puny warfare against the Philistines, compared with the warfare which this Queen of Romance has been waging against them for centuries, and will wage after we are gone?

"Our antagonist is our helper. This amiable conflict with
difficulty obliges us to an intimate acquaintance with our object,
and compels us to consider it in all its relations. It will not
suffer us to be superficial."—BURKE.

THE FUNCTION OF CRITICISM AT THE PRESENT TIME.

MANY objections have been made to a proposition which, in some remarks of mine on translating Homer, I ventured to put forth; a proposition about criticism, and its importance at the present day. I said : "Of the literature of France and Germany, as of the intellect of Europe in general, the main effort, for now many years, has been a critical effort; the endeavour, in all branches of knowledge, theology, philosophy, history, art, science, to see the object as in itself it really is." I added, that owing to the operation in English literature of certain causes, "almost the last thing for which one would come to English literature is just that very thing which now Europe most desires—criticism;" and that the power and value of English literature was thereby impaired. More than one rejoinder declared that the importance I here assigned to criticism was excessive, and asserted the inherent superiority of the creative effort of the human spirit over its critical effort. And the other day, having been led by an.

excellent notice of Wordsworth* published in the *North British Review*, to turn again to his biography, I found, in the words of this great man, whom I, for one, must always listen to with the profoundest respect, a sentence passed on the critic's business, which seems to justify every possible disparagement of it. Wordsworth says in one of his letters :—

" The writers in these publications" (the Reviews), "while they prosecute their inglorious employment, cannot be supposed to be in a state of mind very favourable for being affected by the finer influences of a thing so pure as genuine poetry."

And a trustworthy reporter of his conversation quotes a more elaborate judgment to the same effect :—

" Wordsworth holds the critical power very low, infinitely lower than the inventive; and he said to-day that if the quantity of time consumed in writing critiques on the works of others were given to original composition, of whatever kind it might be, it would be much better employed; it would make a man find out sooner his own level, and it would do infinitely less

* I cannot help thinking that a practice, common in England during the last century, and still followed in France, of printing a notice of this kind,—a notice by a competent critic,—to serve as an introduction to an eminent author's works, might be revived among us with advantage. To introduce all succeeding editions of Wordsworth, Mr. Shairp's notice (it is permitted, I hope, to mention his name) might, it seems to me, excellently serve; it is written from the point of view of an admirer, nay, of a disciple, and that is right; but then the disciple must be also, as in this case he is, a critic, a man of letters, not, as too often happens, some relation or friend with no qualification for his task except affection for his author.

mischief. A false or malicious criticism may do much injury to the minds of others; a stupid invention, either in prose or verse, is quite harmless."

It is almost too much to expect of poor human nature, that a man capable of producing some effect in one line of literature, should, for the greater good of society, voluntarily doom himself to impotence and obscurity in another. Still less is this to be expected from men addicted to the composition of the " false or malicious criticism," of which Wordsworth speaks. However, everybody would admit that a false or malicious criticism had better never have been written. Everybody, too, would be willing to admit, as a general proposition, that the critical faculty is lower than the inventive. But is it true that criticism is really, in itself, a baneful and injurious employment; is it true that all time given to writing critiques on the works of others would be much better employed if it were given to original composition, of whatever kind this may be? Is it true that Johnson had better have gone on producing more *Irenes* instead of writing his *Lives of the Poets;* nay, is it certain that Wordsworth himself was better employed in making his Ecclesiastical Sonnets, than when he made his celebrated Preface, so full of criticism, and criticism of the works of others? Wordsworth was himself a great critic, and it is to be sincerely regretted that he has not left us more criticism; Goethe was one of the greatest of critics, and we may sincerely congratulate ourselves that he has left us so much criticism. Without wasting time over the exaggeration which Wordsworth's judgment on criticism clearly contains, or over an attempt to trace the causes,—not difficult I think to be traced,—which may have led Wordsworth to this exaggeration, a critic may with advantage seize an occasion for trying his own conscience, and for asking himself of what real service, at any given moment, the practice of criticism either is, or may be made, to his own mind and spirit, and to the minds and spirits of others.

The critical power is of lower rank than the creative. True ; but in assenting to this proposition, one or two things are to be kept in mind. It is undeniable that the exercise of a creative power, that a free creative activity, is the true function of man ; it is proved to be so by man's finding in it his true happiness. But it is undeniable, also, that men may have the sense of exercising this free creative activity in other ways than in producing great works of literature or art; if it were not so, all but a very few men would be shut out from the true happiness of all men ; they may have it in well-doing, they may have it in learning, they may have it even in criticising. This is one thing to be kept in mind. Another is, that the exercise of the creative power in the production of great works of literature or art, however high this exercise of it may rank, is not at all epochs and under all conditions possible ; and that therefore labour may be vainly spent in attempting it, which might with more fruit be used in preparing for it, in rendering it possible. This creative power works with elements, with materials ; what if it has not those materials, those elements, ready for its use ? In that case it must surely wait till they are ready. Now in literature,—I will limit myself to literature, for it is about literature that the question arises,—the elements with which the creative power works are ideas ; the best ideas, on every matter which literature touches, current at the time ; at any rate we may lay it down as certain that in modern literature no manifestation of the creative power not working with these can be very important or fruitful. And I say *current* at the time, not merely accessible at the time ; for creative literary genius does not principally show itself in discovering new ideas ; that is rather the business of the philosopher ; the grand work of literary genius is a work of synthesis and exposition, not of analysis and discovery ; its gift lies in the faculty of being happily inspired by a certain intellectual and spiritual atmosphere, by a certain order of ideas, when it finds itself in them ; of dealing divinely with these ideas, presenting them in the most effective and attractive combinations, making beautiful works with them, in short. But it must have the atmosphere, it must find itself amidst the order of ideas, in order to work freely ; and these it is not so easy to command. This is why great creative epochs in literature are so rare ; this is why there is so much that is unsatisfactory in the productions of many men of real genius ; because for the creation of a master-work of literature two powers must concur, the power of the man and the power of the moment, and the man is not enough without the moment ; the creative power has, for its happy exercise, appointed elements, and those elements are not in its own control.

Nay, they are more within the control of the critical power. It is the business of the critical power, as I said in the words already quoted, "in all branches of knowledge, theology, philosophy, history, art, science, to see the object as in itself it really is."   Thus it tends, at last, to make an intellectual situation of which the creative power can profitably avail itself. It tends to establish an order of ideas, if not absolutely true, yet true by comparison with that which it displaces ; to make the best ideas prevail. Presently these new ideas reach society, the touch of truth is the touch of life, and there is a stir and growth everywhere ; out of this stir and growth come the creative epochs of literature.

Or, to narrow our range, and quit these considerations of the general march of genius and of society, considerations which are apt to become too abstract and impalpable,—every one can see that a poet, for instance, ought to know life and the world before dealing with them in poetry ; and life and the world being, in modern times, very complex things, the creation of a modern poet, to be worth much, implies a great critical effort behind it ; else it must be a comparatively poor, barren, and short-lived affair. This is why Byron's poetry had so little endurance in it, and Goethe's so much ; both Byron and Goethe had a great productive power, but Goethe's was nourished by a great critical effort providing the true materials for it, and Byron's was not ; Goethe knew life and the world, the poet's necessary subjects, much more comprehensively and thoroughly than Byron. He knew a great deal more of them, and he knew them much more as they really are.

It has long seemed to me that the burst of creative activity in our literature, through the first quarter of this century, had about it, in fact, something premature ; and that from this cause its productions are doomed, most of them, in spite of the sanguine hopes which accompanied and do still accompany them, to prove hardly more lasting than the productions of far less splendid epochs. And this prematureness comes from its having proceeded without having its proper data, without sufficient materials to work with. In other words, the English poetry of the first quarter of this century, with plenty of energy, plenty of creative force, did not know enough. This makes Byron so empty of matter, Shelley so incoherent, Wordsworth even, profound as he is, yet so wanting in completeness and variety. Wordsworth cared little for books, and disparaged Goethe. I admire Wordsworth, as he is, so much that I cannot wish him different; and it is vain, no doubt, to imagine such a man different from what he is, to suppose that he could have been different; but surely the one thing wanting to make Wordsworth an even greater poet than he is,—his thought richer, and his influence of wider application,—was that he should have read more books, among them, no doubt, those of that Goethe whom he disparaged without reading him.

But to speak of books and reading may easily lead to a misunderstanding here. It was not really books and reading that lacked to our poetry, at this epoch; Shelley had plenty of reading, Coleridge had immense reading. Pindar and Sophocles,—as we all say so glibly, and often with so little discernment of the real import of what we are saying,—had not many books; Shakspeare was no deep reader. True; but in the Greece of Pindar and Sophocles, in the England of Shakspeare, the poet lived in a current of ideas in the highest degree animating and nourishing to the creative power; society was, in the fullest measure, permeated by fresh thought, intelligent and alive; and this state of things is the true basis for the creative power's exercise, in this it finds its data, its materials, truly ready for its hand; all the books and reading in the world are only valuable as they are helps to this. Even when this does not actually exist, books and reading may enable a man to construct a kind of semblance of it in his own mind, a world of knowledge and intelligence in which he may live and work; this is by no means an equivalent, to the artist, for the nationally diffused life and thought of the epochs of Sophocles or Shakspeare, but, besides that it may be a means of preparation for such epochs, it does really constitute, if many share in it, a quickening and sustaining atmosphere of great value. Such an atmosphere the many-sided learning and the long and widely-combined critical effort of Germany formed for Goethe, when he lived and worked. There was no national glow of life and thought there, as in the Athens of Pericles, or the England of Elizabeth. That was the poet's weakness. But there was a sort of equivalent for it in the complete culture and unfettered thinking of a large body of Germans. That was his strength. In the England of the first quarter of this century, there was neither a national glow of life and thought, such as we had in the age of Elizabeth, nor yet a culture and a force of learning and criticism, such as were to be found in Germany. Therefore the creative power of poetry wanted, for success in the highest sense, materials and a basis; a thorough interpretation of the world was necessarily denied to it.

At first sight it seems strange that out of the immense stir of the French Revolution and its age should not have come a crop of works of genius equal to that which came out of the stir of the great productive time of Greece, or out of that of the Renaissance, with its powerful episode the Reformation. But the truth is that the stir of the French Revolution took a character which essentially distinguished it from such movements as these. These were, in the main, disinterestedly intellectual and spiritual movements ; movements in which the human spirit looked for its satisfaction in itself and in the increased play of its own activity : the French Revolution took a political, practical character. The movement which went on in France under the old *régime*, from 1700 to 1789, was far more really akin than that of the Revolution itself to the movement of the Renaissance ; the France of Voltaire and Rousseau told far more powerfully upon the mind of Europe than the France of the Revolution. Goethe reproached this last expressly with having "thrown quiet culture back." Nay, and the true key to how much in our Byron, even in our Wordsworth, is this !—that they had their source in a great movement of feeling, not in a great movement of mind. The French Revolution, however,—that object of so much blind love and so much blind hatred,—found undoubtedly its motive-power in the intelligence of men and not in their practical sense ;—this is what distinguishes it from the English Revolution of Charles the First's time ; this is what makes it a more spiritual event than our Revolution, an event of much more powerful and world-wide interest, though practically less successful ;—it appeals to

an order of ideas which are universal, certain, permanent.
1789 asked of a thing, Is it rational? 1642 asked of a
thing, Is it legal? or, when it went furthest, Is it according
to conscience?   This is the English fashion; a fashion
to be treated, within its own sphere, with the highest
respect; for its success, within its own sphere, has been
prodigious.   But what is law in one place, is not law
in another; what is law here to-day, is not law even here
to-morrow; and as for conscience, what is binding on
one man's conscience is not binding on another's; the
old woman who threw her stool at the head of the
surpliced minister in St. Giles's Church at Edinburgh
obeyed an impulse to which millions of the human race
may be permitted to remain strangers.   But the prescriptions of reason are absolute, unchanging, of universal
validity; *to count by tens is the simplest way of counting,"*—

* A writer in the *Saturday Review*, who has offered me some
counsels about style for which I am truly grateful, suggests that
this should stand as follows:—*To take as your unit an established
base of notation, ten being given as the base of notation, is, except for
numbers under twenty, the simplest way of counting.*   I tried it so,
but I assure him, without jealousy, that the more I looked at his
improved way of putting the thing, the less I liked it.   It seems to
me that the maxim, in this shape, would never make the tour of a
world, where most of us are plain easy-spoken people.   He forgets
that he is a reasoner, a member of a school, a disciple of the great
Bentham, and that he naturally talks in the scientific way of his
school, with exact accuracy, philosophic propriety; I am a mere
solitary wanderer in search of the light, and I talk an artless, un-
studied, every-day, familiar language.   But, after all, this is the
language of the mass of the world.

The mass of Frenchmen who felt the force of that prescription of
the reason which my reviewer, in his purified language, states thus :—
to count by tens has the advantage of taking as your unit the base of an

that is a proposition of which every one, from here to the Antipodes, feels the force ; at least, I should say so, if we did not live in a country where it is not impossible that any morning we may find a letter in the *Times* declaring that a decimal coinage is an absurdity. That a whole nation should have been penetrated with an enthusiasm for pure reason, and with an ardent zeal for making its prescriptions triumph, is a very

established system of notation, certainly rendered this, for themselves, in some such loose language as mine. My point is that they felt the force of a prescription of the reason so strongly that they legislated in accordance with it. They may have been wrong in so doing ; they may have foolishly omitted to take other prescriptions of reason into account ;—the non-English world does not seem to think so, but let that pass ;—what I say is, that by legislating as they did they showed a keen susceptibility to purely rational, intellectual considerations. On the other hand, does my reviewer say that we keep our monetary system unchanged because our nation has grasped the intellectual proposition which he puts, in his masterly way, thus : *to count by twelves has the advantage of taking as your unit a number in itself far more convenient than ten for that purpose!*" Surely not ; but because our system is there, and we are too practical a people to trouble ourselves about its intellectual aspect.

To take a second case. The French Revolutionists abolished the sale of offices, because they thought (my reviewer will kindly allow me to put the thing in my imperfect, popular language) the sale of offices a gross anomaly. We still sell commissions in the army. I have no doubt my reviewer, with his scientific powers, can easily invent some beautiful formula to make us appear to be doing this on the purest philosophical principles ; the principles of Hobbes, Locke, Bentham, Mr. Mill, Mr. Bain, and himself, their worthy disciple. But surely the plain unscientific account of the matter is, that we have the anomalous practice (he will allow it is, in itself, an anomalous practice ?) established, and that (in the words of senatorial wisdom already quoted) " for a thing to be an anomaly we consider to be no objection to it whatever."

remarkable thing, when we consider how little of mind, or anything so worthy and quickening as mind, comes into the motives which alone, in general, impel great masses of men. In spite of the extravagant direction given to this enthusiasm, in spite of the crimes and follies in which it lost itself, the French Revolution derives, from the force, truth, and universality of the ideas which it took for its law, and from the passion with which it could inspire a multitude for these ideas, a unique and still living power; it is,—it will probably long remain,—the greatest, the most animating event in history. And, as no sincere passion for the things of the mind, even though it turn out in many respects an unfortunate passion, is ever quite thrown away and quite barren of good, France has reaped from hers one fruit, the natural and legitimate fruit, though not precisely the grand fruit she expected ; she is the country in Europe where *the people* is most alive.

But the mania for giving an immediate political and practical application to all these fine ideas of the reason was fatal. Here an Englishman is in his element : on this theme we can all go on for hours. And all we are in the habit of saying on it has undoubtedly a great deal of truth. Ideas cannot be too much prized in and for themselves, cannot be too much lived with ; but to transport them abruptly into the world of politics and practice, violently to revolutionise this world to their bidding,—that is quite another thing. There is the world of ideas and there is the world of practice ; the French are often for suppressing the one and the English the other ; but neither is to be suppressed. A member of the House of Commons said to me the other day : " That a thing is an anomaly, I consider to be no objection to it whatever." I venture to think he was wrong; that a thing is an anomaly *is* an objection to it, but absolutely and in the sphere of ideas : it is not necessarily, under such and such circumstances, or at such and such a moment, an objection to it in the sphere of politics and practice. Joubert has said beautifully: " C'est la force et le droit qui règlent toutes choses dans le monde; la force en attendant le droit." Force and right are the governors of this world ; force till right is ready. *Force till right is ready;* and till right is ready, force, the existing order of things, is justified, is the legitimate ruler. But right is something moral, and implies inward recognition, free assent of the will ; we are not ready for right,—*right*, so far as we are concerned, *is not ready*,—until we have attained this sense of seeing it and willing it. The way in which for us it may change and transform force, the existing order of things, and become, in its turn, the legitimate ruler of the world, will depend on the way in which, when our time comes, we see it and will it. Therefore for other people enamoured of their own newly discerned right, to attempt to impose it upon us as ours, and violently to substitute their right for our force, is an act of tyranny, and to be resisted. It sets at nought the second great half of our maxim, *force till right is ready*. This was the grand error of the French Revolution, and its movement of ideas, by quitting the intellectual sphere and rushing furiously into the political sphere, ran, indeed, a prodigious and memorable course, but produced no such intellectual fruit as the movement of ideas of the Renaissance, and created, in opposition to itself, what I may call an *epoch of concentration*. The great force of that epoch of concentration was England ; and the great voice of that epoch of concentration was Burke. It is the fashion to treat Burke's writings on the French Revolution as superannuated and conquered by the event; as the eloquent but unphilosophical tirades of bigotry and prejudice. I will not deny that they are often disfigured by the violence and passion of the moment, and that in some directions Burke's view was bounded, and his observation therefore at fault; but on the whole, and for those who can make the needful corrections, what distinguishes these writings is their profound, permanent, fruitful, philosophical truth ; they contain the true philosophy of an epoch of concentration, dissipate the heavy atmosphere which its own nature is apt to engender round it, and make its resistance rational instead of mechanical.

But Burke is so great because, almost alone in England, he brings thought to bear upon politics, he saturates politics with thought; it is his accident that his ideas were at the service of an epoch of concentration, not of an epoch of expansion ; it is his characteristic that he so lived by ideas, and had such a source of them welling up within him, that he could float even an epoch of concentration and English Tory politics with them. It does not hurt him that Dr. Price and the Liberals were enraged with him ; it does not even hurt him that George the Third and the Tories were enchanted with him. His greatness is that he lived in a world which neither English Liberalism nor English Toryism is apt to enter ;—the world of ideas, not the world of catchwords and party habits. So far is it from being really true of him that he "to party gave up what was meant for mankind," that at the very end of his fierce struggle with the French Revolution, after all his invectives against its false pretensions, hollowness, and madness, with his sincere conviction of its mischievousness, he can close a memorandum on the best means of combating it, some of the last pages he ever wrote,—the *Thoughts on French Affairs*, in December, 1791,—with these striking words :—

"The evil is stated, in my opinion, as it exists. The remedy must be where power, wisdom, and information, I hope, are more united with good intentions than they can be with me. I have done with this subject, I believe, for ever. It has given me many anxious moments for the last two years. *If a great change is to be made in human affairs, the minds of men will be fitted to it; the general opinions and feelings will draw that way. Every fear, every hope will forward it; and then they who persist in opposing this mighty current in human affairs, will appear rather to resist the decrees of Providence itself, than the mere designs of men. They will not be resolute and firm, but perverse and obstinate."*

That return of Burke upon himself has always seemed to me one of the finest things in English literature, or indeed, in any literature. That is what I call living by ideas; when one side of a question has long had your earnest support, when all your feelings are engaged, when you hear all round you no language but one, when your party talks this language like a steam engine and can imagine no other,—still to be able to think, still to be irresistibly carried, if so it be, by the current of thought to the opposite side of the question, and, like Balaam, to be·unable to speak anything *but what the Lord has put in your mouth.* I know nothing more striking, and I must add that I know nothing more un-English.

For the Englishman in general is like my friend the Member of Parliament, and believes, point-blank, that for a thing to be an anomaly is absolutely no objection to it whatever.   He is like the Lord Auckland of Burke's day, who, in a memorandum on the French Revolution, talks of "certain miscreants, assuming the name of philosophers, who have presumed themselves capable of establishing a new system of society."   The Englishman has been called a political animal, and he values what is political and practical so much that ideas easily become objects of dislike in his eyes, and thinkers "miscreants," because ideas and thinkers have rashly meddled with politics and practice. This would be all very well if the dislike and neglect confined themselves to ideas transported out of their own sphere, and meddling rashly with practice; but they are inevitably extended to ideas as such, and to the whole life of intelligence; practice is everything, a free play of the mind is nothing. The notion of the free play of the mind upon all subjects being a pleasure in itself, being an object of desire, being an essential provider of elements without which a nation's spirit, whatever compensations it may have for them, must, in the long run, die of inanition, hardly enters into an Englishman's thoughts. It it noticeable that the word *curiosity,* which in other languages is used in a good sense, to mean, as a high and fine quality of man's nature, just

this disinterested love of a free play of the mind on all
subjects, for its own sake,—it is noticeable, I say, that
this word has in our language no sense of the kind,
no sense but a rather bad and disparaging one. But
criticism, real criticism, is essentially the exercise of this
very quality; it obeys an instinct prompting it to try to
know the best that is known and thought in the world,
irrespectively of practice, politics, and everything of the
kind; and to value knowledge and thought as they
approach this best, without the intrusion of any other
considerations whatever. This is an instinct for which
there is, I think, little original sympathy in the practical
English nature, and what there was of it has undergone
a long benumbing period of blight and suppression in
the epoch of concentration which followed the French
Revolution.

But epochs of concentration cannot well endure for
ever; epochs of expansion, in the due course of things,
follow them. Such an epoch of expansion seems to be
opening in this country. In the first place all danger of
a hostile forcible pressure of foreign ideas upon our
practice has long disappeared; like the traveller in the
fable, therefore, we begin to wear our cloak a little more
loosely. Then, with a long peace, the ideas of Europe
steal gradually and amicably in, and mingle, though in
infinitesimally small quantities at a time, with our own
notions. Then, too, in spite of all that is said about the
absorbing and brutalising influence of our passionate
material progress, it seems to me indisputable that this
progress is likely, though not certain, to lead in the end
to an apparition of intellectual life; and that man, after

he has made himself perfectly comfortable and has now
to determine what to do with himself next, may begin to
remember that he has a mind, and that the mind may be
made the source of great pleasure. I grant it is mainly
the privilege of faith, at present, to discern this end to
our railways, our business, and our fortune-making; but
we shall see if, here as elsewhere, faith is not in the end
the true prophet. Our ease, our travelling, and our unbounded liberty to hold just as hard and securely as
we please to the practice to which our notions have
given birth, all tend to beget an inclination to deal a
little more freely with these notions themselves, to canvass
them a little, to penetrate a little into their real nature.
Flutterings of curiosity, in the foreign sense of the word,
appear amongst us, and it is in these that criticism must
look to find its account. Criticism first; a time of true
creative activity, perhaps,—which, as I have said, must
inevitably be preceded amongst us by a time of criticism,
—hereafter, when criticism has done its work.

It is of the last importance that English criticism
should clearly discern what rule for its course, in order
to avail itself of the field now opening to it, and to produce fruit for the future, it ought to take. The rule may
be summed up in one word,—*disinterestedness*. And how
is criticism to show disinterestedness? By keeping aloof
from practice; by resolutely following the law of its own
nature, which is to be a free play of the mind on all
subjects which it touches; by steadily refusing to lend
itself to any of those ulterior, political, practical considerations about ideas which plenty of people will be
sure to attach to them, which perhaps ought often to be

attached to them, which in this country at any rate are certain to be attached to them quite sufficiently, but which criticism has really nothing to do with. Its business is, as I have said, simply to know the best that is known and thought in the world, and by in its turn making this known, to create a current of true and fresh ideas. Its business is to do this with inflexible honesty, with due ability; but its business is to do no more, and to leave alone all questions of practical consequences and applications, questions which will never fail to have due prominence given to them. Else criticism, besides being really false to its own nature, merely continues in the old rut which it has hitherto followed in this country, and will certainly miss the chance now given to it For what is at present the bane of criticism in this country? It is that practical considerations cling to it and stifle it; it subserves interests not its own; our organs of criticism are organs of men and parties having practical ends to serve, and with them those practical ends are the first thing and the play of mind the second; so much play of mind as is compatible with the prosecution of those practical ends is all that is wanted. An organ like the *Revue des Deux Mondes*, having for its main function to understand and utter the best that is known and thought in the world, existing, it may be said, as just an organ for a free play of the mind, we have not; but we have the *Edinburgh Review*, existing as an organ of the old Whigs, and for as much play of mind as may suit its being that; we have the *Quarterly Review*, existing as an organ of the Tories, and for as much play of mind as may suit its being that; we have the *British Quarterly Review*, existing as an organ of the political Dissenters, and for as much play of mind as may suit its being that ; we have the *Times*, existing as an organ of the common, satisfied, well-to-do Englishman, and for as much play of mind as may suit its being that. And so on through all the various fractions, political and religious, of our society ; every fraction has, as such, its organ of criticism, but the notion of combining all fractions in the common pleasure of a free disinterested play of mind meets with no favour. Directly this play of mind wants to have more scope, and to forget the pressure of practical considerations a little, it is checked, it is made to feel the chain ; we saw this the other day in the extinction, so much to be regretted, of the *Home and Foreign Review ;* perhaps in no organ of criticism in this country was there so much knowledge, so much play of mind ; but these could not save it ; the *Dublin Review* subordinates play of mind to the practical business of English and Irish Catholicism, and lives. It must needs be that men should act in sects and parties, that each of these sects and parties should have its organ, and should make this organ subserve the interests of its action ; but it would be well, too, that there should be a criticism, not the minister of these interests, not their enemy, but absolutely and entirely independent of them. No other criticism will ever attain any real authority or make any real way towards its end,—the creating a current of true and fresh ideas.

It is because criticism has so little kept in the pure intellectual sphere, has so little detached itself from practice, has been so directly polemical and controversial, that it has so ill accomplished, in this country, its best spiritual work ; which is to keep man from a self-satisfaction which is retarding and vulgarising, to lead him towards perfection, by making his mind dwell upon what is excellent in itself, and the absolute beauty and fitness of things. A polemical practical criticism makes men blind even to the ideal imperfection of their practice, makes them willingly assert its ideal perfection, in order the better to secure it against attack ; and clearly this is narrowing and baneful for them. If they were reassured on the practical side, speculative considerations of ideal perfection they might be brought to entertain, and their spiritual horizon would thus gradually widen. Mr. Adderley says to the Warwickshire farmers :—

"Talk of the improvement of breed ! Why, the race we ourselves represent, the men and women, the old Anglo-Saxon race, are the best breed in the whole world. . . . The absence of a too enervating climate, too unclouded skies, and a too luxurious nature, has produced so vigorous a race of people, and has rendered us so superior to all the world."

Mr. Roebuck says to the Sheffield cutlers :—

"I look around me and ask what is the state of England ? Is not property safe ? Is not every man able to say what he likes ? Can you not walk from one end of England to the other in perfect security ? I ask you whether, the world over or in past history, there is anything like it ? Nothing. I pray that our unrivalled happiness may last."

Now obviously there is a peril for poor human nature in words and thoughts of such exuberant self-satisfaction, until we find ourselves safe in the streets of the Celestial City.

> " Das wenige verschwindet leicht dem Blicke
>   Der vorwärts sieht, wie viel noch übrig bleibt—"

says Goethe ; the little that is done seems nothing when we look forward and see how much we have yet to do. Clearly this is a better line of reflection for weak humanity, so long as it remains on this earthly field of labour and trial.   But neither Mr. Adderley nor Mr. Roebuck are by nature inaccessible to considerations of this sort. They only lose sight of them owing to the controversial life we all lead, and the practical form which all speculation takes with us.   They have in view opponents whose aim is not ideal, but practical, and in their zeal to uphold their own practice against these innovators, they go so far as even to attribute to this practice an ideal perfection.   Somebody has been wanting to introduce a six-pound franchise, or to abolish church-rates, or to collect agricultural statistics by force, or to diminish local self-government.   How natural, in reply to such proposals, very likely improper or ill-timed, to go a little beyond the mark, and to say stoutly : "Such a race of people as we stand, so superior to all the world !   The old Anglo-Saxon race, the best breed in the whole world ! I pray that our unrivalled happiness may last !   I ask you whether, the world over or in past history, there is anything like it !"   And so long as criticism answers this dithyramb by insisting that the old Anglo-Saxon race would be still more superior to all others if it had no church-rates, or that our unrivalled happiness would last yet longer with a six-pound franchise, so long will the strain, "The best breed in the whole world!" swell louder and louder, everything ideal and refining will be lost out of sight, and both the assailed and their critics will remain in a sphere, to say the truth, perfectly unvital, a sphere in which spiritual progression is impossible. But let criticism leave church-rates and the franchise alone, and in the most candid spirit, without a single lurking thought of practical innovation, confront with our dithyramb this paragraph on which I stumbled in a newspaper soon after reading Mr. Roebuck :—

"A shocking child murder has just been committed at Nottingham. A girl named Wragg left the workhouse there on Saturday morning with her young illegitimate child. The child was soon afterwards found dead on Mapperly Hills, having been strangled. Wragg is in custody."

Nothing but that; but, in juxtaposition with the absolute eulogies of Mr. Adderley and Mr. Roebuck, how eloquent, how suggestive are those few lines ! "Our old Anglo-Saxon breed, the best in the whole world !"—how much that is harsh and ill-favoured there is in this best ! *Wragg !* If we are to talk of ideal perfection, of "the best in the whole world," has anyone reflected what a touch of grossness in our race, what an original shortcoming in the more delicate spiritual perceptions, is shown by the natural growth amongst us of such hideous names,—Higginbottom, Stiggins, Bugg ! In Ionia and Attica they were luckier in this respect than "the best race in the world ;" by the Ilissus there was no Wragg, poor thing ! And "our unrivalled happiness ;"—what an element of grimness, bareness, and hideousness mixes with it and blurs it ; the workhouse, the dismal Mapperly Hills,—how dismal those who have seen them will remember;—the gloom, the smoke, the cold, the strangled illegitimate child ! " I ask you whether, the world over or in past history, there is anything like it ?" Perhaps not, one is inclined to answer ; but at any rate, in that case, the world is very much to be pitied. And the final touch,—short, bleak, and inhuman : *Wragg is in custody.* The sex lost in the confusion of our unrivalled happiness ; or, shall I say ? the superfluous Christian name lopped off by the straightforward vigour of our old Anglo-Saxon breed ! There is profit for the spirit in such contrasts as this ; criticism serves the cause of perfection by establishing them. By eluding sterile conflict, by refusing to remain in the sphere where alone narrow and relative conceptions have any worth and validity, criticism may diminish its momentary importance, but only in this way has it a chance of gaining admittance for those wider and more perfect conceptions to which all its duty is really owed. Mr. Roebuck will have a poor opinion of an adversary who replies to his defiant songs of triumph only by murmuring under his breath, *Wragg is in custody;* but in no other way will these songs of triumph be induced gradually to moderate themselves, to get rid of what in them is excessive and offensive, and to fall into a softer and truer key.

It will be said that it is a very subtle and indirect action which I am thus prescribing for criticism, and that by embracing in this manner the Indian virtue of detachment and abandoning the sphere of practical life, it condemns itself to a slow and obscure work. Slow and obscure it may be, but it is the only proper work of criticism. The mass of mankind will never have any ardent zeal for seeing things as they are ; very inadequate ideas will always satisfy them. On these inadequate ideas reposes, and must repose, the general practice of the world. That is as much as saying that whoever sets himself to see things as they are will find himself one of a very small circle ; but it is only by this small circle resolutely doing its own work that adequate ideas will ever get current at all. The rush and roar of practical life will always have a dizzying and attracting effect upon the most collected spectator, and tend to draw him into its vortex ; most of all will this be the case where that life is so powerful as it is in England. But it is only by remaining collected, and refusing to lend himself to the point of view of the practical man, that the critic can do the practical man any service ; and it is only by the greatest sincerity in pursuing his own course, and by at last convincing even the practical man of his sincerity, that he can escape misunderstandings which perpetually threaten him.

For the practical man is not apt for fine distinctions, and yet in these distinctions truth and the highest culture greatly find their account. But it is not easy to lead a practical man,—unless you reassure him as to your practical intentions you have no chance of leading him,—to see that a thing which he has always been used to look at from one side only, which he greatly values, and which, looked at from that side, more than deserves, perhaps, all the prizing and admiring which he bestows upon it,—that this thing, looked at from another side, may appear much less beneficent and beautiful, and yet retain all its claims to our practical allegiance. Where shall we find language innocent enough, how shall we make the spotless purity of our intentions evident enough, to enable us to say to the political Englishman that the British Constitution itself, which, seen from the practical side, looks such a magnificent organ of progress and virtue, seen from the speculative side,—with its compromises, its love of facts, its horror of theory, its studied avoidance of clear thoughts,—that, seen from this side, our august Constitution sometimes looks,—forgive me, shade of Lord Somers!—a colossal machine for the manufacture of Philistines! How is Cobbett to say this and not be misunderstood, blackened as he is with the smoke of a life-long conflict in the field of political practice? how is Mr. Carlyle to say it and not be misunderstood, after his furious raid into this field with his *Latter-day Pamphlets?* how is Mr. Ruskin, after his pugnacious political economy? I say, the critic must keep out of the region of immediate practice in the political, social, humanitarian sphere, if he wants to make a beginning for that more free speculative treatment of things, which may perhaps one day make its benefits felt even in this sphere, but in a natural and thence irresistible manner.

Do what he will, however, the critic will still remain exposed to frequent misunderstandings, and nowhere so much as in this country. For here people are particularly indisposed even to comprehend that without this free disinterested treatment of things, truth and the highest culture are out of the question. So immersed are they in practical life, so accustomed to take all their notions from this life and its processes, that they are apt to think that truth and culture themselves can be reached by the processes of this life, and that it is an impertinent singularity to think of reaching them in any other. "We are all *terræ filii*," cries their eloquent advocate; "all Philistines together. Away with the notion of proceeding by any other course than the course dear to the Philistines; let us have a social movement, let us organise and combine a party to pursue truth and new thought, let us call it *the liberal party*, and let us all stick to each other, and back each other up. Let us have no nonsense about independent criticism, and intellectual delicacy, and the few and the many; don't let us trouble ourselves about foreign thought; we shall invent the whole thing for ourselves as we go along; if one of us speaks well, applaud him; if one of us speaks ill, applaud him too; we are all in the same movement, we are all liberals, we are all in pursuit of truth." In this way the pursuit of truth becomes really a social, practical, pleasureable affair, almost requiring a chairman, a secretary, and advertisements; with the excitement of an occasional scandal, with a little resistance to give the happy sense of difficulty overcome; but, in general, plenty of bustle and very little thought. To act is so easy, as Goethe says; to think is so hard! It is true that the critic has many temptations to go with the stream, to make one of the party of movement, one of these *terræ filii;* it seems ungracious to refuse to be a *terræ filius*, when so many excellent people are; but the critic's duty is to refuse, or, if resistance is vain, at least to cry with Obermann: *Périssons en résistant.*

How serious a matter it is to try and resist, I had ample opportunity of experiencing when I ventured some time ago to criticise the celebrated first volume of Bishop Colenso.* The echoes of the storm which was then raised I still, from time to time, hear grumbling round me. That storm arose out of a misunderstanding almost inevitable. It is a result of no little culture to attain to a clear perception that science and religion are two wholly different things; the multitude will for ever confuse them, but happily that is of no great real importance, for while the multitude imagines itself to live by its false science, it does really live by its true religion. Dr. Colenso, however, in his first volume did all he could to strengthen the confusion,† and to make it dangerous.

* So sincere is my dislike to all personal attack and controversy, that I abstain from reprinting, at this distance of time from the occasion which called them forth, the essays in which I criticised the Bishop of Natal's book; I feel bound, however, after all that has passed, to make here a final declaration of my sincere impenitence for having published them. The Bishop of Natal's subsequent volumes are in great measure free from the crying fault of his first; he has at length succeeded in more clearly separating, in his own thoughts, the idea of science from the idea of religion; his mind appears to be opening as he goes along, and he may perhaps end by becoming a useful biblical critic, though never, I think, of the first order.

Still, in here taking leave of him at the moment when he is publishing, for popular use, a cheap edition of his work, I cannot forbear repeating yet once more, for his benefit and that of his readers, this sentence from my original remarks upon him: *There is truth of science and truth of religion; truth of science does not become truth of religion till it is made religious.* And I will add: Let us have all the science there is from the men of science; from the men of religion let us have religion.

† It has been said I make it " a crime against literary criticism

He did this with the best intentions, I freely admit, and with the most candid ignorance that this was the natural effect of what he was doing ; but, says Joubert, " Ignorance, which in matters of morals extenuates the crime, is itself, in intellectual matters, a crime of the first order." I criticised Bishop Colenso's speculative confusion. Immediately there was a cry raised : " What is this ? here is a liberal attacking a liberal. Do not you belong to the movement ? are not you a friend of truth ? Is not Bishop Colenso in pursuit of truth ? then speak with proper respect of his book.   Dr. Stanley is another friend of truth, and you speak with proper respect of his book ; why make these invidious differences ? both books are excellent, admirable, liberal ; Bishop Colenso's perhaps the most so, because it is the boldest, and will have the best practical consequences for the liberal cause.   Do you want to encourage to the attack of a brother liberal his, and your, and our implacable enemies, the *Church and State Review* or the *Record*,—the High Church rhinoceros and the Evangelical hyæna ? Be silent, therefore ; or rather speak, speak as loud as ever you can, and go into ecstasies over the eighty and odd pigeons." But criticism cannot follow this coarse and indiscriminate method.   It is unfortunately possible for a man in pursuit of truth to write a book which reposes upon a false conception.   Even the practical consequences of a book are to genuine criticism no recommendation of it, if the book is, in the highest sense, blundering.   I see that a

and the higher culture to attempt to inform the ignorant." Need I point out that the ignorant are not informed by being confirmed in a confusion ?

lady who herself, too, is in pursuit of truth, and who writes with great ability, but a little too much, perhaps, under the influence of the practical spirit of the English liberal movement, classes Bishop Colenso's book and M. Renan's together, in her survey of the religious state of Europe, as facts of the same order, works, both of them, of "great importance ; " "great ability, power and skill ; " Bishop Colenso's, perhaps, the most powerful ; at least, Miss Cobbe gives special expression to her gratitude that to Bishop Colenso "has been given the strength to grasp, and the courage to teach truths of such deep import." In the same way, more than one popular writer has compared him to Luther. Now it is just this kind of false estimate which the critical spirit is, it seems to me, bound to resist. It is really the strongest possible proof of the low ebb at which, in England, the critical spirit is, that while the critical hit in the religious literature of Germany is Dr. Strauss's book, in that of France M. Renan's book, the book of Bishop Colenso is the critical hit in the religious literature of England. Bishop Colenso's book reposes on a total misconception of the essential elements of the religious problem, as that problem is now presented for solution. To criticism, therefore, which seeks to have the best that is known and thought on this problem, it is, however well meant, of no importance whatever. M. Renan's book attempts a new synthesis of the elements furnished to us by the four Gospels. It attempts, in my opinion, a synthesis, perhaps premature, perhaps impossible, certainly not successful Up to the present time, at any rate, we must acquiesce in Fleury's sentence on such recastings of the Gospel story: *Quiconque s'imagine la pouvoir mieux écrire, ne l'entend pas.* M. Renan had himself passed by anticipation a like sentence on his own work, when he said: " If a new presentation of the character of Jesus were offered to me, I would not have it ; its very clearness would be, in my opinion, the best proof of its insufficiency." His friends may with perfect justice rejoin that at the sight of the Holy Land, and of the actual scene of the Gospel-story, all the current of M. Renan's thoughts may have naturally changed, and a new casting of that story irresistibly suggested itself to him ; and that this is just a case for applying Cicero's maxim : Change of mind is not inconsistency— *nemo doctus unquam mutationem consilii inconstantiam dixit esse.* Nevertheless, for criticism, M. Renan's first thought must still be the truer one, as long as his new casting so fails more fully to commend itself, more fully (to use Coleridge's happy phrase about the Bible) to *find* us. Still M. Renan's attempt is, for criticism, of the most real interest and importance, since, with all its difficulty, a fresh synthesis of the New Testament *data*,— not a making war on them, in Voltaire's fashion, not a leaving them out of mind, in the world's fashion, but the putting a new construction upon them, the taking them from under the old, adoptive, traditional, un-spiritual point of view and placing them under a new one,—is the very essence of the religious problem, as now presented ; and only by efforts in this direction can it receive a solution.

Again, in the same spirit in which she judges Bishop Colenso, Miss Cobbe, like so many earnest liberals of

our practical race, both here and in America, herself
sets vigorously about a positive reconstruction of religion,
about making a religion of the future out of hand, or at
least setting about making it; we must not rest, she and
they are always thinking and saying, in negative criticism, we must be creative and constructive; hence we
have such works as her recent *Religious Duty*, and works
still more considerable, perhaps, by others, which will
be in everyone's mind. These works often have much
ability; they often spring out of sincere convictions,
and a sincere wish to do good; and they sometimes,
perhaps, do good. Their fault is (if I may be permitted
to say so) one which they have in common with the
British College of Health, in the New Road. Everyone
knows the British College of Health; it is that building
with the lion and the statue of the Goddess Hygeia before
it; at least, I am sure about the lion, though I am not
absolutely certain about the Goddess Hygeia. This
building does credit, perhaps, to the resources of Dr.
Morrison and his disciples; but it falls a good deal
short of one's idea of what a British College of Health
ought to be. In England, where we hate public inter-
ference and love individual enterprise, we have a whole
crop of places like the British College of Health; the
grand name without the grand thing. Unluckily, creditable to individual enterprise as they are, they tend to
impair our taste by making us forget what more grandiose,
noble, or beautiful character properly belongs to a public
institution. The same may be said of the religions of
the future of Miss Cobbe and others. Creditable, like
the British College of Health, to the resources of their

authors, they yet tend to make us forget what more grandiose, noble, or beautiful character properly belongs to religious constructions. The historic religions, with all their faults, have had this; it certainly belongs to the religious sentiment, when it truly flowers, to have this; and we impoverish our spirit if we allow a religion of the future without it. What then is the duty of criticism here? To take the practical point of view, to applaud the liberal movement and all its works,—its New Road religions of the future into the bargain,—for their general utility's sake? By no means; but to be perpetually dissatisfied with these works, while they perpetually fall short of a high and perfect ideal.

For criticism, these are elementary laws; but they never can be popular, and in this country they have been very little followed, and one meets with immense obstacles in following them. That is a reason for asserting them again and again. Criticism must maintain its independence of the practical spirit and its aims. Even with well-meant efforts of the practical spirit it must express dissatisfaction, if in the sphere of the ideal they seem impoverishing and limiting. It must not hurry on to the goal because of its practical importance. It must be patient, and know how to wait; and flexible, and know how to attach itself to things and how to withdraw from them. It must be apt to study and praise elements that for the fulness of spiritual perfection are wanted, even though they belong to a power which in the practical sphere may be maleficent. It must be apt to discern the spiritual shortcomings or illusions of powers that in the practical sphere may be beneficent. And this without any notion of favouring or injuring, in the practical sphere, one power or the other; without any notion of playing off, in this sphere, one power against the other. When one looks, for instance, at the English Divorce Court,—an institution which perhaps has its practical conveniences, but which in the ideal sphere is so hideous;*

---

* A critic, already quoted, says that I have no right, on my own principles, to "object to practical measures on theoretical grounds," and that only "when a man has got a theory which will fully explain all the duties of the legislator on the matter of marriage, will he have a right to abuse the Divorce Court." In short, he wants me to produce a plan for a new and improved Divorce Court, before I call the present one hideous. But God forbid that I should thus enter into competition with the Lord Chancellor! It is just this invasion of the practical sphere which is really against my principles; the taking a practical measure into the world of ideas, and seeing how it looks there, is, on the other hand, just what I am recommending. It is because we have not been conversant enough with ideas that our practice now falls so short; it is only by becoming more conversant with them that we shall make it better. Our present Divorce Court is not the result of any legislator's meditations on the subject of marriage; rich people had an anomalous privilege of getting divorced; privileges are odious, and we said everybody should have the same chance. There was no meditation about marriage here; that was just the mischief.

If my practical critic will but himself accompany me, for a little while, into the despised world of ideas;—if, renouncing any attempt to patch hastily up, with a noble disdain for transcendentalists, our present Divorce law, he will but allow his mind to dwell a little, first on the Catholic idea of marriage, which exhibits marriage as indissoluble, and then upon that Protestant idea of marriage, which exhibits it as a union terminable by mutual consent,—if he will meditate well on these, and afterwards on the thought of what married life, according to its idea, really is, of what family life really is, of what social life really is, and national life, and public morals, —he will find, after a while, I do assure him, the whole state of his

an institution which neither makes divorce impossible
nor makes it decent, which allows a man to get rid of
his wife, or a wife of her husband, but makes them drag
one another first, for the public edification, through a
mire of unutterable infamy,—when one looks at this
charming institution, I say, with its crowded benches,
its newspaper-reports, and its money-compensations, this
institution in which the gross unregenerate British Philistine has indeed stamped an image of himself,—one may
be permitted to find the marriage-theory of Catholicism
refreshing and elevating. Or when Protestantism, in
virtue of its supposed rational and intellectual origin,
gives the law to criticism too magisterially, criticism may
and must remind it that its pretensions, in this respect,
are illusive and do it harm ; that the Reformation was a
moral rather than an intellectual event ; that Luther's
theory of grace no more exactly reflects the mind of the
spirit than Bossuet's philosophy of history reflects it ;
and that there is no more antecedent probability of the
Bishop of Durham's stock of ideas being agreeable to
perfect reason than of Pope Pius the Ninth's. But
criticism will not on that account forget the achievements
of Protestantism in the practical and moral sphere ; nor
that, even in the intellectual sphere, Protestantism,

spirit quite changed ; the Divorce Court will then seem to him, if he
looks at it, strangely hideous ; and he will at the same time discover
in himself, as the fruit of his inward discipline, lights and resources
for making it better, of which now he does not dream.

He must make haste, though, for the condition of his "practical
measure" is getting awkward ; even the British Philistine begins to
have qualms as he looks at his offspring ; even his "thrice-battered
God of Palestine" is beginning to roll its eyes convulsively.

though in a blind and stumbling manner, carried forward the Renaissance, while Catholicism threw itself violently across its path.

I lately heard a man of thought and energy contrasting the want of ardour and movement which he now found amongst young men in this country with what he remembered in his own youth, twenty years ago. "What reformers we were then!" he exclaimed; "what a zeal we had! how we canvassed every institution in Church and State, and were prepared to remodel them all on first principles!" He was inclined to regret, as a spiritual flagging, the lull which he saw. I am disposed rather to regard it as a pause in which the turn to a new mode of spiritual progress is being accomplished. Everything was long seen, by the young and ardent amongst us, in inseparable connexion with politics and practical life; we have pretty well exhausted the benefits of seeing things in this connexion, we have got all that can be got by so seeing them. Let us try a more disinterested mode of seeing them; let us betake ourselves more to the serener life of the mind and spirit. This life, too, may have its excesses and dangers; but they are not for us at present. Let us think of quietly enlarging our stock of true and fresh ideas, and not, as soon as we get an idea or half an idea, be running out with it into the street, and trying to make it rule there. Our ideas will, in the end, shape the world all the better for maturing a little. Perhaps in fifty years time it will in the English House of Commons be an objection to an institution that it is an anomaly, and my friend the Member of Parliament will shudder in his grave. But let us in the meanwhile rather endeavour that in twenty years time it may, in English literature, be an objection to a proposition that it is absurd. That will be a change so vast, that the imagination almost fails to grasp it. *Ab integro sæclorum nascitur ordo.*

If I have insisted so much on the course which criticism must take where politics and religion are concerned, it is because, where these burning matters are in question, it is most likely to go astray. In general, its course is determined for it by the idea which is the law of its being; the idea of a disinterested endeavour to learn and propagate the best that is known and thought in the world, and thus to establish a current of fresh and true ideas. By the very nature of things, as England is not all the world, much of the best that is known and thought in the world cannot be of English growth, must be foreign; by the nature of things, again, it is just this that we are least likely to know, while English thought is streaming in upon us from all sides and takes excellent care that we shall not be ignorant of its existence; the English critic, therefore, must dwell much on foreign thought, and with particular heed on any part of it, which, while significant and fruitful in itself, is for any reason specially likely to escape him. Again, judging is often spoken of as the critic's one business; and so in some sense it is; but the judgment which almost insensibly forms itself in a fair and clear mind, along with fresh knowledge, is the valuable one; and thus knowledge, and ever fresh knowledge, must be the critic's great concern for himself; and it is by communicating fresh knowledge, and letting his own judgment pass along with it,—but insensibly, and in the second place not the first, as a sort of companion and clue, not as an abstract law-giver,—that he will generally do most good to his readers. Sometimes, no doubt, for the sake of establishing an author's place in literature, and his relation to a central standard (and if this is not done how are we to get at our *best in the world?*), criticism may have to deal with a subject-matter so familiar that fresh knowledge is out of the question, and then it must be all judgment; an enunciation and detailed application of principles. Here the great safeguard is never to let oneself become abstract, always to retain an intimate and lively consciousness of the truth of what one is saying, and, the moment this fails us, to be sure that something is wrong. Still, under all circumstances, this mere judgment and application of principles is, in itself, not the most satisfactory work to the critic; like mathematics it is tautological, and cannot well give us, like fresh learning, the sense of creative activity.

But stop, some one will say; all this talk is of no practical use to us whatever; this criticism of yours is not what we have in our minds when we speak of criticism; when we speak of critics and criticism, we mean critics and criticism of the current English literature of the day; when you offer to tell criticism its function, it is to this criticism that we expect you to address yourself. I am sorry for it, for I am afraid I must disappoint these expectations. I am bound by my own definition of criticism : *a disinterested endeavour to learn and propagate the best that is known and thought in the world.* How much of current English literature comes into this " best that is known and thought in the world "? Not very much, I fear ; certainly less, at this moment, than of the current literature of France or Germany. Well, then, am I to alter my definition of criticism, in order to meet the requirements of a number of practising English critics, who, after all, are free in their choice of a business ? That would be making criticism lend itself just to one of those alien practical considerations, which, I have said, are so fatal to it. One may say, indeed, to those who have to deal with the mass,—so much better disregarded,—of current English literature, that they may at all events endeavour, in dealing with this, to try it, so far as they can, by the standard of the best that is known and thought in the world ; one may say, that to get anywhere near this standard, every critic should try and possess one great literature, at least, besides his own ; and the more unlike his own, the better. But, after all, the criticism I am really concerned with,—the criticism which alone can much help us for the future, the criticism which, throughout Europe, is at the present day meant, when so much stress is laid on the importance of criticism and the critical spirit,—is a criticism which regards Europe as being, for intellectual and spiritual purposes, one great confederation, bound to a joint action and working to a common result ; and whose members have, for their proper outfit, a knowledge of Greek, Roman, and Eastern antiquity, and of one another. Special, local, and temporary advantages being put out of account, that modern nation will in the intellectual and spiritual sphere make most progress, which most thoroughly carries out this programme. And what is that but saying that we too, all of us, as individuals, the more thoroughly we carry it out, shall make the more progress?

There is so much inviting us! what are we to take! what will nourish us in growth towards perfection? That is the question which, with the immense field of life and of literature lying before him, the critic has to answer; for himself first, and afterwards for others. In this idea of the critic's business the essays brought together in the following pages have had their origin; in this idea, widely different as are their subjects, they have, perhaps, their unity.

I conclude with what I said at the beginning: to have the sense of creative activity is the great happiness and the great proof of being alive, and it is not denied to criticism to have it; but then criticism must be sincere, simple, flexible, ardent, ever widening its knowledge. Then it may have, in no contemptible measure, a joyful sense of creative activity; a sense which a man of insight and conscience will prefer to what he might derive from a poor, starved, fragmentary, inadequate creation. And at some epochs no other creation is possible.

Still, in full measure, the sense of creative activity belongs only to genuine creation; in literature we must never forget that. But what true man of letters ever can forget it? It is no such common matter for a gifted nature to come into possession of a current of true and living ideas, and to produce amidst the inspiration of them, that we are likely to underrate it. The epochs of Æschylus and Shakspeare make us feel their pre-eminence. In an epoch like those is, no doubt, the true life of a literature; there is the promised land, towards which criticism can only beckon. That promised land it will not be ours to enter, and we shall die in the wilderness: but to have desired to enter it, to have saluted it from afar, is already, perhaps, the best distinction among contemporaries; it will certainly be the best title to esteem with posterity.

THE LITERARY INFLUENCE OF ACADEMIES.

IT is impossible to put down a book like the history of
the French Academy, by Pellisson and D'Olivet, which
M. Charles Livet has lately re-edited, without being led
to reflect upon the absence, in our own country, of any
institution like the French Academy, upon the probable
causes of this absence, and upon its results. A thousand
voices will be ready to tell us that this absence is a signal
mark of our national superiority ; that it is in great part
owing to this absence that the exhilarating words of Lord
Macaulay, lately given to the world by his very clever
nephew, Mr. Trevelyan, are so profoundly true : " It may
safely be said that the literature now extant in the English
language is of far greater value than all the literature
which three hundred years ago was extant in all the
languages of the world together." I daresay this is so ;
only, remembering Spinoza's maxim that the two great
banes of humanity are self-conceit and the laziness coming
from self-conceit, I think it may do us good, instead of
resting in our pre-eminence with perfect security, to look
a little more closely why this is so, and whether it is so
without any limitations.

But first of all I must give a very few words to the
outward history of the French Academy. About the year

1629, seven or eight persons in Paris, fond of literature, formed themselves into a sort of little club to meet at one another's houses and discuss literary matters. Their meetings got talked of, and Cardinal Richelieu, then minister and all powerful, heard of them. He himself had a noble passion for letters, and for all fine culture ; he was interested by what he heard of the nascent society. Himself a man in the grand style, if ever man was, he had the insight to perceive what a potent instrument of the grand style was here to his hand. It was the beginning of a great century for France, the seventeenth ; men's minds were working, the French language was forming. Richelieu sent to ask the members of the new society whether they would be willing to become a body with a public character, holding regular meetings. Not without a little hesitation,—for apparently they found themselves very well as they were, and these seven or eight gentlemen of a social and literary turn were not perfectly at their ease as to what the great and terrible minister could want with them,—they consented. The favours of a man like Richelieu are not easily refused, whether they are honestly meant or no ; but this favour of Richelieu's was meant quite honestly. The Parliament, however, had its doubts of this. The Parliament had none of Richelieu's enthusiasm about letters and culture ; it was jealous of the apparition of a new public body in the State ; above all, of a body called into existence by Richelieu. The King's letters patent, establishing and authorising the new society, were granted early in 1635 ; but, by the old constitution of France, these letters patent required the verification of the Parliament. It was two

years and a half,—towards the autumn of 1637,—before
the Parliament would give it ; and it then gave it only
after pressing solicitations, and earnest assurances of the
innocent intentions ·of the young Academy.   Jocose
people said that this society, with its mission to purify
and embellish the language, filled with terror a body of
lawyers like the French Parliament, the stronghold of
barbarous jargon and of chicane.

This improvement of the language was in truth the
declared grand aim for the operations of the Academy.
Its statutes of foundation, approved by Richelieu before
the royal edict establishing it was issued, say expressly :
" The Academy's principal function shall be to work
with all the care and all the diligence possible at giving
sure rules to our language, and rendering it pure, eloquent, and capable of treating the arts and sciences."
This zeal for making a nation's great instrument of
thought,—its language,—correct and worthy, is undoubtedly a sign full of promise, a weighty earnest of future
power.   It is said that Richelieu had it in his mind that
French should succeed Latin in its general ascendancy,
as Latin had succeeded Greek ; if it was so, even this
wish has to some extent been fulfilled.   But, at any rate,
the *ethical* influences of style in language,—its close
relations, so often pointed out, with character,—are most
important.   Richelieu, a man of high culture, and, at
the same time, of great character, felt them profoundly ;
and that he should have sought to regularise, strengthen,
and perpetuate them by an institution for perfecting
language, is alone a striking proof of his governing
spirit and of his genius.

This was not all he had in his mind, however. The new Academy, now enlarged to a body of forty members, and meant to contain all the chief literary men of France, was to be a *literary tribunal*. The works of its members were to be brought before it previous to publication, were to be criticised by it, and finally, if it saw fit, to be published with its declared approbation. The works of other writers, not members of the Academy, might also, at the request of these writers themselves, be passed under the Academy's review. Besides this, in essays and discussions the Academy examined and judged works already published, whether by living or dead authors, and literary matters in general. The celebrated opinion on Corneille's *Cid*, delivered in 1637 by the Academy at Richelieu's urgent request, when this poem, which strongly occupied public attention, had been attacked by M. de Scudéry, shows how fully Richelieu designed his new creation to do duty as a supreme court of literature, and how early it, in fact, began to exercise this function. One * who had known Richelieu declared, after the Cardinal's death, that he had projected a yet greater institution than the Academy, a sort of grand European college of art, science, and literature, a Prytaneum, where the chief authors of all Europe should be gathered together in one central home, there to live in security, leisure, and honour;—that was a dream which will not bear to be pulled about too roughly. But the project of forming a high court of letters for France was no dream ; Richelieu in great measure fulfilled it. This is what the Academy, by its idea, really is ; this is

* La Mesnardière.

what it has always tended to become; this is what it has, from time to time, really been; by being, or tending to be this, far more than even by what it has done for the language, it is of such importance in France. To give the law, the tone to literature, and that tone a high one, is its business. " Richelieu meant it," says M. Sainte-Beuve, " to be a *haut jury*,"—a jury the most choice and authoritative that could be found on all important literary matters in question before the public; to be, as it in fact became in the latter half of the eighteenth century, "a sovereign organ of opinion." " The duty of the Academy is," says M. Renan, " *maintenir la déli-catesse de l'esprit français* "—to keep the fine quality of the French spirit unimpaired; it represents a kind of " *maîtrise en fait de bon ton* "—the authority of a recog-nised master in matters of tone and taste. " All ages," says M. Renan again, " have had their inferior literature; but the great danger of our time is that this inferior literature tends more and more to get the upper place. No one has the same advantages as the Academy for fighting against this mischief;" the Academy, which, as he says elsewhere, has even special facilities for " creating a form of intellectual culture *which shall impose itself on all around.*" M. Sainte-Beuve and M. Renan are, both of them, very keen-sighted critics; and they show it signally by seizing and putting so prominently forward this character of the French Academy.

Such an effort to set up a recognised authority, im-posing on us a high standard in matters of intellect and taste, has many enemies in human nature. We all of us like to go our own way, and not to be forced out of the

atmosphere of commonplace habitual to most of us ;—
" *was uns alle bändigt*," says Goethe, " *das Gemeine*." We
like to be suffered to lie comfortably in the old straw
of our habits, especially of our intellectual habits, even
though this straw may not be very clean and fine. But
if the effort to limit this freedom of our lower nature
finds, as it does and must find, enemies in human nature,
it finds also auxiliaries in it. Out of the four great parts,
says Cicero, of the *honestum*, or good, which forms the
matter on which *officium*, or human duty, finds employment, one is the fixing of a *modus* and an *ordo*, a measure
and an order, to fashion and wholesomely constrain our
action, in order to lift it above the level it keeps if
left to itself, and to bring it nearer to perfection. Man
alone of living creatures, he says, goes feeling after
" *quid sit* ordo, *quid sit quod* deceat, *in factis dictisque
qui* modus "—the discovery of an *order*, a law of *good
taste*, a *measure* for his words and actions. Other creatures
submissively follow the law of their nature ; man alone
has an impulse leading him to set up some other law to
control the bent of his nature.

This holds good, of course, as to moral matters, as well
as intellectual matters : and it is of moral matters that
we are generally thinking when we affirm it. But it holds
good as to intellectual matters too. Now, probably,
M. Sainte-Beuve had not these words of Cicero in his
mind when he made, about the French nation, the
assertion I am going to quote ; but, for all that, the
assertion leans for support, one may say, upon the truth
conveyed in those words of Cicero, and wonderfully
illustrates and confirms them. "In France," says M.

Sainte-Beuve, "the first consideration for us is not whether we are amused and pleased by a work of art or mind, nor is it whether we are touched by it. What we seek above all to learn is, whether *we were right* in being amused with it, and in applauding it, and in being moved by it." Those are very remarkable words, and they are, I believe, in the main quite true. A Frenchman has, to a considerable degree, what one may call a conscience in intellectual matters; he has an active belief that there is a right and a wrong in them, that he is bound to honour and obey the right, that he is disgraced by cleaving to the wrong. All the world has, or professes to have, this conscience in moral matters. The word *conscience* has become almost confined, in popular use, to the moral sphere, because this lively susceptibility of feeling is, in the moral sphere, so far more common than in the intellectual sphere; the livelier, in the moral sphere, this susceptibility is, the greater becomes a man's readiness to admit a high standard of action, an ideal authoritatively correcting his everyday moral habits; here, such willing admission of authority is due to sensitiveness of conscience. And a like deference to a standard higher than one's own habitual standard in intellectual matters, a like respectful recognition of a superior ideal, is caused, in the intellectual sphere, by sensitiveness of intelligence. Those whose intelligence is quickest, openest, most sensitive, are readiest with this deference; those whose intelligence is less delicate and sensitive are less disposed to it. Well, now we are on the road to see why the French have their Academy and we have nothing of the kind.

What are the essential characteristics of the spirit of our nation ? Not, certainly, an open and clear mind, not a quick and flexible intelligence. Our greatest admirers would not claim for us that we have these in a pre-eminent degree ; they might say that we had more of them than our detractors gave us credit for ; but they would not assert them to be our essential characteristics. They would rather allege, as our chief spiritual characteristics, energy and honesty ; and, if we are judged favourably and positively, not invidiously and negatively, our chief characteristics are, no doubt, these ;—energy and honesty, not an open and clear mind, not a quick and flexible intelligence. Openness of mind and flexibility of intelligence were very signal characteristics of the Athenian people in ancient times ; everybody will feel that. Openness of mind and flexibility of intelligence are remarkable characteristics of the French people in modern times ; at any rate, they strikingly characterise them as compared with us ; I think everybody, or almost everybody, will feel that. I will not now ask what more the Athenian or the French spirit has than this, nor what shortcomings either of them may have as a set-off against this; all I want now to point out is that they have this, and that we have it in a much lesser degree.

Let me remark, however, that not only in the moral sphere, but also in the intellectual and spiritual sphere, energy and honesty are most important and fruitful qualities ; that, for instance, of what we call genius, energy is the most essential part. So, by assigning to a nation energy and honesty as its chief spiritual

characteristics,—by refusing to it, as at all eminent characteristics, openness of mind and flexibility of intelligence,—we do not by any means, as some people might
at first suppose, relegate its importance and its power
of manifesting itself with effect from the intellectual to
the moral sphere. We only indicate its probable special
line of successful activity in the intellectual sphere, and,
it is true, certain imperfections and failings to which, in
this sphere, it will always be subject. Genius is mainly
an affair of energy, and poetry is mainly an affair of
genius ; therefore, a nation whose spirit is characterised
by energy may well be eminent in poetry;—and we have
Shakspeare. Again, the highest reach of science is, one
may say, an inventive power, a faculty of divination, akin
to the highest power exercised in poetry ; therefore, a
nation whose spirit is characterised by energy may well
be eminent in science ;—and we have Newton. Shakspeare and Newton : in the intellectual sphere there can
be no higher names. And what that energy, which is
the life of genius, above everything demands and insists
upon, is freedom ; entire independence of all authority,
prescription, and routine,—the fullest room to expand as
it will. Therefore, a nation whose chief spiritual characteristic is energy, will not be very apt to set up, in intellectual matters, a fixed standard, an authority, like an
academy. By this it certainly escapes certain real incon-
veniences and dangers, and it can, at the same time, as
we have seen, reach undeniably splendid heights in
poetry and science. On the other hand, some of the
requisites of intellectual work are specially the affair of
quickness of mind and flexibility of intelligence. The

form, the method of evolution, the precision, the proportions, the relations of the parts to the whole, in an intellectual work, depend mainly upon them. And these are the elements of an intellectual work which are really most communicable from it, which can most be learned and adopted from it, which have, therefore, the greatest effect upon the intellectual performance of others. Even in poetry, these requisites are very important; and the poetry of a nation, not eminent for the gifts on which they depend, will, more or less, suffer by this short-coming. In poetry, however, they are, after all, secondary, and energy is the first thing; but in prose they are of first-rate importance. In its prose literature, therefore, and in the routine of intellectual work generally, a nation, with no particular gifts for these, will not be so successful. These are what, as I have said, can to a certain degree be learned and appropriated, while the free activity of genius cannot. Academies consecrate and maintain them, and, therefore, a nation with an eminent turn for them naturally establishes academies. So far as routine and authority tend to embarrass energy and inventive genius, academies may be said to be obstructive to energy and inventive genius, and, to this extent, to the human spirit's general advance. But then this evil is so much compensated by the propagation, on a large scale, of the mental aptitudes and demands which an open mind and a flexible intelligence naturally engender, genius itself, in the long run, so greatly finds its account in this propagation, and bodies like the French Academy have such power for promoting it, that the general advance of the human spirit is perhaps, on the whole, rather furthered than impeded by their existence.

How much greater is our nation in poetry than prose ! how much better, in general, do the productions of its spirit show in the qualities of genius than in the qualities of intelligence ! One may constantly remark this in the work of individuals ; how much more striking, in general, does any Englishman,—of some vigour of mind, but by no means a poet,—seem in his verse than in his prose ! No doubt his verse suffers from the same defects which impair his prose, and he cannot express himself with real success in it ; but how much more powerful a per- sonage does he appear in it, by dint of feeling, and of originality and movement of ideas, than when he is writing prose ! With a Frenchman of like stamp, it is just the reverse : set him to write poetry, he is limited, artificial, and impotent ; set him to write prose, he is free, natural, and effective.   The power of French litera- ture is in its prose-writers, the power of English literature is in its poets.   Nay, many of the celebrated French poets depend wholly for their fame upon the qualities of intelligence which they exhibit,—qualities which are the distinctive support of prose ; many of the celebrated English prose-writers depend wholly for their fame upon the qualities of genius and imagination which they exhibit, —qualities which are the distinctive support of poetry. But, as I have said, the qualities of genius are less trans- ferable than the qualities of intelligence ; less can be immediately learned and appropriated from their product ; they are less direct and stringent intellectual agencies, though they may be more beautiful and divine.   Shakspeare and our great Elizabethan group were certainly more gifted writers than Corneille and his group; but what was the sequel to this great literature, this literature of genius, as we may call it, stretching from Marlow to Milton? What did it lead up to in English literature? To our provincial and second-rate literature of the eighteenth century. What, on the other hand, was the sequel to the literature of the French "great century," to this literature of intelligence, as, by comparison with our Elizabethan literature, we may call it; what did it lead up to? To the French literature of the eighteenth century, one of the most powerful and pervasive intellectual agencies that have ever existed, the greatest European force of the eighteenth century. In science again, we had Newton, a genius of the very highest order, a type of genius in science, if ever there was one. On the continent, as a sort of counterpart to Newton, there was Leibnitz; a man, it seems to me (though on these matters I speak under correction), of much less creative energy of genius, much less power of divination than Newton, but rather a man of admirable intelligence, a type of intelligence in science, if ever there was one. Well, and what did they each directly lead up to in science? What was the intellectual generation that sprang from each of them? I only repeat what the men of science have themselves pointed out. The man of genius was continued by the English analysts of the eighteenth century, comparatively powerless and obscure followers of the renowned master; the man of intelligence was continued by successors like Bernouilli, Euler, Lagrange, and Laplace, the greatest names in modern mathematics.

What I want the reader to see is, that the question as to the utility of academies to the intellectual life of a nation is not settled when we say, for instance : " Oh, we have never had an academy, and yet we have, confessedly, a very great literature." It still remains to be asked: " What sort of a great literature ? a literature great in the special qualities of genius, or great in the special qualities of intelligence ?" If in the former, it is by no means sure that either our literature, or the general intellectual life of our nation, has got already, without academies, all that academies can give. Both the one and the other may very well be somewhat wanting in those qualities of intelligence, out of a lively sense for which a body like the French Academy, as I have said, springs, and which such a body does a great deal to spread and confirm. Our literature, in spite of the genius manifested in it, may fall short in form, method, precision, proportions, arrangement,—all of them, I have said, things where intelligence proper comes in. It may be comparatively weak in prose, that branch of literature where intelligence proper is, so to speak, all in all. In this branch it may show many grave faults to which the want of a quick, flexible intelligence, and of the strict standard which such an intelligence tends to impose, makes it liable; it may be full of hap-hazard, crudeness, provincialism, eccentricity, violence, blundering. It may be a less stringent and effective intellectual agency, both upon our own nation and upon the world at large, than other literatures which show less genius, perhaps, but more intelligence.

The right conclusion certainly is that we should try,

so far as we can, to make up our shortcomings ; and that to this end, instead of always fixing our thoughts upon the points in which our literature, and our intellectual life generally, are strong, we should, from time to time, fix them upon those in which they are weak, and so learn to perceive clearly what we have to amend.   What is our second great spiritual characteristic,—our honesty, —good for, if it is not good for this ?   But it will,— I am sure it will,—more and more, as time goes on, be found good for this.

Well, then, an institution like the French Academy,— an institution owing its existence to a national bent to- wards the things of the mind, towards culture, towards clearness, correctness, and propriety in thinking and speaking, and, in its turn, promoting this bent,—sets standards in a number of directions, and creates, in all these directions, a force of educated opinion, checking and rebuking those who fall below these standards, or who set them at nought.   Educated opinion exists here as in France ; but in France the Academy serves as a sort of centre and rallying-point to it, and gives it a force which it has not got here.   Why is all the *journey-man-work* of literature, as I may call it, so much worse done here than it is in France ?   I do not wish to hurt any one's feelings ; but surely this is so.   Think of the difference between our books of reference and those of the French, between our biographical dictionaries (to take a striking instance) and theirs ; think of the dif- ference between the translations of the classics turned out for Mr. Bohn's library and those turned out for M. Nisard's collection !   As a general rule, hardly any

one amongst us, who knows French and German well,
would use an English book of reference when he could
get a French or German one; or would look at an
English prose translation of an ancient author when he
could get a French or German one.   It is not that there
do not exist in England, as in France, a number of
people perfectly well able to discern what is good, in
these things, from what is bad, and preferring what is
good; but they are isolated, they form no powerful
body of opinion, they are not strong enough to set a
standard, up to which even the journeyman-work of
literature must be brought, if it is to be vendible.
Ignorance and charlatanism in work of this kind are
always trying to pass off their wares as excellent, and to
cry down criticism as the voice of an insignificant, over-
fastidious minority; they easily persuade the multitude
that this is so when the minority is scattered about as it
is here; not so easily when it is banded together as in
the French Academy.   So, again, with freaks in dealing
with language; certainly all such freaks tend to impair
the power and beauty of language; and how far more
common they are with us than with the French!   To
take a very familiar instance.   Every one has noticed
the way in which the *Times* chooses to spell the word
" diocese;" it always spells it dioce*ss*, deriving it, I
suppose, from *Zeus* and *census*.   The *Journal des Débats*
might just as well write " diocess " instead of " diocèse,"
but imagine the *Journal des Débats* doing so!   Imagine
an educated Frenchman indulging himself in an ortho-
graphical antic of this sort, in face of the grave respect
with which the Academy and its dictionary invest the

French language! Some people will say these are little
things; they are not; they are of bad example. They
tend to spread the baneful notion that there is no such
thing as a high, correct standard in intellectual matters;
that every one may as well take his own way; they are
at variance with the severe discipline necessary for all
real culture; they confirm us in habits of wilfulness and
eccentricity, which hurt our minds, and damage our
credit with serious people. The late Mr. Donaldson
was certainly a man of great ability, and I, who am not
an Orientalist, do not pretend to judge his *Jashar;* but
let the reader observe the form which a foreign Orientalist's judgment of it naturally takes. M. Renan calls
it a *tentative malheureuse*, a failure, in short; this it may
be, or it may not be; I am no judge. But he goes on:
"It is astonishing that a recent article" (in a French
periodical, he means) "should have brought forward as
the last word of German exegesis a work like this,
composed by a doctor of the University of Cambridge,
and universally condemned by German critics." You
see what he means to imply: an extravagance of this
sort could never have come from Germany, where there
is a great force of critical opinion controlling a learned
man's vagaries, and keeping him straight; it comes from
the native home of intellectual eccentricity of all kinds,*
—from England, from a doctor of the University of

---

* A critic declares I am wrong in saying that M. Renan's language
implies this. I still think that there is a shade, a *nuance* of expression, in M. Renan's language, which does imply this; but, I confess,
the only person who can really settle such a question is M. Renan
himself.

Cambridge ;—and I daresay he would not expect much
better things from a doctor of the University of Oxford.
Again, after speaking of what Germany and France
have done for the history of Mahomet : " America and
England," M. Renan goes on, " have also occupied
themselves with Mahomet." He mentions Washington
Irving's " Life of Mahomet," which does not, he says,
evince much of an historical sense, a *sentiment historique
fort élevé;* " but," he proceeds, " this book shows a real
progress, when one thinks that in 1829 Mr. Charles
Forster published two thick volumes, which enchanted
the English *reverends*, to make out that Mahomet was
the little horn of the he-goat that figures in the eighth
chapter of Daniel, and that the Pope was the great
horn. Mr. Forster founded on this ingenious parallel a
whole philosophy of history, according to which the
Pope represented the Western corruption of Christianity,
and Mahomet the Eastern ; thence the striking resem-
blances between Mahometanism and Popery." And in
a note M. Renan adds : " This is the same Mr. Charles
Forster who is the author of a mystification about the
Sinaitic inscriptions, in which he declares he finds the
primitive language." As much as to say : " It is an
Englishman, be surprised at no extravagance." If these
innuendoes had no ground, and were made in hatred
and malice, they would not be worth a moment's attention ;
but they come from a grave Orientalist, on his own
subject, and they point to a real fact ;—the absence, in
this country, of any force of educated literary and
scientific opinion, making aberrations like those of the
author of *The One Primeval Language* out of the

question.   Not only the author of such aberrations, often a very clever man, suffers by the want of check, by the not being kept straight, and spends force in vain on a false road, which, under better discipline, he might have used with profit on a true one; but all his adherents, both " reverends " and others, suffer too, and the general rate of information and judgment is in this way kept low.

In a production which we have all been reading lately, a production stamped throughout with a literary quality very rare in this country, and of which I shall have a word to say presently,—*urbanity;* in this production, the work of a man never to be named by any son of Oxford without sympathy, a man who alone in Oxford of his generation, alone of many generations, conveyed to us in his genius that same charm, that same ineffable senti-ment, which this exquisite place itself conveys,—I mean Dr. Newman,—an expression is frequently used which is more common in theological than in literary language, but which seems to me fitted to be of general service; the *note* of so and so, the note of catholicity, the note of antiquity, the note of sanctity, and so on.   Adopting this expressive word, I say that in the bulk of the intellectual work of a nation which has no centre, no intellectual metropolis like an academy, like M. Sainte-Beuve's " sovereign organ of opinion," like M. Renan's "re-cognised authority in matters of tone and taste,"—there is observable a *note of provinciality.*   Now to get rid of provinciality is a certain stage of culture; a stage the positive result of which we must not make of too much importance, but which is, nevertheless, indispensable;

for it brings us on to the platform where alone the best and highest intellectual work can be said fairly to begin. Work done after men have reached this platform is *classical;* and that is the only work which, in the long run, can stand. All the *scoriæ* in the work of men of great genius who have not lived on this platform, are due to their not having lived on it. Genius raises them to it by moments, and the portions of their work which are immortal are done at these moments; but more of it would have been immortal if they had not reached this platform at moments only, if they had had the culture which makes men live there.

The less a literature has felt the influence of a supposed centre of correct information, correct judgment, correct taste, the more we shall find in it this note of provinciality. I have shown the note of provinciality as caused by remoteness from a centre of correct information. Of course, the note of provinciality from the want of a centre of correct taste is still more visible, and it is also still more common. For here great,—even the greatest,— powers of mind most fail a man. Great powers of mind will make him inform himself thoroughly, great powers of mind will make him think profoundly, even with ignorance and platitude all round him; but not even great powers of mind will keep his taste and style per- fectly sound and sure, if he is left too much to himself, with no "sovereign organ of opinion," in these matters, near him. Even men like Jeremy Taylor and Burke suffer here. Take this passage from Taylor's funeral sermon on Lady Carbery :—

"So have I seen a river, deep and smooth, passing

with a still foot and a sober face, and paying to the *fiscus*, the great exchequer of the sea, a tribute large and full ; and hard by it, a little brook, skipping and making a noise upon its unequal and neighbour bottom ; and after all its talking and bragged motion, it paid to its common audit no more than the revenues of a little cloud or a contemptible vessel : so have I sometimes compared the issues of her religion to the solemnities and famed outsides of another's piety."

That passage has been much admired, and, indeed, the genius in it is undeniable. I should say, for my part, that genius, the ruling divinity of poetry, had been too busy in it, and intelligence, the ruling divinity of prose, not busy enough. But can any one, with the best models of style in his head, help feeling the note of provinciality there, the want of simplicity, the want of measure, the want of just the qualities that make prose classical ? If he does not feel what I mean, let him place beside the passage of Taylor this passage from the Panegyric of St. Paul, by Taylor's contemporary, Bossuet :—

" Il ira, cet ignorant dans l'art de bien dire, avec cette locution rude, avec cette phrase qui sent l'étranger, il ira en cette Grèce polie, la mère des philosophes et des orateurs ; et malgré la résistance du monde, il y établira plus d'Églises que Platon n'y a gagné de disciples par cette éloquence qu'on a crue divine."

There we have prose without the note of provinciality, —classical prose, prose of the centre.

Or take Burke, our greatest English prose-writer, as I think ; take expressions like this :—

" Blindfold themselves, like bulls that shut their eyes

when they push, they drive, by the point of their bayonets, their slaves, blindfolded, indeed, no worse than their lords, to take their fictions for currencies, and to swallow down paper pills by thirty-four millions sterling at a dose."

Or this :—

"They used it" (the royal name) "as a sort of navel-string, to nourish their unnatural offspring from the bowels of royalty itself.   Now that the monster can purvey for its own subsistence, it will only carry the mark about it, as a token of its having torn the womb it came from."

Or this :—

"Without one natural pang, he" (Rosseau) "casts away, as a sort of offal and excrement, the spawn of his disgustful amours, and sends his children to the hospital of foundlings."

Or this :—

"I confess, I never liked this continual talk of resistance and revolution, or the practice of making the extreme medicine of the constitution its daily bread.   It renders the habit of society dangerously valetudinary ; it is taking periodical doses of mercury sublimate, and swallowing down repeated provocatives of cantharides to our love of liberty."

I say, that is extravagant prose ; prose too much suffered to indulge its caprices ; prose at too great a distance from the centre of good taste ; prose, in short, with the note of provinciality.   People may reply, it is rich and imaginative ; yes, that is just it, it is *Asiatic* prose, as the ancient critics would have said ; prose somewhat barbarously rich and overloaded.   But the true prose is Attic prose.

Well, but Addison's prose is Attic prose. Where, then, it may be asked, is the note of provinciality in Addison? I answer, in the commonplace of his ideas.* This is a matter worth remarking. Addison claims to take leading rank as a moralist. To do that, you must have ideas of the first order on your subject,—the best ideas, at any rate, attainable in your time,—as well as be able to express them in a perfectly sound and sure style. Else you show your distance from the centre of ideas by your matter; you are provincial by your matter, though you may not be provincial by your style. It is comparatively a small matter to express oneself well, if one will be content with not expressing much, with expressing only trite ideas; the problem is to express new and profound ideas in a perfectly sound and classical style. He is the true classic, in every age, who does that. Now Addison has not, on his subject of morals, the force of ideas of the moralists of the first class,—the classical moralists;

* A critic says this is paradoxical, and urges that many second-rate French academicians have uttered the most commonplace ideas possible. I detest paradox, and I agree that many second-rate French academicians have uttered the most commonplace ideas possible; but Addison is not a second-rate man. He is a man of the order, I will not say of Pascal, but, at any rate, of La Bruyère and Vauvenargues; why does he not equal them? I say, because of the medium in which he finds himself, the atmosphere in which he lives and works; an atmosphere which tells unfavourably, or rather *tends* to tell unfavourably (for that is the truer way of putting it) either upon style or else upon ideas; tends to make even a man of great ability either a Mr. Carlyle or else a Lord Macaulay.

It is to be observed, however, that Lord Macaulay's style has in its turn suffered by his failure in ideas, and this cannot be said of Addison's.

he has not the best ideas attainable in or about his time, and which were, so to speak, in the air then, to be seized by the finest spirits ; he is not to be compared, for power, searchingness, or delicacy of thought, to Pascal, or La Bruyère, or Vauvenargues; he is rather on a level, in this respect, with a man like Marmontel; therefore, I say, he has the note of provinciality as a moralist; he is provincial by his matter, though not by his style.

To illustrate what I mean by an example. Addison, writing as a moralist on fixedness in religious faith, says :—

"Those who delight in reading books of controversy do very seldom arrive at a fixed and settled habit of faith.   The doubt which was laid revives again, and shows itself in new difficulties ; and that generally for this reason, — because the mind, which is perpetually tossed in controversies and disputes, is apt to forget the reasons which had once set it at rest, and to be disquieted with any former perplexity when it appears in a new shape, or is started by a different hand."

It may be said, that is classical English, perfect in lucidity, measure, and propriety.   I make no objection ; but, in my turn, I say that the idea expressed is perfectly trite and barren, and that it is a note of provinciality in Addison, in a man whom a nation puts forward as one of its great moralists, to have no profounder and more striking idea to produce on this great subject.   Compare, on the same subject, these words of a moralist really of the first order, really at the centre by his ideas,—Joubert :—

" L'expérience de beaucoup d'opinions donne à l'esprit

beaucoup de flexibilité, et l'affermit dans celles qu'il croit les meilleures."

With what a flash of light that touches the subject! how it sets us thinking! what a genuine contribution to moral science it is!

In short, where there is no centre like an academy, if you have genius and powerful ideas, you are apt not to have the best style going; if you have precision of style and not genius, you are apt not to have the best ideas going.

The provincial spirit, again, exaggerates the value of its ideas, for want of a high standard at hand by which to try them.   Or rather, for want of such a standard, it gives one idea too much prominence at the expense of others; it orders its ideas amiss; it is hurried away by fancies; it likes and dislikes too passionately, too exclusively.   Its admiration weeps hysterical tears, and its disapprobation foams at the mouth.   So we get the *eruptive* and the *aggressive* manner in literature; the former prevails most in our criticism, the latter in our newspapers.   For, not having the lucidity of a large and centrally placed intelligence, the provincial spirit has not its graciousness; it does not persuade, it makes war; it has not urbanity, the tone of the city, of the centre, the tone which always aims at a spiritual and intellectual effect, and not excluding the use of banter, never disjoins banter itself from politeness, from felicity.   But the provincial tone is more violent, and seems to aim rather at an effect upon the blood and senses than upon the spirit and intellect; it loves hard-hitting rather than persuading.   The newspaper, with its party spirit, its thorough-goingness, its resolute avoidance of shades and distinctions, its short, highly-charged, heavy-shotted articles, its style so unlike that style *lenis minimèque pertinax*,—easy and not too violently insisting,—which the ancients so much admired, is its true literature; the provincial spirit likes in the newspaper just what makes the newspaper such bad food for it,—just what made Goethe say, when he was pressed hard about the immorality of Byron's poems, that, after all, they were not so immoral as the newspapers. The French talk of the *brutalité des journaux anglais*. What strikes them comes from the necessary inherent tendencies of newspaper-writing not being checked in England by any centre of intelligent and urbane spirit, but rather stimulated by coming in contact with a provincial spirit. Even a newspaper like the *Saturday Review*, that old friend of all of us, a newspaper expressly aiming at an immunity from the common newspaper-spirit, aiming at being a sort of organ of reason,—and, by thus aiming, it merits great gratitude and has done great good,—even the *Saturday Review*, replying to some foreign criticism on our precautions against invasion, falls into a strain of this kind :—

"To do this" (to take these precautions) "seems to us eminently worthy of a great nation, and to talk of it as unworthy of a great nation, seems to us eminently worthy of a great fool."

There is what the French mean when they talk of the *brutalité des journaux anglais*; there is a style certainly as far removed from urbanity as possible,—a style with what I call the note of provinciality. And the same note may not unfrequently be observed even in the ideas of this newspaper, full as it is of thought and cleverness : certain ideas allowed to become fixed ideas, to prevail too absolutely. I will not speak of the immediate present, but, to go a little while back, it had the critic who so disliked the Emperor of the French ; it had the critic who so disliked the subject of my present remarks —academies ; it had the critic who was so fond of the German element in our nation, and, indeed, everywhere ;. who ground his teeth if one said *Charlemagne*, instead of *Charles the Great*, and, in short, saw all things in Teutonism, as Malebranche saw all things in God. Certainly any one may fairly find faults in the Emperor Napoleon or in academies, and merit in the German element ; but it is a note of the provincial spirit not to hold ideas of this kind a little more easily, to be so devoured by them, to suffer them to become crotchets.

In England there needs a miracle of genius like Shakspeare's to produce balance of mind, and a miracle of intellectual delicacy like Dr. Newman's to produce urbanity of style. How prevalent all round us is the want of balance of mind and urbanity of style ! How much, doubtless, it is to be found in ourselves,—in each of us ! but, as human nature is constituted, every one can see it clearest in his contemporaries. There, above all, we should consider it, because they and we are exposed to the same influences ; and it is in the best of one's contemporaries that it is most worth considering, because one then most feels the harm it does, when one sees. what they would be without it. Think of the difference between Mr. Ruskin exercising his genius, and Mr. Ruskin exercising his intelligence ; consider the truth and beauty of this :—

"Go out, in the spring-time, among the meadows that slope from the shores of the Swiss lakes to the roots of their lower mountains. There, mingled with the taller gentians and the white narcissus, the grass grows deep and free ; and as you follow the winding mountain paths, beneath arching boughs all veiled and dim with blossom, —paths that for ever droop and rise over the green banks and mounds sweeping down in scented undulation, steep to the blue water, studded here and there with new-mown heaps, filling all the air with fainter sweetness,—look up towards the higher hills, where the waves of everlasting green roll silently into their long inlets among the shadows of the pines. . . . . ."

There is what the genius, the feeling, the temperament in Mr. Ruskin, the original and incommunicable part, has to do with ; and how exquisite it is ! All the critic could possibly suggest, in the way of objection, would be, perhaps, that Mr. Ruskin is there trying to make prose do more than it can perfectly do ; that what he is there attempting he will never, except in poetry, be able to accomplish to his own entire satisfaction : but he accomplishes so much that the critic may well hesitate to suggest even this. Place beside this charming passage another,—a passage about Shakspeare's names, where the intelligence and judgment of Mr. Ruskin, the acquired, trained, communicable part in him, are brought into play, —and see the difference :—

"Of Shakspeare's names I will afterwards speak at more length ; they are curiously—often barbarously—

mixed out of various traditions and languages. Three
of the clearest in meaning have been already noticed.
Desdemona—'δυσδαιμονία,' *miserable fortune*—is also
plain enough. Othello is, I believe, 'the careful;' all
the calamity of the tragedy arising from the single flaw
and error in his magnificently collected strength. Ophelia,
'serviceableness,' the true, lost wife of Hamlet, is marked
as having a Greek name by that of her brother, Laertes;
and its signification is once exquisitely alluded to in that
brother's last word of her, where her gentle preciousness
is opposed to the uselessness of the churlish clergy:—
'A *ministering* angel shall my sister be, when thou liest
howling.' Hamlet is, I believe, connected in some way
with 'homely,' the entire event of the tragedy turning on
betrayal of home duty. Hermione (ἕρμα), 'pillar-like'
(ἣ εἶδος ἔχε χρυσῆς Ἀφροδίτης); Titania (τιτήνη), 'the
queen'; Benedict and Beatrice, 'blessed and blessing';
Valentine and Proteus, 'enduring or strong' (*valens*),
and 'changeful.' Iago and Iachimo have evidently the
same root—probably the Spanish Iago, Jacob, 'the
supplanter.'"

Now, really, what a piece of extravagance all that is!
I will not say that the meaning of Shakspeare's names
(I put aside the question as to the correctness of Mr.
Ruskin's etymologies) has no effect at all, may be entirely
lost sight of; but to give it that degree of prominence is
to throw the reins to one's whim, to forget all modera-
tion and proportion, to lose the balance of one's mind
altogether. It is to show in one's criticism, to the highest
excess, the note of provinciality.

Again, there is Mr. Palgrave, certainly endowed with a

very fine critical tact; his *Golden Treasury* abundantly proves it. The plan of arrangement which he devised for that work, the mode in which he followed his plan out, nay, one might even say, merely the juxtaposition, in pursuance of it, of two such pieces as those of Wordsworth and Shelley which form the 285th and 286th in his collection, show a delicacy of feeling in these matters which is quite indisputable and very rare. And his notes are full of remarks which show it too. All the more striking, conjoined with so much justness of perception, are certain freaks and violences in Mr. Palgrave's criticism, mainly imputable, I think, to the critic's isolated position in this country, to his feeling himself too much left to take his own way, too much without any central authority representing high culture and sound judgment, by which he may be, on the one hand, confirmed as against the ignorant, on the other, held in respect when he himself is inclined to take liberties. I mean such things as this note on Milton's line,—

"The great Emathian conqueror bade spare" . . .

" When Thebes was destroyed, Alexander ordered the house of Pindar to be spared. *He was as incapable of appreciating the poet as Louis XIV. of appreciating Racine; but even the narrow and barbarian mind of Alexander could understand the advantage of a showy act of homage to poetry.*" A note like that I call a freak or a violence ; if this disparaging view of Alexander and Louis XIV., so unlike the current view, is wrong,—if the current view is, after all, the truer one of them,—the note is a freak. But, even if its disparaging view is right, the note is a violence; for, abandoning the true mode of intellectual action — persuasion, the instilment of conviction,—it simply astounds and irritates the hearer by contradicting without a word of proof or preparation, his fixed and familiar notions; and this is mere violence. In either case, the fitness, the measure, the centrality, which is the soul of all good criticism, is lost, and the note of provinciality shows itself.

Thus in the famous *Handbook*, marks of a fine power of perception are everywhere discernible, but so, too, are marks of the want of sure balance, of the check and support afforded by knowing one speaks before good and severe judges. When Mr. Palgrave dislikes a thing, he feels no pressure constraining him either to try his dislike closely or to express it moderately; he does not mince matters, he gives his dislike all its own way; both his judgment and his style would gain if he were under more restraint. "The style which has filled London with the dead monotony of Gower or Harley Streets, or the pale commonplace of Belgravia, Tyburnia and Kensington; which has pierced Paris and Madrid with the feeble frivolities of the Rue Rivoli and the Strada de Toledo." He dislikes the architecture of the Rue Rivoli, and he puts it on a level with the architecture of Belgravia and Gower Street; he lumps them all together in one condemnation, he loses sight of the shade, the distinction, which is everything here; the distinction, namely, that the architecture of the Rue Rivoli expresses show, splendour, pleasure,—unworthy things, perhaps, to express alone and for their own sakes, but it expresses them; whereas the architecture of Gower Street and

Belgravia merely expresses the impotence of the architect to express anything. Then, as to style : "sculpture which stands in a contrast with Woolner hardly more shameful than diverting," . . . "passing from Davy or Faraday to the art of the mountebank or the science of the spirit-rapper." . . . "it is the old, old story with Marochetti, the frog trying to blow himself out to bull dimensions. He may puff and be puffed, but he will never do it." We all remember that shower of amenities on poor M. Marochetti. Now, here Mr. Palgrave himself . enables us to form a contrast which lets us see just what the presence of an academy does for style ; for he quotes a criticism by M. Gustave Planche on this very M. Maro-chetti. M. Gustave Planche was a critic of the very first order, a man of strong opinions, which he expressed with severity; he, too, condemns M. Marochetti's work, and Mr. Palgrave calls him as a witness to back what he has himself said ; certainly Mr. Palgrave's translation will not exaggerate M. Planche's urbanity in dealing with M. Marochetti, but, even in this translation, see the difference in sobriety, in measure, between the critic writing in Paris and the critic writing in London :—

"These conditions are so elementary, that I am at a perfect loss to comprehend how M. Marochetti has neglected them. There are soldiers here like the leaden playthings of the nursery : it is almost impossible to guess whether there is a body beneath the dress. We have here no question of style, not even of grammar ; it is nothing beyond mere matter of the alphabet of art. To break these conditions is the same as to be ignorant of spelling."

That is really more formidable criticism than Mr. Palgrave's, and yet in how perfectly temperate a style ! M. Planche's advantage is, that he feels himself to be speaking before competent judges, that there is a force of cultivated opinion for him to appeal to.   Therefore, he must not be extravagant, and he need not storm; he must satisfy the reason and taste,—that is his business. Mr. Palgrave, on the other hand, feels himself to be speaking before a promiscuous multitude, with the few good judges so scattered through it as to be powerless; therefore, he has no calm confidence and no self-control ; he relies on the strength of his lungs ; he knows that big words impose on the mob, and that, even if he is out-rageous, most of his audience are apt to be a great deal more so.*

Again, the most successful English book of last season was certainly Mr. Kinglake's *Invasion of the Crimea.*   Its style was one of the most renowned things about it, and yet how conspicuous a fault in Mr. Kinglake's style is this over-charge of which I have been speaking ! Mr. James Gordon Bennett, of the *New York Herald,* says, I believe, that the highest achievement of the human intellect is what he calls "a good editorial." This is not quite so; but, if it were so, on what a height would Mr. Kinglake stand ! I have already spoken of the Attic and the Asiatic styles ; besides these, there is the Corinthian style. That is the style for "a good editorial," and Mr. Kinglake has really reached perfec-

* When I wrote this I had before me the first edition of Mr. Palgrave's *Handbook.* I am bound to say that in the second edition much strong language has been expunged, and what remains, softened.

tion in it. It has not the warm glow, blithe movement, and soft pliancy of life, as the Attic style has ; it has not the over-heavy richness and encumbered gait of the Asiatic style ; it has glitter without warmth, rapidity without ease, effectiveness without charm. Its characteristic is, that it has no soul ; all it exists for, is to get its ends, to make its points, to damage its adversaries, to be admired, to triumph. "His features put on that glow which, seen in men of his race—race known by the kindling gray eye, and the light, stubborn, crisping hair —discloses the rapture of instant fight." How glittering that is, but how perfectly frosty ! "There was a salient point of difference between the boulevards and the hillsides of the Alma. The Russians were armed." How trenchant that is, but how perfectly unscrupulous ! This is the Corinthian style ; the glitter of the East with the hardness of the West ; "the passion for tinsel,"—some one, himself a Corinthian, said of Mr. Kinglake's style,— "of a sensuous Jew, with the savage spleen of a dyspeptic Englishman." I do not say this of Mr. Kinglake's style, —I am very far from saying it. To say it is to fall into just that hard, brassy, over-stretched style which Mr. Kinglake himself employs so far too much, and which I, for my part, reprobate. But when a brother Corinthian of Mr. Kinglake's says it, I feel what he means.

A style so bent on effect at the expense of soul, simplicity, and delicacy ; a style so little studious of the charm of the great models ; so far from classic truth and grace, must surely be said to have the note of provinciality. Yet Mr. Kinglake's talent is a really eminent one, and so in harmony with our intellectual habits and tendencies, that, to the great bulk of English people, the faults of his style seem its merits; all the more needful that criticism should not be dazzled by them, but should try closely this, the form of his work. The matter of the work is a separate thing; and, indeed, this has been, I believe, withdrawn from discussion, Mr. Kinglake declaring that this must and shall stay as it is, and that he is resolved, like Pontius Pilate, to stand by what he has written. And here, I must say, he seems to me to be quite right. On the breast of the huge Mississippi of falsehood called *history*, a foam-bell more or less is of no consequence. But he may, at any rate, ease and soften his style.

We must not compare a man of Mr. Kinglake's literary talent with writers like M. de Bazancourt. We must compare him with M. Thiers. And what a superiority in style has M. Thiers from being formed in a good school, with severe traditions, wholesome restraining influences ! Even in this age of Mr. James Gordon Bennett, his style has nothing Corinthian about it; its lightness and brightness make it almost Attic. It is not quite Attic, however; it has not the infallible sureness of Attic taste. Sometimes his head gets a little hot with the fumes of patriotism, and then he crosses the line, he loses perfect measure, he declaims, he raises a momentary smile. France condemned "à être l'effroi du monde *dont elle pourrait être l'amour*,"—Cæsar, whose exquisite simplicity M. Thiers so admires, would not have written like that. There is, if I may be allowed to say so, the slightest possible touch of fatuity in such language,—of that failure in good sense which comes from too warm a self-satisfaction. But compare this language with Mr. Kinglake's Marshal St. Arnaud—"dismissed from the presence" of Lord Raglan or Lord Stratford, "cowed and pressed down" under their "stern reproofs," or under "the majesty of the great Elchi's Canning brow and tight, merciless lips!" The failure in good sense and good taste there reaches far beyond what the French mean by *fatuity;* they would call it by another word,—a word expressing blank defect of intelligence,—a word for which we have no exact equivalent in English ; *bête.* It is the difference between a venial, momentary, good-tempered excess, in a man of the world, of an amiable and social weakness,— vanity; and a serious, settled, fierce, narrow, provincial misconception of the whole relative value of one's own things and the things of others. So baneful to the style of even the cleverest man may be the total want of checks.

In all I have said, I do not pretend that the examples given prove my rule as to the influence of academies; they only illustrate it. Examples in plenty might very likely be found to set against them ; the truth of the rule depends, no doubt, on whether the balance of all the examples is in its favour or not ; but actually to strike this balance is always out of the question. Here, as every- where else, the rule, the idea, if true, commends itself to the judicious, and then the examples make it clearer still to them. This is the real use of examples, and this alone is the purpose which I have meant mine to serve. There is also another side to the whole question,—as to the limiting and prejudicial operation which academies may have ; but this side of the question it rather behoves the French, not us, to study.

The reader will ask for some practical conclusion about the establishment of an Academy in this country, and perhaps I shall hardly give him the one he expects. But nations have their own modes of acting, and these modes are not easily changed; they are even consecrated, when great things have been done in them. When a literature has produced Shakspeare and Milton, when it has even produced Barrow and Burke, it cannot well abandon its traditions; it can hardly begin, at this late time of day, with an institution like the French Academy. I think academies with a limited, special, scientific scope, in the various lines of intellectual work,—academies like that of Berlin, for instance,—we with time may, and probably shall, establish. And no doubt they will do good; no doubt the presence of such influential centres of correct information will tend to raise the standard amongst us for what I have called the *journeyman-work* of literature, and to free us from the scandal of such biographical dictionaries as Chalmers's, or such translations as a recent one of Spinoza, or, perhaps, such philological freaks as Mr. Forster's about the one primeval language. But an academy quite like the French Academy, a sovereign organ of the highest literary opinion, a recognised authority in matters of intellectual tone and taste, we shall hardly have, and perhaps we ought not to wish to have it. But then every one amongst us with any turn for literature will do well to remember to what short-comings and excesses, which such an academy tends to correct, we are liable; and the more liable, of course, for not having it. He will do well constantly to try himself in respect of these, steadily to widen his culture, severely to check in himself the provincial spirit ; and he will do this the better the more he keeps in mind that all mere glorification by ourselves of ourselves or our literature, in the strain of what, at the beginning of these remarks, I quoted from Lord Macaulay, is both vulgar, and, besides being vulgar, retarding.

MAURICE DE GUÉRIN.

I WILL not presume to say that I now know the French
language well ; but at a time when I knew it even less
well than at present,—some fifteen years ago,—I remember
pestering those about me with this sentence, the rhythm
of which had lodged itself in my head, and which, with
the strangest pronunciation possible, I kept perpetually
declaiming : " Les dieux jaloux ont enfoui quelque part
les témoignages de la descendance des choses ; mais au
bord de quel Océan ont ils roulé la pierre qui les couvre,
ô Macarée ! "

These words come from a short composition called
the *Centaur*, of which the author, Georges-Maurice de
Guérin, died in the year 1839, at the age of twenty-
eight, without having published anything.   In 1840,
Madame Sand brought out the *Centaur* in the *Revue
des Deux Mondes*, with a short notice of its author, and a
few extracts from his letters.   A year or two afterwards
she reprinted these at the end of a volume of her novels ;
and there it was that I fell in with them.   I was so much
struck with the *Centaur* that I waited anxiously to hear
something more of its author, and of what he had left ;
but it was not till the other day—twenty years after the
first publication of the *Centaur* in the *Revue des Deux*

Mondes, that my anxiety was satisfied. At the end of
1860 appeared two volumes with the title, *Maurice de
Guérin, Reliquiæ*, containing the *Centaur*, several poems
of Guérin, his journals, and a number of his letters, collected and edited by a devoted friend, M. Trebutien, and
preceded by a notice of Guérin by the first of living
critics, M. Sainte-Beuve.

The grand power of poetry is its interpretative power ;
by which I mean, not a power of drawing out in black
and white an explanation of the mystery of the universe,
but the power of so dealing with things as to awaken in
us a wonderfully full, new, and intimate sense of them,
and of our relations with them. When this sense is
awakened in us, as to objects without us, we feel ourselves
to be in contact with the essential nature of those objects,
to be no longer bewildered and oppressed by them, but
to have their secret, and to be in harmony with them ;
and this feeling calms and satisfies us as no, other can.
Poetry, indeed, interprets in another way besides this ;
but one of its two ways of interpreting, of exercising its
highest power, is by awakening this sense in us. I will
not now inquire whether this sense is illusive, whether it
can be proved not to be illusive, whether it does absolutely make us possess the real nature of things ; all I
say is, that poetry can awaken it in us, and that to
awaken it is one of the highest powers of poetry. The
interpretations of science do not give us this intimate
sense of objects as the interpretations of poetry give it ;
they appeal to a limited faculty, and not to the whole
man. It is not Linnæus, or Cavendish, or Cuvier who
gives us the true sense of animals, or water, or plants,

who seizes their secret for us, who makes us participate
in their life ; it is Shakspeare, with his

> " daffodils
> That come before the swallow dares, and take
> The winds of March with beauty ; "

it is Wordsworth, with his

> " voice . . . heard
> In spring-time from the cuckoo-bird,
> Breaking the silence of the seas
> Among the farthest Hebrides ; "

it is Keats, with his

> "moving waters at their priestlike task
> Of cold ablution round Earth's human shores ; "

it is Chateaubriand, with his "*cîme indéterminée des forêts;*"
it is Senancour, with his mountain birch-tree : " *Cette écorce
blanche, lisse et crevassée; cette tige agreste; ces branches
qui s'inclinent vers la terre; la mobilité des feuilles, et tout
cet abandon, simplicité de la nature, attitude des déserts.*"

Eminent manifestations of this magical power of poetry
are very rare and very precious : the compositions of
Guérin manifest it, I think, in singular eminence.   Not
his poems, strictly so called,—his verse,—so much as his
prose ; his poems in general take for their vehicle that
favourite metre of French poetry, the Alexandrine ; and,
in my judgment, I confess they have thus, as compared
with his prose, a great disadvantage to start with.   In
prose, the character of the vehicle for the composer's
thoughts is not determined beforehand ; every composer
has to make his own vehicle ; and who has ever done this

more admirably than the great prose-writers of France,—
Pascal, Bossuet, Fénelon, Voltaire? But in verse the
composer has (with comparatively narrow liberty of
modification) to accept his vehicle ready-made; it is
therefore of vital importance to him that he should find
at his disposal a vehicle adequate to convey the highest
matters of poetry. We may even get a decisive test of
the poetical power of a language and nation by ascertain-
ing how far the principal poetical vehicle which they
have employed, how far (in plainer words) the established
national metre for high poetry, is adequate or inadequate.
It seems to me that the established metre of this kind
in France,—the Alexandrine,—is inadequate; that as a
vehicle for high poetry it is greatly inferior to the hexa-
meter 'or to the iambics of Greece (for example), or to
the blank verse of England. Therefore the man of
genius who uses it is at a disadvantage as compared
with the man of genius who has for conveying his
thoughts a more adequate vehicle, metrical or not.
Racine is at a disadvantage as compared with Sophocles
or Shakspeare, and he is likewise at a disadvantage as
compared with Bossuet. The same may be said of our
own poets of the eighteenth century, a century which
gave them as the main vehicle for their high poetry a
metre inadequate (as much as the French Alexandrine,
and nearly in the same way) for this poetry,—the ten-
syllable couplet. It is worth remarking, that the English
poet of the eighteenth century whose compositions wear
best and give one the most entire satisfaction,—Gray,—
does not use that couplet at all: this abstinence, however,
limits Gray's productions to a few short compositions,

and (exquisite as these are) he is a poetical nature repressed and without free issue. For English poetical production on a great scale, for an English poet deploying all the forces of his genius, the ten-syllable couplet was, in the eighteenth century, the established, one may almost say the inevitable, channel. Now this couplet, admirable (as Chaucer uses it) for story-telling not of the epic pitch, and often admirable for a few lines even in poetry of a very high pitch, is for continuous use in poetry of this latter kind inadequate. Pope, in his *Essay on Man*, is thus at a disadvantage compared with Lucretius in his poem on Nature : Lucretius has an adequate vehicle, Pope has not. Nay, though Pope's genius for didactic poetry was not less than that of Horace, while his satirical power was certainly greater, still one's taste receives, I cannot but think, a certain satisfaction when one reads the Epistles and Satires of Horace, which it fails to receive when one reads the Satires and Epistles of Pope. Of such avail is the superior adequacy of the vehicle used to compensate even an inferiority of genius in the user I In the same way Pope is at a disadvantage as compared with Addison : the best of Addison's composition (the " Coverley Papers " in the *Spectator*, for instance) wears better than the best of Pope's, because Addison has in his prose an intrinsically better vehicle for his genius than Pope in his couplet. But Bacon has no such advantage over Shakspeare ; nor has Milton, writing prose (for no contemporary English prose-writer must be matched with Milton except Milton himself), any such advantage over Milton writing verse : indeed, the advantage here is all the other way.

It is in the prose remains of Guérin,—his journals, his letters, and the striking composition which I have already mentioned, the *Centaur*,—that his extraordinary gift manifests itself. He has a truly interpretative faculty; the most profound and delicate sense of the life of Nature, and the most exquisite felicity in finding expressions to render that sense. To all who love poetry, Guérin deserves to be something more than a name; and I shall try, in spite of the impossibility of doing justice to such a master of expression by translations, to make my English readers see for themselves how gifted an organization his was, and how few artists have received from Nature a more magical faculty of interpreting her.

In the winter of the year 1832 there was collected in Brittany, around the well-known Abbé Lamennais, a singular gathering. At a lonely place, La Chênaie, he had founded a religious retreat, to which disciples, attracted by his powers or by his reputation, repaired. Some came with the intention of preparing themselves for the ecclesiastical profession; others merely to profit by the society and discourse of so distinguished a master. Among the inmates were men whose names have since become known to all Europe,—Lacordaire and M. de Montalembert; there were others, who have acquired a reputation, not European, indeed, but considerable,—the Abbé Gerbet, the Abbé Rohrbacher; others, who have never quitted the shade of private life. The winter of 1832 was a period of crisis in the religious world of France: Lamennais's rupture with Rome, the condemnation of his opinions by the Pope, and his revolt against that condemnation, were imminent. Some of his followers, like

Lacordaire, had already resolved not to cross the Rubicon with their leader, not to go into rebellion against Rome ; they were preparing to separate from him. The society of La Chênaie was soon to dissolve ; but, such as it is shown to us for a moment, with its voluntary character, its simple and severe life in common, its mixture of lay and clerical members, the genius of its chiefs, the sincerity of its disciples,—above all, its paramount fervent interest in matters of spiritual and religious concernment,—it offers a most instructive spectacle. It is not the spectacle we most of us think to find in France, the France we have imagined from common English notions, from the streets of Paris, from novels : it shows us how, wherever there is greatness like that of France, there are, as its foundation, treasures of fervour, pure-mindedness, and spirituality somewhere, whether we know of them or not ;—a store of that which Goethe calls *Halt ;*—since greatness can never be founded upon frivolity and corruption.

On the evening of the 18th of December in this year 1832, M. de Lamennais was talking to those assembled in the sitting-room of La Chênaie of his recent journey to Italy. He talked with all his usual animation ; " but," writes one of his hearers, a Breton gentleman, M. de Marzan, " I soon became inattentive and absent, being struck with the reserved attitude of a young stranger some twenty-two years old, pale in face, his black hair already thin over his temples, with a southern eye, in which brightness and melancholy were mingled. He kept himself somewhat aloof, seeming to avoid notice rather than to court it. All the old faces of friends which I found about me at this my re-entry into the circle of La

Chênaie, failed to occupy me so much as the sight of
this stranger, looking on, listening, observing, and saying
nothing."

The unknown was Maurice de Guérin. Of a noble
but poor family, having lost his mother at six years old,
he had been brought up by his father, a man saddened
by his wife's death, and austerely religious, at the château
of Le Cayla, in Languedoc. His childhood was not
gay; he had not the society of other boys; and solitude,
the sight of his father's gloom, and the habit of accompanying the curé of the parish on his rounds among the
sick and dying, made him prematurely grave and familiar
with sorrow. He went to school first at Toulouse, then
at the Collège Stanislas at Paris, with a temperament
almost as unfit as Shelley's for common school life. His
youth was ardent, sensitive, agitated, and unhappy. In
1832 he procured admission to La Chênaie to brace his
spirit by the teaching of Lamennais, and to decide
whether his religious feelings would determine themselves
into a distinct religious vocation. Strong and deep
religious feelings he had, implanted in him by nature,
developed in him by the circumstances of his childhood;
but he had also (and here is the key to his character)
that temperament which opposes itself to the fixedness
of a religious vocation, or of any vocation of which
fixedness is an essential attribute; a temperament
mobile, inconstant, eager, thirsting for new impressions,
abhorring rules, aspiring to a "renovation without end;"
a temperament common enough among artists, but with
which few artists, who have it to the same degree as
Guérin, unite a seriousness and a sad intensity like his.

After leaving school, and before going to La Chênaie,
he had been at home at Le Cayla with his sister Eugénie
(a wonderfully gifted person, whose genius so competent
a judge as M. Sainte-Beuve is inclined to pronounce
even superior to her brother's) and his sister Eugénie's
friends. With one of these friends he had fallen in love,
—a slight and transient fancy, but which had already
called his poetical powers into exercise ; and his poems
and fragments, in a certain green note-book (*le Cahier
Vert*) which he long continued to make the depository
of his thoughts, and which became famous among his
friends, he brought with him to La Chênaie. There he
found among the younger members of the Society several
who, like himself, had a secret passion for poetry and
literature ; with these he became intimate, and in his
letters and journal we find him occupied, now with a
literary commerce established with these friends, now
with the fortunes, fast coming to a crisis, of the Society,
and now with that for the sake of which he came to
La Chênaie,—his religious progress and the state of his
soul.

On Christmas-day, 1832, having then been three
weeks at La Chênaie, he writes thus of it to a friend
of his family, M. de Bayne :—

"La Chênaie is a sort of oasis in the midst of the
steppes of Brittany. In front of the château stretches
a very large garden, cut in two by a terrace with a lime
avenue, at the end of which is a tiny chapel. I am
extremely fond of this little oratory, where one breathes
a twofold peace,—the peace of solitude and the peace
of the Lord. When spring comes we shall walk to

prayers between two borders of flowers. On the east side, and only a few yards from the château, sleeps a small mere between two woods, where the birds in warm weather sing all day long; and then,—right, left, on all sides,—woods, woods, everywhere woods. It looks desolate just now that all is bare and the woods are rustcolour, and under this Brittany sky, which is always clouded and so low that it seems as if it were going to fall on your head; but as soon as spring comes the sky raises itself up, the woods come to life again, and everything will be full of charm."

Of what La Chênaie will be when spring comes he has a foretaste on the 3d of March.

"To-day" (he writes in his journal) "has enchanted me. For the first time for a long while the sun has shown himself in all his beauty. He has made the buds of the leaves and flowers swell, and he has waked up in me a thousand happy thoughts. The clouds assume more and more their light and graceful shapes, and are sketching, over the blue sky, the most charming fancies. The woods have not yet got their leaves, but they are taking an indescribable air of life and gaiety, which gives them quite a new physiognomy. Everything is getting ready for the great festival of Nature."

Storm and snow adjourn this festival a little longer. On the 11th of March he writes :—

" It has snowed all night. I have been to look at our primroses; each of them had its small load of snow, and was bowing its head under its burden. These pretty flowers, with their rich yellow colour, had a charming effect under their white hoods. I saw whole

tufts of them roofed over by a single block of snow; all
these laughing flowers thus shrouded and leaning one
upon another, made one think of a group of young
girls surprised by a wave, and sheltering under a white
cloth."

The burst of spring comes at last, though late. On
the 5th of April we find Guérin "sitting in the sun to
penetrate himself to the very marrow with the divine
spring." On the 3d of May, "one can actually *see* the
progress of the green; it has made a start from the
garden to the shrubberies, it is getting the upper hand
all along the mere; it leaps, one may say, from tree to
tree, from thicket to thicket, in the fields and on the
hill-sides; and I can see it already arrived at the forest ·
edge and beginning to spread itself over the broad back
of the forest. Soon it will have overrun everything as far
as the eye can reach, and all those wide spaces between
here and the horizon will be moving and sounding like
one vast sea, a sea of emerald."

Finally, on the 16th of May, he writes to M. de Bayne
that "the gloomy and bad days,—bad because they bring
temptation by their gloom,—are, thanks to God and the
spring, over; and I see approaching a long file of shining
and happy days, to do me all the good in the world.
This Brittany of ours," he continues, "gives one the idea
of the greyest and most wrinkled old woman possible
suddenly changed back by the touch of a fairy's wand
into a girl of twenty, and one of the loveliest in the
world; the fine weather has so decked and beautified the
dear old country." He felt, however, the cloudiness and
cold of the "dear old country" with all the sensitiveness

of a child of the South. "What a difference," he cries, "between the sky of Brittany, even on the finest day, and the sky of our South ! Here the summer has, even on its highdays and holidays, something mournful, overcast, and stinted about it. It is like a miser who is making a show; there is a niggardliness in his magnificence. Give me our Languedoc sky, so bountiful of light, so blue, so largely vaulted !" And somewhat later, complaining of the short and dim sunlight of a February day in Paris, "What a sunshine," he exclaims, "to gladden eyes accustomed to all the wealth of light of the South ! —*aux larges et libérales effusions de lumière du ciel du Midi.*"

In the long winter of La Chênaie his great resource was literature. One has often heard that an educated Frenchman's reading seldom goes much beyond French and Latin, and that he makes the authors in these two languages his sole literary standard. This may or may not be true of Frenchmen in general, but there can be no question as to the width of the reading of Guérin and his friends, and as to the range of their literary sympathies. One of the circle, Hippolyte la Morvonnais,—a poet who published a volume of verse, and died in the prime of life,—had a passionate admiration for Wordsworth, and had even, it is said, made a pilgrimage to Rydal Mount to visit him ; and in Guérin's own reading I find, besides the French names of Bernardin de St. Pierre, Chateaubriand, Lamartine, and Victor Hugo, the names of Homer, Dante, Shakspeare, Milton, and Goethe ; and he quotes both from Greek and from English authors in the original. His literary tact is beautifully fine and true.

" Every poet," he writes to his sister, "has his own art of
poetry written on the ground of his own soul ; there is no
other. Be constantly observing Nature in her smallest
details, and then write as the current of your thoughts
guides you ;—that is all." But with all this freedom from
the bondage of forms and rules, Guérin marks with perfect
precision the faults of the *free* French literature of his
time,—the *littérature facile*,—and judges the romantic
school and its prospects like a master : " that youthful
literature which has put forth all its blossom prematurely,
and has left itself a helpless prey to the returning frost,
stimulated as it has been by the burning sun of our
century, by this atmosphere charged with a perilous heat,
which has over-hastened every sort of development, and
will most likely reduce to a handful of grains the harvest
of our age." And the popular authors,—those " whose
name appears once and disappears for ever, whose books,
unwelcome to all serious people, welcome to the rest of
the world, to novelty-hunters and novel-readers, fill with
vanity these vain souls, and then, falling from hands
heavy with the languor of satiety, drop for ever into the
gulf of oblivion ;" and those, more noteworthy, " the
writers of books celebrated, and, as works of art, deserving celebrity, but which have in them not one grain of
that hidden manna, not one of those sweet and wholesome thoughts which nourish the human soul and refresh
it when it is weary,"—these he treats with such severity
that he may in some sense be described, as he describes
himself, as " invoking with his whole heart a classical
restoration." He is best described, however, not as a
partisan of any school, but as an ardent seeker for that

mode of expression which is the most natural, happy, and true.   He writes to his sister Eugénie :—

" I want you to reform your system of composition ; it is too loose, too vague, too Lamartinian.   Your verse is too sing-song ; it does not *talk* enough.   Form for yourself a style of your own, which shall be your real expression.   Study the French language by attentive reading, making it your care to remark constructions, turns of expression, delicacies of style, but without ever adopting the manner of any master.   In the works of these masters we must learn our language, but we must use it each in our own fashion."*

It was not, however, to perfect his literary judgment that Guérin came to La Chênaie.   The religious feeling, which was as much a part of his essence as the passion for Nature and the literary instinct, shows itself at moments jealous of these its rivals, and alarmed at their predominance.   Like all powerful feelings, it wants to exclude every other feeling and to be absolute.   One Friday in April, after he has been delighting himself with the shapes of the clouds and the progress of the spring, he suddenly bethinks himself that the day is Good Friday, and exclaims in his diary :—

" My God, what is my soul about that it can thus go running after such fugitive delights on Good Friday, on this day all filled with thy death and our redemption 1 There is in me I know not what damnable spirit, that

* Part of these extracts date from a time a little after Guérin's residence at La Chênaie; but already, amidst the readings and conversations of La Chênaie, his literary judgment was perfectly formed.

awakens in me strong discontents, and is for ever prompting me to rebel against the holy exercises and the devout collectedness of soul which are the meet preparation for these great solemnities of our faith. Oh how well can I trace here the old leaven, from which I have not yet perfectly cleared my soul!"

And again, in a letter to M. de Marzan : "Of what, my God, are we made," he cries, "that a little verdure and a few trees should be enough to rob us of our tranquillity and to distract us from thy love!" And writing, three days after Easter Sunday, in his journal, he records the reception at La Chênaie of a fervent neophyte, in words which seem to convey a covert blame of his own want of fervency :—

" Three days have passed over our heads since the great festival. One anniversary the less for us yet to spend of the death and resurrection of our Saviour! Every year thus bears away with it its solemn festivals; when will the everlasting festival be here? I have been witness of a most touching sight; François has brought us one of his friends whom he has gained to the faith. This neophyte joined us in our exercises during the Holy week, and on Easter day he received the communion with us. François was in raptures. It is a truly good work which he has thus done. François is quite young, hardly twenty years old; M. de la M. is thirty, and is married. There is something most touching and beautifully simple in M. de la M. letting himself thus be brought to God by quite a young man; and to see friendship, on François's side, thus doing the work of an Apostle, is not less beautiful and touching."

Admiration for Lamennais worked in the same direction with this feeling. Lamennais never appreciated Guérin ; his combative, rigid, despotic nature, of which the characteristic was energy, had no affinity with Guérin's elusive, undulating, impalpable nature, of which the characteristic was delicacy. He set little store by his new disciple, and could hardly bring himself to understand what others found so remarkable in him, his own genuine feeling towards him being one of indulgent compassion. But the intuition of Guérin, more discerning than the logic of his master, instinctively felt what there was commanding and tragic in Lamennais's character, different as this was from his own ; and some of his notes are among the most interesting records of Lamennais which remain.

"'Do you know what it is,' M. Féli* said to us on the evening of the day before yesterday, 'which makes man the most suffering of all creatures? It is that he has one foot in the finite and the other in the infinite, and that he is torn asunder, not by four horses, as in the horrible old times, but between two worlds.' Again he said to us as we heard the clock strike : 'If that clock knew that it was to be destroyed the next instant, it would still keep striking its hour until that instant arrived. My children, be as the clock ; whatever may be going to happen to you, strike always your hour.'"

Another time Guérin writes,

"To-day M. Féli startled us. He was sitting behind the chapel, under the two Scotch firs ; he took his stick

* The familiar name given to M. de Lamennais by his followers at La Chênaie.

and marked out a grave on the turf, and said to Elie,
' It is there I wish to be buried, but no tombstone ! only
a simple hillock of grass. Oh, how well I shall be
there !' Elie thought he had a presentiment that his
end was near. This is not the first time he has been
visited by such a presentiment ; when he was setting out
for Rome, he said to those here : ' I do not expect ever
to come back to you ; you must do the good which I
have failed to do.' He is impatient for death."

Overpowered by the ascendancy of Lamennais, Guérin,
in spite of his hesitations, in spite of his confession to
himself that "after a three weeks' close scrutiny of his
soul, in the hope of finding the pearl of a religious vocation
hidden in some corner of it," he had failed to find what
he sought, took, at the end of August, 1833, a decisive
step. He joined the religious order which Lamennais
had founded. But at this very moment the deepening
displeasure of Rome with Lamennais determined the
Bishop of Rennes to break up, in so far as it was a
religious congregation, the Society of La Chênaie, to
transfer the novices to Ploërmel, and to place them
under other superintendence. In September, Lamennais,
"who had not yet ceased," writes M. de Marzan, a fervent
Catholic, "to be a Christian and a priest, took leave of
his beloved colony of La Chênaie, with the anguish of a
general who disbands his army down to the last recruit,
and withdraws annihilated from the field of battle."
Guérin went to Ploërmel. But here, in the seclusion of
a real religious house, he instantly perceived how alien
to a spirit like his,—a spirit which, as he himself says
somewhere, "had need of the open air, wanted to see

the sun and the flowers,"—was the constraint and monotony of a monastic life, when Lamennais's genius was no
longer present to enliven this life for him.   On the 7th
of October he renounced the novitiate, believing himself
a partisan of Lamennais in his quarrel with Rome, re-
proaching the life he had left with demanding passive
obedience instead of trying "to put in practice the
admirable alliance of order with liberty, and of variety
with unity," and declaring that, for his part, he preferred
taking the chances of a life of adventure to submitting
himself to be "*garotté par un réglement,*—tied hand and
foot by a set of rules." In real truth, a life of adventure,
or rather a life free to wander at its own will, was that to
which his nature irresistibly impelled him.

For a career of adventure, the inevitable field was
Paris.   But before this career began, there came a stage,
the smoothest, perhaps, and the most happy in the short
life of Guérin.   M. la Morvonnais, one of his La Chênaie
friends,—some years older than Guérin, and married to
a wife of singular sweetness and charm,—had a house by
the seaside at the mouth of one of the beautiful rivers of
Brittany, the Arguenon.   He asked Guérin, when he left
Ploërmel, to come and stay with him at this place, called
Le Val de l'Arguenon, and Guérin spent the winter of
1833-4 there.   I grudge every word about Le Val and
its inmates which is not Guérin's own, so charming is
the picture he draws of them, so truly does his talent
find itself in its best vein as he draws it.

"How full of goodness" (he writes in his journal of
the 7th of December) "is Providence to me I For fear
the sudden passage from the mild and temperate air of a

religious life to the torrid clime of the world should be too trying for my soul, it has conducted me, after I have left my sacred shelter, to a house planted on the frontier between the two regions, where, without being in solitude, one is not yet in the world; a house whose windows look on the one side towards the plain where the tumult of men is rocking, on the other towards the wilderness where the servants of God are chanting. I intend to write down the record of my sojourn here, for the days here spent are full of happiness, and I know that in the time to come I shall often turn back to the story of these past felicities. A man, pious, and a poet; a woman, whose spirit is in such perfect sympathy with his that you would say they had but one being between them; a child, called Marie like her mother, and who sends, like a star, the first rays of her love and thought through the white cloud of infancy; a simple life in an old-fashioned house; the ocean, which comes morning and evening to bring us its harmonies; and lastly, a wanderer who descends from Carmel and is going on to Babylon, and who has laid down at this threshold his staff and his sandals, to take his seat at the hospitable table;—here is matter to make a biblical poem of, if I could only describe things as I can feel them!"

Every line written by Guérin during this stay at Le Val is worth quoting, but I have only room for one extract more :—

"Never" (he writes, a fortnight later, on the 20th of December), "never have I tasted so inwardly and deeply the happiness of home-life. All the little details of this life which in their succession make up the day, are to me so many stages of a continuous charm carried from one end of the day to the other. The morning greeting, which in some sort renews the pleasure of the first arrival, for the words with which one meets are almost the same, and the separation at night, through the hours of darkness and uncertainty, does not ill represent longer separations; then breakfast, during which you have the fresh enjoyment of having met together again; the stroll afterwards, when we go out and bid Nature good-morning; the return, and setting to work in an old panelled chamber looking out on the sea, inaccessible to all the stir of the house, a perfect sanctuary of labour; dinner, to which we are called, not by a bell, which reminds one too much of school or a great house, but by a pleasant voice; the gaiety, the merriment, the talk flitting from one subject to another and never dropping so long as the meal lasts; the crackling fire of dry branches to which we draw our chairs directly afterwards, the kind words that are spoken round the warm flame which sings while we talk; and then, if it is fine, the walk by the seaside, when the sea has for its visitors a mother with her child in her arms, this child's father and a stranger, each of these two last with a stick in his hand; the rosy lips of the little girl, which keep talking at the same time with the waves,—now and then tears shed by her and cries of childish fright at the edge of the sea; our thoughts, the father's and mine, as we stand and look at the mother and child smiling at one another, or at the child in tears and the mother trying to comfort it by her caresses and exhortations; the Ocean, going on all the while rolling up his waves and noises; the dead

boughs which we go and cut, here and there, out of the
copse-wood, to make a quick and bright fire when we
get home,—this little taste of the woodman's calling
which brings us closer to Nature and makes us think of
M. Féli's eager fondness for the same work; the hours
of study and poetical flow which carry us to supper-
time; this meal, which summons us by the same gentle
voice as its predecessor, and which is passed amid the
same joys, only less loud, because evening sobers everything, tones everything down; then our evening, ushered
in by the blaze of a cheerful fire, and which with its
alternations of reading and talking brings us at last to
bed-time :—to all the charms of a day so spent add the
dreams which follow it, and your imagination will still fall
far short of these home-joys in their delightful reality."

I said the foregoing should be my last extract, but
who could resist this picture of a January evening on
the coast of Brittany?—

"All the sky is covered over with grey clouds just
silvered at the edges. The sun, who departed a few
minutes ago, has left behind him enough light to temper
for awhile the black shadows, and to soften down, as it
were, the approach of night. The winds are hushed,
and the tranquil ocean sends up to me, when I go out
on the doorstep to listen, only a melodious murmur,
which dies away in the soul like a beautiful wave on the
beach. The birds, the first to obey the nocturnal influence, make their way towards the woods, and you
hear the rustle of their wings in the clouds. The copses
which cover the whole hill-side of Le Val, which all the
day-time are alive with the chirp of the wren, the laughing

whistle of the woodpecker,* and the different notes of a
multitude of birds, have no longer any sound in their
paths and thickets, unless it be the prolonged high call
of the blackbirds at play with one another and chasing
one another, after all the other birds have their heads safe
under their wings. The noise of man, always the last
to be silent, dies gradually out over the face of the fields.
The general murmur fades away, and one hears hardly
a sound except what comes from the villages and hamlets, in which, up till far into the night, there are cries of
children and barking of dogs. Silence wraps me round;
everything seeks repose except this pen of mine, which
perhaps disturbs the rest of some living atom asleep in
a crease of my notebook, for it makes its light scratching
as it puts down these idle thoughts. Let it stop, then!
for all I write, have written, or shall write, will never be
worth setting against the sleep of an atom."

On the 1st of February we find him in a lodging at
Paris. "I enter the world" (such are the last words
written in his journal at Le Val) "with a secret horror."
His outward history for the next five years is soon told.
He found himself in Paris, poor, fastidious, and with
health which already, no doubt, felt the obscure presence
of the malady of which he died,—consumption. One
of his Brittany acquaintances introduced him to editors,
tried to engage him in the periodical literature of
Paris ; and so unmistakeable was Guérin's talent, that
even his first essays were immediately accepted. But
Guérin's genius was of a kind which unfitted him to get

* "The woodpecker *laughs*," says White of Selborne : and here
is Guérin, in Brittany, confirming his testimony.

his bread in this manner. At first he was pleased with
the notion of living by his pen ; "*je n'ai qu'à écrire*," he
says to his sister,—"I have only got to write." But to
a nature like his, endued with the passion for perfection,
the necessity to produce, to produce constantly, to produce whether in the vein or out of the vein, to produce
something good or bad or middling, as it may happen,
but at all events *something*,—is the most intolerable of
tortures. To escape from it he betook himself to that
common but most perfidious refuge of men of letters,
that refuge to which Goldsmith and poor Hartley Coleridge had betaken themselves before him,—the profession
of teaching. In September, 1834, he procured an
engagement at the Collège Stanislas, where he had himself been educated. It was vacation-time, and all he
had to do was to teach a small class composed of boys
who did not go home for the holidays,—in his own
words, "scholars left like sick sheep in the fold, while
the rest of the flock are frisking in the fields." After
the vacation he was kept on at the College as a super-
numerary. "The master of the fifth class has asked for
a month's leave of absence ; I am taking his place, and
by this work I get one hundred francs (4*l.*). I have
been looking about for pupils to give private lessons to,
and I have found three or four. Schoolwork and private
lessons together fill my day from half-past seven in the
morning till half-past nine at night. The college dinner
serves me for breakfast, and I go and dine in the evening
at twenty-four *sous*, as a young man beginning life should."
To better his position in the hierarchy of public teachers,
it was necessary that he should take the degree of *agrégé*-

ès-lettres, corresponding to our degree of Master of Arts; and to his heavy work in teaching, there was thus added that of preparing for a severe examination. The drudgery of this life was very irksome to him, although less insupportable than the drudgery of the profession of letters; inasmuch as to a sensitive man, like Guérin, to silence his genius is more tolerable than to hackney it. Still the yoke wore him deeply, and he had moments of bitter revolt: he continued, however, to bear it with resolution, and on the whole with patience, for four years. On the 15th of November, 1838, he married a young Creole lady of some fortune, Mademoiselle Caroline de Gervain, "whom," to use his own words, "Destiny, who loves these surprises, has wafted from the farthest Indies into my arms." The marriage was happy, and it ensured to Guérin liberty and leisure; but now "the blind Fury with the abhorred shears" was hard at hand. Consumption declared itself in him: "I pass my life," he writes, with his old playfulness and calm, to his sister, on the 8th of April, 1839, "within my bed curtains, and wait patiently enough, thanks to Caro's * goodness, books, and dreams, for the recovery which the sunshine is to bring with it." In search of this sunshine he was taken to his native country, Languedoc, but in vain. He died at Le Cayla on the 19th of July, 1839.

The vicissitudes of his inward life during these five years were more considerable. His opinions and tastes underwent great, or what seem to be great, changes. He came to Paris the ardent partisan of Lamennais: even

* His wife.

in April, 1834, after Rome had finally condemned Lamennais,—"To-night there will go forth from Paris," he
writes, "with his face set to the west, a man whose every
step I would fain follow, and who returns to the desert
for which I sigh. M. Féli departs this evening for La
Chênaie." But in October, 1835,—"I assure you," he
writes to his sister, "I am at last weaned from M. de
Lamennais; one does not remain a babe and suckling
for ever; I am perfectly freed from his influence." There
was a greater change than this. In 1834 the main cause
of Guérin's aversion to the literature of the French
romantic school, was that this literature, having had a
religious origin had ceased to be religious : "it has forgotten," he says, "the house and the admonitions of
its Father." But his friend, M. de Marzan, tells us of a
"deplorable revolution" which, by 1836, had taken place
in him. Guérin had become intimate with the chiefs
of this very literature; he no longer went to church.;
"the bond of a common faith, in which our friendship
had its birth, existed between us no longer." Then,
again, "this interregnum was not destined to last."
Reconverted to his old faith by suffering and by the
pious efforts of his sister Eugénie, Guérin died a Catholic.
His feelings about society underwent a like change.
After "entering the world with a secret horror," after
congratulating himself when he had been some months
at Paris on being "disengaged from the social tumult,
out of the reach of those blows which, when I live in
the thick of the world, bruise me, irritate me, or utterly
crush me," M. Sainte-Beuve tells us of him, two years
afterwards, appearing in society "a man of the world,

elegant, even fashionable; a talker who could hold his
own against the most brilliant talkers of Paris."

In few natures, however, is there really such essential
consistency as in Guérin's.   He says of himself, in the
very beginning of his journal: "I owe everything to
poetry, for there is no other name to give to the sum
total of my thoughts; I owe to it whatever I now have
pure, lofty, and solid in my soul; I owe to it all my
consolations in the past; I shall probably owe to it my
future."   Poetry, the poetical instinct, was indeed the
basis of his nature; but to say so thus absolutely is not
quite enough.   One aspect of poetry fascinated Guérin's
imagination and held it prisoner.   Poetry is the interpretress of the natural world, and she is the interpretress
of the moral world; it was as the interpretress of the
natural world that she had Guérin for her mouthpiece.
To make magically near and real the life of Nature, and
man's life only so far as it is a part of that Nature, was
his faculty; a faculty of naturalistic, not of moral interpretation.   This faculty always has for its basis a peculiar
temperament, an extraordinary delicacy of organization
and susceptibility to impressions; in exercising it the
poet is in a great degree passive (Wordsworth thus
speaks of a *wise passiveness*); he aspires to be a sort
of human Æolian-harp, catching and rendering every
rustle of Nature.   To assist at the evolution of the
whole life of the world is his craving, and intimately to
feel it all:

> "the glow, the thrill of life,
> Where, where do these abound?"

is what he asks: he resists being riveted and held

stationary by any single impression, but would be borne
on for ever down an enchanted stream. He goes into
religion and out of religion, into society and out of
society, not from the motives which impel men in
general, but to feel what it is all like ; he is thus hardly
a moral agent, and, like the passive and ineffectual
Uranus of Keats's poem, he may say :

> "I am but a voice ;
> My life is but the life of winds and tides ;
> No more than winds and tides can I avail."

He hovers over the tumult of life, but does not really
put his hand to it.

No one has expressed the aspirations of this temperament better than Guérin himself. In the last year of
his life he writes :—

"I return, as you see, to my old brooding over the
world of Nature, that line which my thoughts irresistibly
take ; a sort of passion which gives me enthusiasm,
tears, bursts of joy, and an eternal food for musing ;
and yet I am neither philosopher, nor naturalist, nor
anything learned whatsoever. There is one word which
is the God of my imagination, the tyrant, I ought rather
to say, that fascinates it, lures it onward, gives it work to
do without ceasing, and will finally carry it I know not
where ; the word *life*."

And in one place in his journal he says :—

"My imagination welcomes every dream, every impression, without attaching itself to any, and goes on for
ever seeking something new."

And again, in another :—

"The longer I live, and the clearer I discern between true and false in society, the more does the inclination to live, not as a savage or a misanthrope, but as a solitary man on the frontiers of society, on the outskirts of the world, gain strength and grow in me. The birds come and go and make nests around our habitations, they are fellow-citizens of our farms and hamlets with us; but they take their flight in a heaven which is boundless, but the hand of God alone gives and measures to them their daily food, but they build their nests in the heart of the thick bushes, or hang them in the height of the trees. So would I, too, live, hovering round society, and having always at my back a field of liberty vast as the sky."

In the same spirit he longed for travel. "When one is a wanderer," he writes to his sister, "one feels that one fulfils the true condition of humanity." And the last entry in his journal is—"The stream of travel is full of delight. Oh, who will set me adrift on this Nile!"

Assuredly it is not in this temperament that the active virtues have their rise. On the contrary, this temperament, considered in itself alone, indisposes for the discharge of them. Something morbid and excessive, as manifested in Guérin, it undoubtedly has. In him, as in Keats, and as in another youth of genius, whose name, but the other day unheard of, Lord Houghton has so gracefully written in the history of English poetry,— David Gray,—the temperament, the talent itself, is deeply influenced by their mysterious malady; the temperament is *devouring;* it uses vital power too hard and too fast, paying the penalty in long hours of unutterable exhaustion and in premature death. The intensity of Guérin's depression is described to us by Guérin himself with the same incomparable touch with which he describes happier feelings; far oftener than any pleasurable sense of his gift he has " the sense profound, near, immense, of my misery, of my inward poverty." And again : " My inward misery gains upon me; I no longer dare look within." And on another day of gloom he does look within, and here is the terrible analysis :—

" Craving, unquiet, seeing only by glimpses, my spirit is stricken by all those ills which are the sure fruit of a youth doomed never to ripen into manhood. I grow old and wear myself out in the most futile mental strainings, and make no progress. My head seems dying, and when the wind blows I fancy I feel it, as if I were a tree, blowing through a number of withered branches in my top. Study is intolerable to me, or rather it is quite out of my power. Mental work brings on, not drowsiness, but an irritable and nervous disgust which drives me out, I know not where, into the streets and public places. The Spring, whose delights used to come every year stealthily and mysteriously to charm me in my retreat, crushes me this year under a weight of sudden hotness. I should be glad of any event which delivered me from the situation in which I am. If I were free I would embark for some distant country where I could begin life anew."

Such is this temperament in the frequent hours when the sense of its own weakness and isolation crushes it to the ground. Certainly it was not for Guérin's happiness, or for Keats's, as men count happiness, to be as they were. Still the very excess and predominance of their temperament has given to the fruits of their genius an unique brilliancy and flavour. I have said that poetry interprets in two ways; it interprets by expressing with magical felicity the physiognomy and movement of the outward world, and it interprets by expressing, with inspired conviction, the ideas and laws of the inward world of man's moral and spiritual nature. In other words, poetry is interpretative both by having *natural magic* in it, and by having *moral profundity*. In both ways it illuminates man; it gives him a satisfying sense of reality; it reconciles him with himself and the universe. Thus Æschylus's " δράσαντι παθεῖν " and his " ἀνήριθμον γέλασμα " are alike interpretative. Shakspeare interprets both when he says,

> " Full many a glorious morning have I seen,
>   Flatter the mountain-tops with sovran eye ;"

and when he says,

> " There's a divinity that shapes our ends,
>   Rough-hew them as we will."

These great poets unite in themselves the faculty of both kinds of interpretation, the naturalistic and the moral. But it is observable that in the poets who unite both kinds, the latter (the moral) usually ends by making itself the master. In Shakspeare the two kinds seem wonderfully to balance one another; but even in him the balance leans; his expression tends to become too little sensuous and simple, too much intellectualised. The same thing may be yet more strongly affirmed of Lucretius and of Wordsworth. In Shelley there is not a balance of the two gifts, nor even a co-existence of them, but there is a passionate straining after them both, and this is what makes Shelley, as a man, so interesting; I will not now inquire how much Shelley achieves as a poet, but whatever he achieves, he in general fails to achieve natural magic in his expression; in Mr. Palgrave's charming *Treasury* may be seen a gallery of his failures.* But in Keats and Guérin, in whom the faculty of naturalistic interpretation is overpoweringly predominant, the natural magic is perfect; when they speak of the world they speak like Adam naming by divine inspiration the creatures; their expression corresponds with the thing's essential reality. Even between Keats and Guérin, however, there is a distinction to be drawn. Keats has, above all, a sense of what is pleasureable and open in the life of Nature; for him she is the *Alma Parens:* his expression has, therefore, more than Guérin's, something genial, outward, and sensuous. Guérin has above all a sense of what there is adorable and secret in the life of Nature; for him she is the *Magna Parens;* his expression has, therefore, more than Keats's, something mystic, inward, and profound.

* Compare, for example, his "Lines Written in the Euganean Hills," with Keats's "Ode to Autumn" (*Golden Treasury*, pp. 256, 284). The latter piece *renders* Nature; the former *tries to render* her. I will not deny, however, that Shelley has natural magic in his rhythm; what I deny is, that he has it in his language. It always seems to me that the right sphere for Shelley's genius was the sphere of music, not of poetry; the medium of sounds he can master, but to master the more difficult medium of words he has neither intellectual force enough nor sanity enough.

So he lived like a man possessed; with his eye not on his own career, not on the public, not on fame, but on the Isis whose veil he had uplifted. He published nothing: "There is more power and beauty," he writes, "in the well-kept secret of one's-self and one's thoughts, than in the display of a whole heaven that one may have inside one." "My spirit," he answers the friends who urge him to write, "is of the home-keeping order, and has no fancy for adventure; literary adventure is above all distasteful to it; for this, indeed (let me say so without the least self-sufficiency), it has a contempt. The literary career seems to me unreal, both in its own essence and in the rewards which one seeks from it, and therefore fatally marred by a secret absurdity." His acquaintances, and among them distinguished men of letters, full of admiration for the originality and delicacy of his talent, laughed at his self-depreciation, warmly assured him of his powers. He received their assurances with a mournful incredulity, which contrasts curiously with the self-assertion of poor David Gray, whom I just now mentioned. "It seems to me intolerable," he writes, "to appear to men other than one appears to God. My worst torture at this moment is the overestimate which generous friends form of me. We are told that at the last judgment the secret of all consciences will be laid bare to the universe; would that mine were so this day, and that every passer-by could see me as I am!" "High above my head," he says at another time, "far, far away, I seem to hear the murmur of that world of thought and feeling to which I aspire so often, but where I can never attain. I think of those of

my own age who have wings strong enough to reach it,
but I think of them without jealousy, and as men on
earth contemplate the elect and their felicity." And,
criticising his own composition, "When I begin a subject,
my self-conceit" (says this exquisite artist) "imagines
I am doing wonders; and when I have finished, I see
nothing but a wretched made-up imitation, composed of
odds and ends of colour stolen from other people's
palettes, and tastelessly mixed together on mine." Such
was his *passion for perfection*, his disdain for all poetical
work not perfectly adequate and felicitous. The magic
of expression to which by the force of this passion he
won his way, will make the name of Maurice de Guérin
remembered in literature.

I have already mentioned the *Centaur*, a sort of
prose poem by Guérin, which Madame Sand published
after his death. The idea of this composition came to
him, M. Sainte-Beuve says, in the course of some visits
which he made with his friend, M. Trebutien, a learned
antiquarian, to the Museum of Antiquities in the Louvre.
The free and wild life which the Greeks expressed by
such creations as the Centaur had, as we might well
expect, a strong charm for him; under the same inspiration he composed a *Bacchante*, which was meant by him
to form part of a prose poem on the adventures of
Bacchus in India. Real as was the affinity which
Guérin's nature had for these subjects, I doubt whether,
in treating them, he would have found the full and
final employment of his talent. But the beauty of his
Centaur is extraordinary; in its whole conception and
expression this piece has in a wonderful degree that

natural magic of which I have said so much, and the
rhythm has a charm which bewitches even a foreigner.
An old Centaur on his mountain, is supposed to relate
to Melampus, a human questioner, the life of his youth.
Untranslateable as the piece is, I shall conclude with
some extracts from it :—

"THE CENTAUR.

"I had my birth in the caves of these mountains.
Like the stream of this valley, whose first drops trickle
from some weeping rock in a deep cavern, the first
moment of my life fell in the darkness of a remote abode,
and without breaking the silence. When our mothers
draw near to the time of their delivery, they withdraw to
the caverns, and in the depth of the loneliest of them,
in the thickest of its gloom, bring forth, without uttering
a plaint, a fruit silent as themselves. Their puissant
milk makes us surmount, without weakness or dubious
struggle, the first difficulties of life ; and yet we leave our
caverns later than you your cradles. The reason is that
we have a doctrine that the early days of existence
should be kept apart and enshrouded, as days filled with
the presence of the gods. Nearly the whole term of
my growth was passed in the darkness where I was born.
The recesses of my dwelling ran so far under the mountain, that I should not have known on which side was
the exit, had not the winds, when they sometimes made
their way through the opening, sent fresh airs in, and a

sudden trouble. Sometimes, too, my mother came back to me, having about her the odours of the valleys, or streaming from the waters which were her haunt. Her returning thus, without a word said of the valleys or the rivers, but with the emanations from them hanging about her, troubled my spirit, and I moved up and down restlessly in my darkness. 'What is it,' I cried, 'this outside world whither my mother is borne, and what reigns there in it so potent as to attract her so often?' At these moments my own force began to make me unquiet. I felt in it a power which could not remain idle; and betaking myself either to toss my arms or to gallop backwards and forwards in the spacious darkness of the cavern, I tried to make out from the blows which I dealt in the empty space, or from the transport of my course through it, in what direction my arms were meant to reach, or my feet to bear me. Since that day, I have wound my arms round the bust of Centaurs, and round the body of heroes, and round the trunk of oaks; my hands have assayed the rocks, the waters, plants without number, and the subtlest impressions of the air,—for I uplift them in the dark and still nights to catch the breaths of wind, and to draw signs whereby I may augur my road; my feet,—look, O Melampus, how worn they are! And yet, all benumbed as I am in this extremity of age, there are days when, in broad sunlight, on the mountain-tops, I renew these gallopings of my youth in the cavern, and with the same object, brandishing my arms and employing all the fleetness which yet is left to me.

*   *   *   *

murmur of night, or words inarticulate as the bubbling of the rivers.

"'O Macareus,' one day said the great Chiron to me, whose old age I tended; 'we are, both of us, Centaurs of the mountain ; but how different are our lives!   Of my days all the study is (thou seest it) the search for plants; thou, thou art like those mortals who have picked up on the waters or in the woods, and carried to their lips, some pieces of the reed-pipe thrown away by the god Pan. From that hour these mortals, having caught from their relics of the god a passion for wild life, or perhaps smitten with some secret madness, enter into the wilderness, plunge among the forests, follow the course of the streams, bury themselves in the heart of the mountains, restless, and haunted by an unknown purpose. The mares beloved of the winds in the farthest Scythia, are not wilder than thou, nor more cast down at nightfall, when the North Wind has departed. Seekest thou to know the gods, O Macareus, and from what source men, animals, and the elements of the universal fire have their origin ? But the aged Ocean, the father of all things, keeps locked within his own breast these secrets ; and the nymphs who stand around sing as they weave their eternal dance before him, to cover any sound which might escape from his lips half-opened by slumber. The mortals, dear to the gods for their virtue, have received from their hands lyres to give delight to man, or the seeds of new plants to make him rich ; but from their inexorable lips, nothing!'

*   *   *   *

" Such were the lessons which the old Chiron gave

me. Waned to the very extremity of life, the Centaur yet nourished in his spirit the most lofty discourse.

* * * *

"For me, O Melampus, I decline into my last days, calm as the setting of the constellations. I still retain enterprise enough to climb to the top of the rocks, and there I linger late, either gazing on the wild and restless clouds, or to see come up from the horizon the rainy Hyades, the Pleiades, or the great Orion; but I feel myself perishing and passing quickly away, like a snow-wreath floating on the stream; and soon I shall be mingled with the waters which flow in the vast bosom of Earth."

EUGÉNIE DE GUÉRIN.

Who that had spoken of Maurice de Guérin could refrain from speaking of his sister Eugénie, the most devoted of sisters, one of the rarest and most beautiful of souls? "There is nothing fixed, no duration, no vitality in the sentiments of women towards one another; their attachments are mere pretty bows of ribbon, and no more. In all the friendships of women I observe this slightness of the tie. I know no instance to the contrary, even in history. Orestes and Pylades have no sisters." So she herself speaks of the friendships of her own sex. But Electra can attach herself to Orestes, if not to Chrysothemis. And to her brother Maurice, Eugénie de Guérin was Pylades and Electra in one.

The name of Maurice de Guérin,—that young man so gifted, so attractive, so careless of fame, and so early snatched away; who died at twenty-nine; who, says his sister, "let what he did be lost with a carelessness so unjust to himself, set no value on any of his own productions, and departed hence without reaping the rich harvest which seemed his due;" who, in spite of his immaturity, in spite of his fragility, exercised such a charm, "furnished to others so much of that which all live by," that some years after his death his sister found in a country-house where he used to stay, in the journal of a young girl who had not known him, but who heard her family speak of him, his name, the date of his death, and these words, "*il était leur vie*" (he was their life); whose talent, exquisite as that of Keats, with less of sunlight, abundance, and facility in it than that of Keats, but with more of distinction and power, had "that winning, delicate, and beautifully happy turn of expression" which is the stamp of the master,—is beginning to be well known to all lovers of literature. This establishment of Maurice's name was an object for which his sister Eugénie passionately laboured. While he was alive, she placed her whole joy in the flowering of this gifted nature; when he was dead, she had no other thought than to make the world know him as she knew him. She outlived him nine years, and her cherished task for those years was to rescue the fragments of her brother's composition, to collect them, to get them published. In pursuing this task she had at first cheering hopes of success; she had at last baffling and bitter disappointment. Her earthly business was at an end; she died. Ten years afterwards, it was permitted to the love of a friend, M. Trebutien, to effect for Maurice's memory what the love of a sister had failed to accomplish. But those who read, with delight and admiration, the journal and letters of Maurice de Guérin, could not but be attracted and touched by this sister Eugénie, who met them at every page. She seemed hardly less gifted, hardly less interesting, than Maurice himself. And presently M. Trebutien did for the sister what he had done for the brother. He published the journal of Mdlle. Eugénie de Guérin, and a few (too few, alas!) of her letters.* The book has made a profound impression in France; and the fame which she sought only for her brother now crowns the sister also.

Parts of Mdlle. de Guérin's journal were several years ago printed for private circulation, and a writer in the *National Review* had the good fortune to fall in with them. The bees of our English criticism do not often roam so far afield for their honey, and this critic deserves thanks for having flitted in his quest of blossom to foreign parts, and for having settled upon a beautiful flower found there. He had the discernment to see that Mdlle. de Guérin was well worth speaking of, and he spoke of her with feeling and appreciation. But that, as I have said, was several years ago; even a true and feeling homage needs to be from time to time renewed, if the memory of its object is to endure; and criticism must not lose the occasion offered by Mdlle. de Guérin's journal being for the first time published to the world, of directing notice once more to this religious and beautiful character.

Eugénie de Guérin was born in 1805, at the château of Le Cayla, in Languedoc. Her family, though reduced in circumstances, was noble; and even when one is a saint one cannot quite forget that one comes of the stock of the Guarini of Italy, or that one counts among one's ancestors a Bishop of Senlis, who had the marshalling of

* A volume of these, also, has just been brought out by M. Trebutien. One good book, at least, in the literature of the year 1865!

revolts; somewhere in the depths of that strong nature there is a struggle, an impatience, an inquietude, an ennui, which endures to the end, and which leaves one, when one finally closes her journal, with an impression of profound melancholy. "There are days," she writes to her brother, "when one's nature rolls itself up, and becomes a hedgehog. If I had you here at this moment, here close by me, how I should prick you! how sharp and hard!" "Poor soul, poor soul," she cries out to herself another day, "what is the matter, what would you have? Where is that which will do you good? Everything is green, everything is in bloom, all the air has a breath of flowers. How beautiful it is! well, I will go out. No, I should be alone, and all this beauty, when one is alone, is worth nothing. What shall I do then? Read, write, pray, take a basket of sand on my head like that hermit-saint, and walk with it? Yes, work, work! keep busy the body which does mischief to the soul! I have been too little occupied to-day, and that is bad for one, and it gives a certain ennui which I have in me time to ferment."

A certain ennui which I have in me: her wound is there. In vain she follows the counsel of Fénelon: "If God tires you, *tell Him that He tires you.*" No doubt she obtained great and frequent solace and restoration from prayer: "This morning I was suffering; well, at present I am calm, and this I owe to faith, simply to faith, to an act of faith. I can think of death and eternity without trouble, without alarm. Over a deep of sorrow there floats a divine calm, a suavity which is the work of God only. In vain have I tried other things at

a time like this: nothing human comforts the soul,
nothing human upholds it :—.

> ' A l'enfant il faut sa mère,
> A mon âme il faut mon Dieu.' "

Still the ennui reappears, bringing with it hours of unutterable forlornness, and making her cling to her one
great earthly happiness,—her affection for her brother,—
with an intenseness, an anxiety, a desperation in which
there is something morbid, and by which she is occasion-
ally carried into an irritability, a jealousy, which she
herself is the first, indeed, to censure, which she severely
represses, but which nevertheless leaves a sense of pain.

Mdlle. de Guérin's admirers have compared her to
Pascal, and in some respects the comparison is just.
But she cannot exactly be classed with Pascal, any more
than with Saint François de Sales. Pascal is a man, and
the inexhaustible power and activity of his mind leave
him no leisure for ennui. He has not the sweetness and
serenity of the perfect saint; he is, perhaps, " der strenge,
kranke Pascal—*the severe, morbid Pascal*,"—as Goethe
(and, strange to say, Goethe at twenty-three, an age
which usually feels Pascal's charm most profoundly) calls
him ; but the stress and movement of the lifelong conflict
waged in him between his soul and his reason keep him
full of fire, full of agitation, and keep his reader, who
witnesses this conflict, animated and excited ; the sense
of forlornness and dejected weariness which clings to
Eugénie de Guérin does not belong to Pascal. Eugénie
de Guérin is a woman, and longs for a state of firm
happiness, for an affection in which she may repose ; the

the power of religion; religion was the master-influence of her life; she derived immense consolations from religion, she earnestly strove to conform her whole nature to it; if there was an element in her which religion could not perfectly reach, perfectly transmute, she groaned over this element in her, she chid it, she made it bow. Almost every thought in her was brought into harmony with religion; and what few thoughts were not thus brought into harmony were brought into subjection.

Then she had her affection for her brother; and this, too, though perhaps there might be in it something a little over-eager, a little too absolute, a little too susceptible, was a pure, a devoted affection. It was not only passionate, it was tender. It was tender, pliant, and self-sacrificing to a degree that not in one nature out of a thousand,—of natures with a mind and will like hers, —is found attainable. She thus united extraordinary power of intelligence, extraordinary force of character, and extraordinary strength of affection; and all these under the control of a deep religious feeling.

This is what makes her so remarkable, so interesting. I shall try and make her speak for herself, that she may show us the characteristic sides of her rare nature with her own inimitable touch.

It must be remembered that her journal is written for Maurice only; in her lifetime no eye but his ever saw it. *" Ceci n'est pas pour le public,"* she writes; *"c'est de l'intime, c'est de l'âme, c'est pour un."* " This is not for the public; it contains my inmost thoughts, my very soul; it is for *one*." And Maurice, this *one*, was a kind of second self to her. "We see things with the same eyes; what you find beautiful, I find beautiful; God has made our souls of one piece." And this genuine confidence in her brother's sympathy gives to the entries in her journal a naturalness and simple freedom rare in such compositions. She felt that he would understand her, and be interested in all that she wrote.

One of the first pages of her journal relates an incident of the home-life of Le Cayla, the smallest detail of which Maurice liked to hear; and in relating it she brings this simple life before us. She is writing in November, 1834 :—

"I am furious with the grey cat. The mischievous beast has made away with a little half-frozen pigeon, which I was trying to thaw by the side of the fire. The poor little thing was just beginning to come round; I meant to tame him; he would have grown fond of me; and there is my whole scheme eaten up by a cat ! This event, and all the rest of to-day's history, has passed in the kitchen. Here I take up my abode all the morning and a part of the evening, ever since I am without Mimi.* I have to superintend the cook; sometimes papa comes down and I read to him by the oven, or by the fireside, some bits out of the *Antiquities of the Anglo-Saxon Church*. This book struck Pierril † with astonishment. ' *Que de mouts aqui dédins !* What a lot of words there are inside it;' This boy is a real original. One evening he asked me if the soul was immortal; then afterwards, what a philosopher was ? We had got upon

<hr>

* The familiar name of her sister Marie.
† A servant-boy at Le Cayla.

great questions, as you see. When I told him that a philosopher was a person who was wise and learned : ' Then, mademoiselle, you are a philosopher.' This was said with an air of simplicity and sincerity which might have made even Socrates take it as a compliment ; but it made me laugh so much that my gravity as catechist was gone for that evening. A day or two ago Pierril left us, to his great sorrow : his time with us was up on Saint Brice's day. Now he goes about with his little dog, truffle-hunting. If he comes this way I shall go and ask him if he still thinks I look like a philosopher."

Her good sense and spirit made her discharge with alacrity her household tasks in this patriarchal life of Le Cayla, and treat them as the most natural thing in the world. She sometimes complains, to be sure, of burning her fingers at the kitchen-fire. But when a literary friend of her brother expresses enthusiasm about her and her poetical nature : " The poetess," she says, " whom this gentleman believes me to be, is an ideal being, infinitely removed from the life which is actually mine—a life of occupations, a life of household-business, which takes up all my time. How could I make it otherwise ? I am sure I do not know ; and, besides, my duty is in this sort of life, and I have no wish to escape from it."

Among these occupations of the patriarchal life of the châtelaine of Le Cayla intercourse with the poor fills a prominent place :—

" To-day," she writes on the 9th of December, 1834, " I have been warming myself at every fireside in the village. It is a round which Mimi and I often make, and in which I take pleasure. To-day we have been seeing sick people, and holding forth on doses and sick-room drinks. ' Take this, do that ;' and they attend to us just as if we were the doctor. We prescribed shoes for a little thing who was amiss from having gone bare-foot ; to the brother, who, with a bad headache, was lying quite flat, we prescribed a pillow ; the pillow did him good, but I am afraid it will hardly cure him. He is at the beginning of a bad feverish cold, and these poor people live in the filth of their hovels like animals in their stable ; the bad air poisons them. When I come home to Le Cayla I seem to be in a palace."

She had books, too ; not in abundance, not for the fancying them ; the list of her library is small, and it is enlarged slowly and with difficulty. The *Letters of Saint Theresa*, which she had long wished to get, she sees in the hands of a poor servant girl, before she can procure them for herself. "What then ?" is her comment : "very likely she makes a better use of them than I could." But she has the *Imitation*, the *Spiritual Works* of Bossuet and Fénelon, the *Lives of the Saints*, Corneille, Racine, André Chénier, and Lamartine ; Madame de Staël's book on Germany, and French translations of Shakspeare's plays, Ossian, the *Vicar of Wakefield*, Scott's *Old Mortality* and *Redgauntlet*, and the *Promessi Sposi* of Manzoni. Above all, she has her own mind ; her medi-tations in the lonely fields, on the oak-grown hill-side of "The Seven Springs ;" her meditations and writing in her own room, her *chambrette*, her *délicieux chez moi*, where every night, before she goes to bed, she opens the window to look out upon the sky,—the balmy moon-lit sky of Languedoc. This life of reading, thinking, and writing, was the life she liked best, the life that most truly suited her. "I find writing has become almost a necessity to me. Whence does it arise, this impulse to give utterance to the voice of one's spirit, to pour out my thoughts before God and one human being? I say one human being, because I always imagine that you are present, that you see what I write. In the stillness of a life like this my spirit is happy, and, as it were, dead to all that goes on upstairs or downstairs, in the house or out of the house. But this does not last long. 'Come, my poor spirit,' I then say to myself, 'we must go back to the things of this world. And I take my spinning, or a book, or a saucepan, or I play with Wolf or Trilby. Such a life as this I call heaven upon earth."

Tastes like these, joined with a talent like Mdlle. de Guérin's, naturally inspire thoughts of literary composition. Such thoughts she had, and perhaps she would have been happier if she had followed them; but she never could satisfy herself that to follow them was quite consistent with the religious life, and her projects of composition were gradually relinquished :—

"Would to God that my thoughts, my spirit, had never taken their flight beyond the narrow round in which it is my lot to live! In spite of all that people say to the contrary, I feel that I cannot go beyond my needlework and my spinning without going too far: I feel it, I believe it : well, then, I will keep in my proper sphere; however much I am tempted, my spirit shall not be allowed to occupy itself with great matters until it occupies itself with them in Heaven."

And again :—

"My journal has been untouched for a long while. Do you want to know why? It is because the time seems to me misspent which I spend in writing it. We owe God an account of every minute; and is it not a wrong use of our minutes to employ them in writing a history of our transitory days?"

She overcomes her scruples, and goes on writing the journal; but again and again they return to her. Her brother tells her of the pleasure and comfort something she has written gives to a friend of his in affliction. She answers:—

" It is from the Cross that those thoughts come, which your friend finds so soothing, so unspeakably tender. None of them come from me. I feel my own aridity; but I feel, too, that God, when he will, can make an ocean flow upon this bed of sand. It is the same with so many simple souls, from which proceed the most admirable things; because they are in direct relation with God, without false science and without pride. And thus I am gradually losing my taste for books; I say to myself : ' What can they teach me which I shall not one day know in Heaven? let God be my master and my study here !' I try to make him so, and I find myself the better for it. I read little ; I go out little ; I plunge myself in the inward life. How infinite are the sayings, doings, feelings, events of that life ! Oh, if you could but see them ! But what avails it to make them known ? God alone should be admitted to the sanctuary of the soul."

Beautifully as she says all this, one cannot, I think, read it without a sense of disquietude, without a presentiment that this ardent spirit is forcing itself from its natural bent, that the beatitude of the true mystic will never be its earthly portion. And yet how simple and charming is her picture of the life of religion which she chose as her ark of refuge, and in which she desired to place all her happiness :—

"Cloaks, clogs, umbrellas, all the apparatus of winter, went with us this morning to Andillac, where we have passed the whole day; some of it at the curé's house, the rest in church. How I like this life of a country Sunday, with its activity, its journeys to church, its liveliness! You find all your neighbours on the road; you have a curtsey from every woman you meet, and then, as you go along, such a talk about the poultry, the sheep and cows, the good man and the children! My great delight is to give a kiss to these children, and see them run away and hide their blushing faces in their mother's gown. They are alarmed at *las doumaïsélos*,* as at a being of another world. One of these little things said the other day to its grandmother, who was talking of coming to see us: '*Minino*, you mustn't go to that castle ; there is a black hole there.' What is the reason that in all ages the noble's château has been an object of terror? Is it because of the horrors that were committed there in old times? I suppose so."

This vague horror of the château, still lingering in the mind of the French peasant fifty years after he has stormed it, is indeed curious, and is one of the thousand indications how unlike aristocracy on the Continent has been to aristocracy in England. But this is one of the great

* The young lady.

matters with which Mdlle. de Guérin would not have us occupied; let us pass to the subject of Christmas in Languedoc :—

"Christmas is come; the beautiful festival, the one I love most, and which gives me the same joy as it gave the shepherds of Bethlehem.   In real truth, one's whole soul sings with joy at this beautiful coming of God upon earth,—a coming which here is announced on all sides of us by music and by our charming *nadalet.*   Nothing at Paris can give you a notion of what Christmas is with us. You have not even the midnight-mass.   We all of us went to it, papa at our head, on the most perfect night possible.   Never was there a finer sky than ours was that midnight ;—so fine that papa kept perpetually throwing back the hood of his cloak, that he might look up at the sky.   The ground was white with hoar-frost, but we were not cold ; besides, the air, as we met it, was warmed by the bundles of blazing torchwood which our servants carried in front of us to light us on our way.   It was delightful, I do assure you ; and I should like you to have seen us there on our road to church, in those lanes with the bushes along their banks as white as if they were in flower.   The hoar-frost makes the most lovely flowers. We saw a long spray so beautiful that we wanted to take it with us as a garland for the communion-table, but it melted in our hands : all flowers fade so soon !   I was very sorry about my garland ; it was mournful to see it drip away, and get smaller and smaller every minute."

* A peculiar peal rung at Christmas-time by the church-bells of Languedoc.

The religious life is at bottom everywhere alike ; but it is curious to note the variousness of its setting and outward circumstance. Catholicism has these so different from Protestantism ! and in Catholicism these accessories have, it cannot be denied, a nobleness and amplitude which in Protestantism is often wanting to them. In Catholicism they have, from the antiquity of this form of religion, from its pretensions to universality, from its really wide-spread prevalence, from its sensuousness, something European, august, and imaginative : in Protestantism they often have, from its inferiority in all these respects, something provincial, mean, and prosaic. In revenge, Protestantism has a future before it, a prospect of growth in alliance with the vital movement of modern society ; while Catholicism appears to be bent on widening the breach between itself and the modern spirit, to be fatally losing itself in the multiplication of dogmas, Mariolatry, and miracle-mongering. But the style and circumstance of actual Catholicism is grander than its present tendency, and the style and circumstance of Protestantism is meaner than its tendency. While I was reading the journal of Mdlle. de Guérin, there came into my hands the memoir and poems of a young Englishwoman, Miss Emma Tatham ; and one could not but be struck with the singular contrast which the two lives,—in their setting rather than in their inherent quality,—present. Miss Tatham had not, certainly, Mdlle. de Guérin's talent, but she had a sincere vein of poetic feeling, a genuine aptitude for composition. Both were fervent Christians, and, so far, the two lives have a real resemblance ; but, in the setting of them, what a difference ! The Frenchwoman

is a Catholic in Languedoc; the Englishwoman is a
Protestant at Margate; Margate, that brick-and-mortar
image of English Protestantism, representing it in all its
prose, all its uncomeliness,—let me add, all its salubrity.
Between the external form and fashion of these two lives,
between the Catholic Mdlle. de Guérin's *nadalet* at the
Languedoc Christmas, her chapel of moss at Easter-
time, her daily reading of the life of a saint, carrying
her to the most diverse times, places, and peoples,—her
quoting, when she wants to fix her mind upon the stanch-
ness which the religious aspirant needs, the words of
Saint Macedonius to a hunter whom he met in the
mountains, "I pursue after God, as you pursue after
game,"—her quoting, when she wants to break a village
girl of disobedience to her mother, the story of the ten
disobedient children whom at Hippo St. Augustine saw
palsied ;—between all this and the bare, blank, narrowly
English setting of Miss Tatham's Protestantism, her
"union in church-fellowship with the worshippers at
Hawley-Square Chapel, Margate;" her "singing with
soft, sweet voice, the animating lines—

> ' My Jesus to know, and feel his blood flow,
> 'Tis life everlasting, 'tis heaven below;'"

her "young female teachers belonging to the Sunday-
school," and her "Mr. Thomas Rowe, a venerable class-
leader,"—what a dissimilarity! In the ground of the
two lives, a likeness; in all their circumstance, what unlikeness! An unlikeness, it will be said, in that which
is non-essential and indifferent. Non-essential,—yes;
indifferent,—no. The signal want of grace and charm in

English Protestantism's setting of its religious life is not an indifferent matter; it is a real weakness. *This ought ye to have done, and not to have left the other undone.*

I have said that the present tendency of Catholicism, —the Catholicism of the main body of the Catholic clergy and laity,—seems likely to exaggerate rather than to remove all that in this form of religion is most repugnant to reason; but this Catholicism was not that of Mdlle. de Guérin. The insufficiency of her Catholicism comes from a doctrine which Protestantism, too, has adopted, although Protestantism, from its inherent element of freedom, may find it easier to escape from it; a doctrine with a certain attraction for all noble natures, but, in the modern world at any rate, incurably sterile,—the doctrine of the emptiness and nothingness of human life, of the superiority of renouncement to activity, of quietism to energy; the doctrine which makes effort for things on this side of the grave a folly, and joy in things on this side of the grave a sin. But her Catholicism is remarkably free from the faults which Protestants commonly think inseparable from Catholicism; the relation to the priest, the practice of confession, assume, when she speaks of them, an aspect which is not that under which Exeter Hall knows them, but which,—unless one is of the number of those who prefer regarding that by which men and nations die to regarding that by which they live,—one is glad to study. "*La confession,*" she says twice in her journal, "*n'est qu'une expansion du repentir dans l'amour;*" and her weekly journey to the confessional in the little church of Cahuzac is her "*cher*

pèlerinage;" the little church is the place where she has
" *laissé tant de misères.*"

"This morning," she writes, one 28th of November,
"I was up before daylight, dressed quickly, said my
prayers, and started with Marie for Cahuzac. When we
got there, the chapel was occupied, which I was not
sorry for. I like not to be hurried, and to have time,
before I go in, to lay bare my soul before God. This
often takes me a long time, because my thoughts are apt
to be flying about like these autumn leaves. At ten
o'clock I was on my knees, listening to words the most
salutary that were ever spoken; and I went away, feeling
myself a better being. Every burden thrown off leaves
us with a sense of brightness; and when the soul has
laid down the load of its sins at God's feet, it feels as if
it had wings. What an admirable thing is confession!
What comfort, what light, what strength is given me
every time after I have said, *I have sinned.*"

This blessing of confession is the greater, she says,
"the more the heart of the priest to whom we confide
our repentance is like that divine heart which 'has so
loved us.' This is what attaches me to M. Bories." M.
Bories was the curé of her parish, a man no longer
young, and of whose loss, when he was about to leave
them, she thus speaks :—

"What a grief for me! how much I lose in losing
this faithful guide of my conscience, heart, and mind, of
my whole self, which God had appointed to be in his
charge, and which let itself be in his charge so gladly!
He knew the resolves which God had put in my heart,
and I had need of his help to follow them. Our new

curé cannot supply his place; he is so young! and then he seems so inexperienced, so undecided! It needs firmness to pluck a soul out of the midst of the world, and to uphold it against the assaults of flesh and blood. It is Saturday, my day for going to Cahuzac; I am just going there, perhaps I shall come back more tranquil. God has always given me some good thing there, in that chapel where I have left behind me so many miseries."

Such is confession for her when the priest is worthy; and, when he is not worthy, she knows how to separate the man from the office :—

"To-day I am going to do something which I dislike; but I will do it, with God's help. Do not think I am on my way to the stake; it is only that I am going to confess to a priest in whom I have not confidence, but who is the only one here. In this act of religion the man must always be separated from the priest, and sometimes the man must be annihilated."

The same clear sense, the same freedom from superstition, shows itself in all her religious life. She tells us, to be sure, how once, when she was a little girl, she stained a new frock, and on praying, in her alarm, to an image of the Virgin which hung in her room, saw the stains vanish: even the austerest Protestant will not judge such Mariolatry as this very harshly. But, in general, the Virgin Mary fills, in the religious parts of her journal, no prominent place; it is Jesus, not Mary. "Oh, how well has Jesus said : 'Come unto me, all ye that labour and are heavy laden.' It is only there, only in the bosom of God, that we can rightly weep, rightly rid ourselves of our burden." And again : " The mystery of suffering makes one grasp the belief of something to be expiated, something to be won. I see it in Jesus Christ, the Man of Sorrow. *It was necessary that the Son of Man should suffer.* That is all we know in the troubles and calamities of life."

And who has ever spoken of justification more impressively and piously than Mdlle. Guérin speaks of it, when, after reckoning the number of minutes she has lived, she exclaims :—

"My God, what have we done with all these minutes of ours, which thou, too, wilt one day reckon 1 Will there be any of them to count for eternal life 1 will there be many of them 1 will there be one of them 1 'If thou, O Lord, wilt be extreme to mark what is done amiss, O Lord, who may abide it 1' This close scrutiny of our time may well make us tremble, all of us who have advanced more than a few steps in life ; for God will judge us otherwise than as he judges the lilies of the field. I have never been able to understand the security of those who place their whole reliance, in presenting themselves before God, upon a good conduct in the ordinary relations of human life. As if all our duties were confined within the narrow sphere of this world ! To be a good parent, a good child, a good citizen, a good brother or sister, is not enough to procure entrance into the kingdom of heaven. God demands other things besides these kindly social virtues, of him whom he means to crown with an eternity of glory."

And, with this zeal for the spirit and power of religion, what prudence in her counsels of religious practice.;

what discernment, what measure! She has been speaking
of the charm of the *Lives of the Saints*, and she goes
on :—

" Notwithstanding this, the *Lives of the Saints* seem to
me, for a great many people, dangerous reading. I
would not recommend them to a young girl, or even to
some women who are no longer young. What one reads
has such power over one's feelings ; and these, even in
seeking God, sometimes go astray. Alas, we have seen
it in poor C.'s case. What care one ought to take with
a young person ; with what she reads, what she writes,
her society, her prayers,—all of them matters which
demand a mother's tender watchfulness ! I remember
many things I did at fourteen, which my mother, had
she lived, would not have let me do. I would have
done anything for God's sake ; I would have cast myself
into an oven, and assuredly things like that are not God's
will ; he is not pleased by the hurt one does to one's
health through that ardent but ill-regulated piety which,
while it impairs the body, often leaves many a fault
flourishing. And, therefore, Saint François de Sales
used to say to the nuns who asked his leave to go bare-
foot : ' Change your brains and keep your shoes.' "   .

Meanwhile Maurice, in a five years' absence, and amid
the distractions of Paris, lost, or seemed to his sister to
lose, something of his fondness for his home and its
inmates ; he certainly lost his early religious habits and
feelings. It is on this latter loss that Mdlle. de Guérin's
journal oftenest touches,—with infinite delicacy, but with
infinite anguish :—

"Oh, the agony of being in fear for a soul's salvation,

who can describe it! That which caused our Saviour
the keenest suffering, in the agony of his Passion, was
not so much the thought of the torments he was to
endure, as the thought that these torments would be of
no avail for a multitude of sinners; for all those who set
themselves against their redemption, or who do not care
for it. The mere anticipation of this obstinacy and this
heedlessness had power to make sorrowful, even unto
death, the divine Son of Man. And this feeling all
Christian souls, according to the measure of faith and
love granted them, more or less share."

Maurice returned to Le Cayla in the summer of 1837,
and passed six months there. This meeting entirely
restored the union between him and his family. "These
six months with us," writes his sister, "he ill, and finding
himself so loved by us all, had entirely reattached him to
us. Five years without seeing us, had perhaps made him
a little lose sight of our affection for him; having found
it again, he met it with all the strength of his own. He
had so firmly renewed, before he left us, all family-ties,
that nothing but death could have broken them." The
separation in religious matters between the brother and
sister gradually diminished, and before Maurice died it
had ceased. I have elsewhere spoken of Maurice's
religious feeling and its character. It is probable that
his divergence from his sister in this sphere of religion
was never so wide as she feared, and that his reunion
with her was never so complete as she hoped. "His
errors were passed," she says, "his illusions were cleared
away; by the call of his nature, by original disposition,
he had come back to sentiments of order. I knew all,

I followed each of his steps; out of the fiery sphere of the passions (which held him but a little moment) I saw him pass into the sphere of the Christian life. It was a beautiful soul, the soul of Maurice." But the illness which had caused his return to Le Cayla reappeared after he got back to Paris in the winter of 1837-8. Again he seemed to recover; and his marriage with a young Creole lady, Mdlle. Caroline de Gervain, took place in the autumn of 1838. At the end of September in that year Mdlle. de Guérin had joined her brother in Paris; she was present at his marriage, and stayed with him and his wife for some months afterwards. Her journal recommences in April, 1839; zealously as she had promoted her brother's marriage, cordial as were her relations with her sister-in-law, it is evident that a sense of loss, of loneliness, invades her, and sometimes weighs her down. She writes in her journal on the 4th of May:—

"God knows when we shall see one another again! My own Maurice, must it be our lot to live apart, to find that this marriage, which I had so much share in bringing about, which I hoped would keep us so much together, leaves us more asunder than ever? For the present and for the future, this troubles me more than I can say. My sympathies, my inclinations, carry me more towards you than towards any other member of our family. I have the misfortune to be fonder of you than of anything else in the world, and my heart had from of old built in you its happiness. Youth gone and life declining, I looked forward to quitting the scene with Maurice. At any time of life a great affection is a great happiness; the spirit comes to take refuge in it entirely. O delight and joy which will never be your sister's portion! Only in the direction of God shall I find an issue for my heart to love as it has the notion of loving, as it has the power of loving."

From such complainings, in which there is undoubtedly something morbid,—complainings which she herself blamed, to which she seldom gave way, but which, in presenting her character, it is not just to put wholly out of sight,—she was called by the news of an alarming return of her brother's illness. For some days the entries in the journal show her agony of apprehension. "He coughs, he coughs still! Those words keep echoing for ever in my ears, and pursue me wherever I go; I cannot look at the leaves on the trees without thinking that the winter will come, and that then the consumptive die." Then she went to him and brought him back by slow stages to Le Cayla, dying. He died on the 19th of July, 1839.

Thenceforward the energy of life ebbed in her; but the main chords of her being, the chord of affection, the chord of religious longing, the chord of intelligence, the chord of sorrow, gave, so long as they answered to the touch at all, a deeper and finer sound than ever. Always she saw before her, "that beloved pale face;" "that beautiful head, with all its different expressions, smiling, speaking, suffering, dying," regarded her always:—

" I have seen his coffin in the same room, in the same spot where I remember seeing, when I was a very little girl, his cradle, when I was brought home from Gaillac, where I was then staying, for his christening. This christening was a grand one, full of rejoicing, more than that of any of the rest of us ; specially marked. I enjoyed myself greatly, and went back to Gaillac next day, charmed with my new little brother. Two years afterwards I came home, and brought with me for him a frock of my own making. I dressed him in the frock, and took him out with me along by the warren at the north of the house, and there he walked a few steps alone,—his first walking alone,—and I ran with delight to tell my mother the news : ' Maurice, Maurice has begun to walk by himself!'—Recollections which, coming back to-day, break one's heart !"

The shortness and suffering of her brother's life filled her with an agony of pity. "Poor beloved soul, you have had hardly any happiness here below ; your life has been so short, your repose so rare. O God, uphold me, stablish my heart in thy faith! Alas, I have too little of this supporting me! How we have gazed at him and loved him, and kissed him,—his wife, and we, his sisters; he lying lifeless in his bed, his head on the pillow as if he were asleep! Then we followed him to the churchyard, to the grave, to his last resting-place, and prayed over him, and wept over him ; and we are here again, and I am writing to him again, as if he were staying away from home, as if he were in Paris. My beloved one, can it be, shall we never see one another again on earth ?"

But in heaven!—and here, though love and hope finally prevailed, the very passion of the sister's longing sometimes inspired torturing inquietudes :—

"I am broken down with misery. I want to see him.

Every moment I pray to God to grant me this grace.
Heaven, the world of spirits, is it so far from us? O
depth, O mystery of the other life which separates us!
I, who was so eagerly anxious about him, who wanted so
to know all that happened to him,—wherever he may be
now, it is over! I follow him into the three abodes: I
stop wistfully in the place of bliss; I pass on to the place
of suffering;—to the gulf of fire. My God, my God, no!
Not there let my brother be! not there! And he is not:
his soul, the soul of Maurice, among the lost . . . .
horrible fear, no! But in purgatory, where the soul is
cleansed by suffering, where the failings of the heart are
expiated, the doubtings of the spirit, the half-yieldings to
evil? Perhaps my brother is there and suffers, and calls
to us amidst his anguish of repentance, as he used to call
to us amidst his bodily suffering: 'Help me, you who
love me.' Yes, beloved one, by prayer. I will go and
pray; prayer has been such a power to me, and I will
pray to the end. Prayer! Oh! and prayer for the dead!
it is the dew of purgatory."

Often, alas, the gracious dew would not fall; the air
of her soul was parched; the arid wind, which was
somewhere in the depths of her being, blew. She marks
in her journal the first of May, "this return of the
loveliest month in the year," only to keep up the old
habit; even the month of May can no longer give her
any pleasure: "Tout est changé—*all is changed.*" She
is crushed by "the misery which has nothing good in it,
the tearless, dry misery, which bruises the heart like a
hammer."

"I am dying to everything. I am dying of a slow

moral agony, a condition of unutterable suffering. Lie there, my poor journal! be forgotten with all this world which is fading away from me. I will write here no more until I come to life again, until God re-awakens me out of this tomb in which my soul lies buried. Maurice, my beloved! it was not thus with me when I had *you!* The thought of Maurice could revive me from the most profound depression: to have him in the world was enough for me. With Maurice, to be buried alive would have not seemed dull to me."

And, as a burden to this funereal strain, the old *vide et néant* of Bossuet, profound, solemn, sterile :—

"So beautiful in the morning, and in the evening, *that!* how the thought disenchants one, and turns one from the world! I can understand that Spanish grandee, who, after lifting up the winding-sheet of a beautiful queen, threw himself into a cloister and became a great saint. I would have all my friends at La Trappe, in the interest of their eternal welfare. Not that in the world one cannot be saved, not that there are not in the world duties to be discharged as sacred and as beautiful as there are in the cloister, but . . . ."

And there she stops, and a day or two afterwards her journal comes to an end. A few fragments, a few letters carry us on a little later, but after the 22nd of August, 1845, there is nothing. To make known her brother's genius to the world was the one task she set herself after his death; in 1840 came Madame Sand's noble tribute to him in the *Revue des Deux Mondes;* then followed projects of raising a yet more enduring monument to his fame, by collecting and publishing his scattered compositions; these projects, I have already said, were baffled;—Mdlle. de Guérin's letter of the 22nd of August, 1845, relates to this disappointment.   In silence, during nearly three years more, she faded away at Le Cayla.   She died on the 31st of May, 1848.

M. Trebutien has accomplished the pious task in which Mdlle. de Guérin was baffled, and has established Maurice's fame; by publishing this journal he has established Eugénie's also.   She was very different from her brother; but she too, like him, had that in her which preserves a reputation.   Her soul has the same characteristic quality as his talent,—*distinction*.   Of this quality the world is impatient; it chafes against it, rails at it, insults it, hates it: it ends by receiving its influence, and by undergoing its law.   This quality at last inexorably corrects the world's blunders, and fixes the world's ideals. It procures that the popular poet shall not finally pass for a Pindar, nor the popular historian for a Tacitus, nor the popular preacher for a Bossuet.   To the circle of spirits marked by this rare quality, Maurice and Eugénie de Guérin belong; they will take their place in the sky which these inhabit, and shine close to one another, *lucida sidera*.

HEINRICH HEINE.

"I KNOW not if I deserve that a laurel-wreath should one day be laid on my coffin. Poetry, dearly as I have loved it, has always been to me but a divine plaything. I have never attached any great value to poetical fame : and I trouble myself very little whether people praise my verses or blame them. But lay on my coffin a *sword :* for I was a brave soldier in the war of liberation of humanity."

Heine had his full share of love of fame, and cared quite as much as his brethren of the *genus irritabile* whether people praised his verses or blamed them. And he was very little of a hero. Posterity will certainly decorate his tomb with the emblem of the laurel rather than with the emblem of the sword. Still, for his contemporaries, for us, for the Europe of the present century, he is significant chiefly for the reason which he himself in the words just quoted assigns. He is significant because he was, if not pre-eminently a brave, yet a brilliant, a most effective soldier in the war of liberation of humanity.

To ascertain the master-current in the literature of an epoch, and to distinguish this from all minor currents, is one of the critic's highest functions ; in discharging it he

shows how far he possesses the most indispensable quality
of his office,—justness of spirit. The living writer who
has done most to make England acquainted with German
authors, a man of genius, but to whom precisely this one
quality of justness of spirit is perhaps wanting,—I mean
Mr. Carlyle,—seems to me in the result of his labours
on German literature to afford a proof how very necessary
to the critic this quality is. Mr. Carlyle has spoken
admirably of Goethe; but then Goethe stands before
all men's eyes, the manifest centre of German literature;
and from this central source many rivers flow. Which
of these rivers is the main stream? which of the courses
of spirit which we see active in Goethe is the course
which will most influence the future, and attract and be
continued by the most powerful of Goethe's successors?
—that is the question. Mr. Carlyle attaches, it seems to
me, far too much importance to the romantic school of
Germany,—Tieck, Novalis, Jean Paul Richter,—and
gives to these writers, really gifted as two, at any rate,
of them are, an undue prominence. These writers, and
others with aims and a general tendency the same as
theirs, are not the real inheritors and continuators of
Goethe's power; the current of their activity is not the
main current of German literature after Goethe. Far
more in Heine's works flows this main current; Heine,
far more than Tieck or Jean Paul Richter, is the continuator of that which, in Goethe's varied activity, is the
most powerful and vital; on Heine, of all German authors
who survived Goethe, incomparably the largest portion
of Goethe's mantle fell. I do not forget that when
Mr. Carlyle was dealing with German literature, Heine,

though he was clearly risen above the horizon, had not
shone forth with all his strength ; I do not forget, too,
that after ten or twenty years many things may come out
plain before the critic which before were hard to be
discerned by him ; and assuredly no one would dream
of imputing it as a fault to Mr. Carlyle that twenty years
ago he mistook the central current in German literature,
overlooked the rising Heine, and attached undue importance to that romantic school which Heine was to
destroy; one may rather note it as a misfortune, sent
perhaps as a delicate chastisement to a critic, who,—
man of genius as he is, and no one recognises his genius
more admiringly than I do,—has, for the functions of
the critic, a little too much of the self-will and eccentricity
of a genuine son of Great Britain.

Heine is noteworthy, because he is the most important
German successor and continuator of Goethe in Goethe's
most important line of activity.   And which of Goethe's
lines of activity is this?—His line of activity as " a
soldier in the war of liberation of humanity."

Heine himself would hardly have admitted this
affiliation, though he was far too powerful-minded a
man to decry, with some of the vulgar German liberals,
Goethe's genius.   " The wind of the Paris Revolution,"
he writes after the three days of 1830, " blew about the
candles a little in the dark night of Germany, so that the
red curtains of a German throne or two caught fire ; but
the old watchmen, who do the police of the German
kingdoms, are already bringing out the fire-engines, and
will keep the candles closer snuffed for the future.   Poor,
fast-bound German people, lose not all heart in thy

bonds ! The fashionable coating of ice melts off from my heart, my soul quivers and my eyes burn, and that is a disadvantageous state of things for a writer, who should control his subject-matter and keep himself beautifully objective, as the artistic school would have us, and as Goethe has done ; he has come to be eighty years old doing this, and minister, and in good condition ;—poor German people ! that is thy greatest man !"

But hear Goethe himself: "If I were to say what I had really been to the Germans in general, and to the young German poets in particular, I should say I had been their *liberator*."

Modern times find themselves with an immense system of institutions, established facts, accredited dogmas, customs, rules, which have come to them from times not modern.　In this system their life has to be carried forward ; yet they have a sense that this system is not of their own creation, that it by no means corresponds exactly with the wants of their actual life, that, for them, it is customary, not rational.　The awakening of this sense is the awakening of the modern spirit.　The modern spirit is now awake almost everywhere ; the sense of want of correspondence between the forms of modern Europe and its spirit, between the new wine of the eighteenth and nineteenth centuries, and the old bottles of the eleventh and twelfth centuries, or even of the sixteenth and seventeenth, almost every one now perceives ; it is no longer dangerous to affirm that this want of correspondence exists ; people are even beginning to be shy of denying it.　To remove this want of correspondence is beginning to be the settled

endeavour of most persons of good sense. Dissolvents
of the old European system of dominant ideas and
facts we must all be, all of us who have any power of
working; what we have to study is that we may not be
acrid dissolvents of it.

And how did Goethe, that grand dissolvent in an age
when there were fewer of them than at present, proceed
in his task of dissolution, of liberation of the modern
European from the old routine? He shall tell us himself.
"Through me the German poets have become aware
that, as man must live from within outwards, so the
artist must work from within outwards, seeing that, make
what contortions he will, he can only bring to light his
own individuality. I can clearly mark where this influence of mine has made itself felt; there arises out of
it a kind of poetry of Nature, and only in this way is it
possible to be original."

My voice shall never be joined to those which decry
Goethe, and if it is said that the foregoing is a lame and
impotent conclusion to Goethe's declaration that he had
been the liberator of the Germans in general, and of the
young German poets in particular, I say it is not.
Goethe's profound, imperturbable naturalism is absolutely fatal to all routine thinking; he puts the standard,
once for all, inside every man instead of outside him;
when he is told, such a thing must be so, there is immense authority and custom in favour of its being so, it
has been held to be so for a thousand years, he answers
with Olympian politeness, "But *is* it so? is it so to *me?*"
Nothing could be more really subversive of the founda-
tions on which the old European order rested; and it

may be remarked that no persons are so radically detached from this order, no persons so thoroughly modern,
as those who have felt Goethe's influence most deeply.
If it is said that Goethe professes to have in this way
deeply influenced but a few persons, and those persons
poets, one may answer that he could have taken no
better way to secure, in the end, the ear of the world ; for
poetry is simply the most beautiful, impressive, and widely
effective mode of saying things, and hence its importance.   Nevertheless the process of liberation, as Goethe
worked it, though sure, is undoubtedly slow ; he came,
as Heine says, to be eighty years old in thus working it,
and at the end of that time the old Middle-Age machine
was still creaking on, the thirty German courts and their
chamberlains subsisted in all their glory ; Goethe himself
was a minister, and the visible triumph of the modern
spirit over prescription and routine seemed as far off as
ever.   It was the year 1830 ; the German sovereigns had
passed the preceding fifteen years in breaking the pro-
mises of freedom they had made to their subjects when
they wanted their help in the final struggle with Napoleon.   Great events were happening in France ; the
revolution, defeated in 1815, had arisen from its defeat,
and was wresting from its adversaries the power.   Heinrich Heine, a young man of genius, born at Hamburg,
and with all the culture of Germany, but by race a Jew ;
with warm sympathies for France, whose revolution had
given to his race the rights of citizenship, and whose rule
had been, as is well known, popular in the Rhine pro-
vinces, where he passed his youth ; with a passionate
admiration for the great French Emperor, with a passion-

ate contempt for the sovereigns who had overthrown him, for their agents, and for their policy,—Heinrich Heine was in 1830 in no humour for any such gradual process of liberation from the old order of things as that which Goethe had followed. His counsel was for open war. With that terrible modern weapon, the pen, in his hand, he passed the remainder of his life in one fierce battle. What was that battle? the reader will ask. It was a life and death battle with Philistinism.

Philistinism !—we have not the expression in English. Perhaps we have not the word because we have so much of the thing. At Soli, I imagine, they did not talk of solecisms ; and here, at the very head-quarters of Goliath, nobody talks of Philistinism. The French have adopted the term *épicier* (grocer), to designate the sort of being whom the Germans designate by the term Philistine ; but the French term,—besides that it casts a slur upon a respectable class, composed of living and susceptible members, while the original Philistines are dead and buried long ago,—is really, I think, in itself much less apt and expressive than the German term. Efforts have been made to obtain in English some term equivalent to *Philister* or *épicier;* Mr. Carlyle has made several such efforts : " respectability with its thousand gigs," he says ; —well, the occupant of every one of those gigs is, Mr. Carlyle means, a Philistine. However, the word *respectable* is far too valuable a word to be thus perverted from its proper meaning ; if the English are ever to have a word for the thing we are speaking of,—and so prodigious are the changes which the modern spirit is introducing, that even we English shall perhaps one day come to want such a word,—I think we had much better take the term *Philistine* itself.

Philistine must have originally meant, in the mind of those who invented the nickname, a strong, dogged, unenlightened opponent of the chosen people, of the children of the light. The party of change, the would-be remodellers of the old traditional European order, the invokers of reason against custom, the representatives of the modern spirit in every sphere where it is applicable, regarded themselves, with the robust self-confidence natural to reformers, as a chosen people, as children of the light. They regarded their adversaries as humdrum people, slaves to routine, enemies to light ; stupid and oppressive, but at the same time very strong. This explains the love which Heine, that Paladin of the modern spirit, has for France ; it explains the preference which he gives to France over Germany : " the French," he says, " are the chosen people of the new religion, its first gospels and dogmas have been drawn up in their language ; Paris is the new Jerusalem, and the Rhine is the Jordan which divides the consecrated land of freedom from the land of the Philistines." He means that the French, as a people, have shown more accessibility to ideas than any other people ; that prescription and routine have had less hold upon them than upon any other people ; that they have shown most readiness to move and to alter at the bidding (real or supposed) of reason. This explains, too, the detestation which Heine had for the English : " I might settle in England," he says, in his exile, " if it were not that I should find there two things, coal-smoke and Englishmen ; I cannot abide either." What he hated in the English was the "ächt-brittische Beschränktheit," as he calls it,—the *genuine British narrowness*. In truth, the English, profoundly as they have modified the old Middle-Age order, great as is the liberty which they have secured for themselves, have in all their changes proceeded, to use a familiar expression, by the rule of thumb ; what was intolerably inconvenient to them they have suppressed, and as they have suppressed it, not because it was irrational, but because it was practically inconvenient, they have seldom in suppressing it appealed to reason, but always, if possible, to some precedent, or form, or letter, which served as a convenient instrument for their purpose, and which saved them from the necessity of recurring to general principles. They have thus become, in a certain sense, of all people the most inaccessible to ideas and the most impatient of them ; inaccessible to them, because of their want of familiarity with them ; and im-patient of them because they have got on so well without them, that they despise those who, not having got on as well as themselves, still make a fuss for what they them-selves have done so well without. But there has certainly followed from hence, in this country, somewhat of a general depression of pure intelligence : Philistia has come to be thought by us the true Land of Promise, and it is anything but that ; the born lover of ideas, the born hater of commonplaces, must feel in this country, that the sky over his head is of brass and iron. The enthusiast for the idea, for reason, values reason, the idea, in and for themselves ; he values them, irrespectively of the practical conveniences which their triumph may obtain for him ; and the man who regards the possession of these practical conveniences as something sufficient in itself, something which compensates for the absence or surrender of the idea, of reason, is, in his eyes, a Philistine. This is why Heine so often and so mercilessly attacks the liberals; much as he hates conservatism he hates Philistinism even more, and whoever attacks conservatism itself ignobly, not as a child of light, not in the name of the idea, is a Philistine. Our Cobbett is thus for him, much as he disliked our clergy and aristocracy whom Cobbett attacked, a Philistine with six fingers on every hand and on every foot six toes, four-and-twenty in number : a Philistine, the staff of whose spear is like a weaver's beam. Thus he speaks of him :—

" While I translate Cobbett's words, the man himself comes bodily before my mind's eye, as I saw him at that uproarious dinner at the Crown and Anchor Tavern, with his scolding red face and his radical laugh, in which venomous hate mingles with a mocking exultation at his enemies' surely approaching downfall. He is a chained cur, who falls with equal fury on every one whom he does not know, often bites the best friend of the house in his calves, barks incessantly, and just because of this incessantness of his barking cannot get listened to, even when he barks at a real thief. Therefore, the distinguished thieves who plunder England do not think it necessary to throw the growling Cobbett a bone to stop his mouth. This makes the dog furiously savage, and he shows all his hungry teeth. Poor old Cobbett ! England's dog ! I have no love for thee, for every vulgar nature my soul abhors ; but thou touchest me to the

inmost soul with pity, as I see how thou strainest in vain
to break loose and to get at those thieves, who make off
with their booty before thy very eyes, and mock at thy
fruitless springs and thine impotent howling."

There is balm in Philistia as well as in Gilead. A
chosen circle of children of the modern spirit, perfectly
emancipated from prejudice and commonplace, regarding
the ideal side of things in all its efforts for change, passionately despising half-measures and condescension to
human folly and obstinacy,—with a bewildered, timid,
torpid multitude behind,—conducts a country to the
ministry of Herr von Bismarck. A nation regarding the
practical side of things in its efforts for change, attacking
not what is irrational, but what is pressingly inconvenient,
and attacking this as one body, "moving altogether if
it move at all," and treating children of light like the
very harshest of step-mothers, comes to the prosperity
and liberty of modern England. For all that, however,
Philistia (let me say it again) is not the true promised
land, as we English commonly imagine it to be ; and our
excessive neglect of the idea, and consequent inaptitude
for it, threatens us, at a moment when the idea is beginning
to exercise a real power in human society, with serious
future inconvenience, and, in the meanwhile, cuts us off
from the sympathy of other nations, which feel its power
more than we do.

But, in 1830, Heine very soon found that the fire-
engines of the German governments were too much for
his direct efforts at incendiarism. "What demon drove
me," he cries, "to write my *Reisebilder*, to edit a newspaper, to plague myself with our time and its interests,

to try and shake the poor German Hodge out of his
thousand years' sleep in his hole ?   What good did I get
by it ?   Hodge opened his eyes, only to shut them again
immediately ; he yawned, only to begin snoring again
the next minute louder than ever ; he stretched his stiff
ungainly limbs, only to sink down again directly afterwards, and lie like a dead man in the old bed of his
accustomed habits.   I must have rest ; but where am
I to find a resting-place ?   In Germany I can no longer
stay."

This is Heine's jesting account of his own efforts to
rouse Germany : now for his pathetic account of them ;
it is because he unites so much wit with so much pathos
that he is so effective a writer :—

"The Emperor Charles the Fifth sate in sore straits,
in the Tyrol, encompassed by his enemies.   All his
knights and courtiers had forsaken him ; not one came
to his help.   I know not if he had at that time the
cheese face with which Holbein has painted him for us.
But I am sure that under-lip of his, with its contempt for
mankind, stuck out even more than it does in his portraits.   How could he but contemn the tribe which in
the sunshine of his prosperity had fawned on him so
devotedly, and now, in his dark distress, left him all
alone ?   Then suddenly his door opened, and there came
in a man in disguise, and, as he threw back his cloak,
the Kaiser recognised in him his faithful Conrad von
der Rosen, the court jester.   This man brought him
comfort and counsel, and he was the court jester !

"O German fatherland ! dear German people ! I am
thy Conrad von der Rosen.   The man whose proper

business was to amuse thee, and who in good times should have catered only for thy mirth, makes his way into thy prison in time of need; here, under my cloak, I bring thee thy sceptre and crown; dost thou not recognise me, my Kaiser? If I cannot free thee, I will at least comfort thee, and thou shalt at least have one with thee who will prattle with thee about thy sorest affliction, and whisper courage to thee, and love thee, and whose best joke and best blood shall be at thy service. For thou, my people, art the true Kaiser, the true lord of the land; thy will is sovereign, and more legitimate far than that purple *Tel est notre plaisir*, which invokes a divine right with no better warrant than the anointings of shaven and shorn jugglers; thy will, my people, is the sole rightful source of power. Though now thou liest down in thy bonds, yet in the end will thy rightful cause prevail; the day of deliverance is at hand, a new time is beginning. My Kaiser, the night is over, and out there glows the ruddy dawn.

" ' Conrad von der Rosen, my fool, thou art mistaken; perhaps thou takest a headsman's gleaming axe for the sun, and the red of dawn is only blood.'

" ' No, my Kaiser, it is the sun, though it is rising in the west; these six thousand years it has always risen in the east; it is high time there should come a change.'

" ' Conrad von der Rosen, my fool, thou hast lost the bells out of thy red cap, and it has now such an odd look, that red cap of thine!'

" ' Ah, my Kaiser, thy distress has made me shake my head so hard and fierce, that the fool's bells have dropped off my cap; the cap is none the worse for that.

"'Conrad von der Rosen, my fool, what is that noise of breaking and cracking outside there?'

"'Hush! that is the saw and the carpenter's axe, and soon the doors of thy prison will be burst open, and thou wilt be free, my Kaiser!'

"'Am I then really Kaiser? Ah, I forgot, it is the fool who tells me so!'

"'Oh, sigh not, my dear master, the air of thy prison makes thee so desponding: when once thou hast got thy rights again, thou wilt feel once more the bold imperial blood in thy veins, and thou wilt be proud like a Kaiser, and violent, and gracious, and unjust, and smiling, and ungrateful, as princes are.'

"'Conrad von der Rosen, my fool, when I am free, what wilt thou do then?'

"'I will then sew new bells on to my cap.'

"'And how shall I recompense thy fidelity?'

"'Ah, dear master, by not leaving me to die in a ditch!'"

I wish to mark Heine's place in modern European literature, the scope of his activity, and his value. I cannot attempt to give here a detailed account of his life, or a description of his separate works. In May, 1831, he went over his Jordan, the Rhine, and fixed himself in his new Jerusalem, Paris. There, henceforward, he lived, going in general to some French watering-place in the summer, but making only one or two short visits to Germany during the rest of his life. His works, in verse and prose, succeeded each other without stopping; a collected edition of them, filling seven closely-printed octavo volumes, has been published in America;* in the

* A complete edition has at last appeared in Germany.

collected editions of few people's works is there so little
to skip. Those who wish for a single good specimen of
him should read his first important work, the work which
made his reputation, the *Reisebilder*, or "Travelling
Sketches:" prose and verse, wit and seriousness, are
mingled in it, and the mingling of these is characteristic
of Heine, and is nowhere to be seen practised more
naturally and happily than in his *Reisebilder*. In 1847
his health, which till then had always been perfectly good,
gave way. He had a kind of paralytic stroke. His
malady proved to be a softening of the spinal marrow:
it was incurable; it made rapid progress. In May, 1848,
not a year after his first attack, he went out of doors for
the last time; but his disease took more than eight years
to kill him. For nearly eight years he lay helpless on a
couch, with the use of his limbs gone, wasted almost to
the proportions of a child, wasted so that a woman could
carry him about; the sight of one eye lost, that of the
other greatly dimmed, and requiring, that it might be
exercised, to have the palsied eyelid lifted and held up
by the finger; all this, and suffering, besides this, at short
intervals, paroxysms of nervous agony. I have said he
was not pre-eminently brave; but in the astonishing force
of spirit with which he retained his activity of mind, even
his gaiety, amid all this suffering, and went on composing
with undiminished fire to the last, he was truly brave.
Nothing could clog that aërial lightness. " Pouvez-vous
siffler ?" his doctor asked him one day, when he was
almost at his last gasp ;—" siffler," as every one knows,
has the double meaning of *to whistle* and *to hiss.*—
" Hélas ! non," was his whispered answer; " pas même

une comédie de M. Scribe!"   M. Scribe is, or was, the favourite dramatist of the French Philistine. "My nerves," he said to some one who asked him about them in 1855, the year of the Great Exhibition in Paris, " my nerves are of that quite singularly remarkable miserableness of nature, that I am convinced they would get at the Exhibition the grand medal for pain and misery."   He read all the medical books which treated of his complaint. " But," said he to some one who found him thus engaged, " what good this reading is to do me I don't know, except that it will qualify me to give lectures in heaven on the ignorance of doctors on earth about diseases of the spinal marrow."   What a matter of grim seriousness are our own ailments to most of us ! yet with this gaiety Heine treated his to the end. That end, so long in coming, came at last.   Heine died on the 17th of February, 1856, at the age of fifty-eight.   By his will he forbade that his remains should be transported to Germany.   He lies buried in the cemetery of Montmartre, at Paris.

His direct political action was null, and this is neither to be wondered at nor regretted ; direct political action is not the true function of literature, and Heine was a born man of letters. Even in his favourite France the turn taken by public affairs was not at all what he wished, though he read French politics by no means as we in England, most of us, read them. He thought things were tending there to the triumph of communism ; and to a champion of the idea like Heine, what there is gross and narrow in communism was very repulsive. "It is all of no use," he cried on his death-bed, " the future belongs to our enemies, the Communists, and Louis

Napoleon is their John the Baptist." "And yet,"—he added with all his old love for that remarkable entity, so full of attraction for him, so profoundly unknown in England, the French people,—"do not believe that God lets all this go forward merely as a grand comedy. Even though the Communists deny him to-day, he knows better than they do, that a time will come when they will learn to believe in him." After 1831 his hopes of soon upsetting the German governments had died away, and his propagandism took another, a more truly literary, character. It took the character of an intrepid application of the modern spirit to literature. To the ideas with which the burning questions of modern life filled him, he made all his subject-matter minister. He touched all the great points in the career of the human race, and here he but followed the tendency of the wide culture of Germany; but he touched them with a wand which brought them all under a light where the modern eye cares most to see them, and here he gave a lesson to the culture of Germany,—so wide, so impartial, that it is apt to become slack and powerless, and to lose itself in its materials for want of a strong central idea round which to group all its other ideas. So the mystic and romantic school of Germany lost itself in the Middle Ages, was overpowered by their influence, came to ruin by its vain dreams of renewing them. Heine, with a far profounder sense of the mystic and romantic charm of the Middle Age than Görres, or Brentano, or Arnim, Heine the chief romantic poet of Germany, is yet also much more than a romantic poet; he is a great modern poet, he is not conquered by the Middle Age, he has a talisman by

which he can feel,—along with but above the power of
the fascinating Middle Age itself,—the power of modern
ideas.

A French critic of Heine thinks he has said enough
in saying that Heine proclaimed in German countries,
with beat of drum, the ideas of 1789, and that at the
cheerful noise of his drum the ghosts of the Middle
Age took to flight. But this is rather too French an
account of the matter. Germany, that vast mine of
ideas, had no need to import ideas, as such, from any
foreign country ; and if Heine had carried ideas, as such,
from France into Germany, he would but have been
carrying coals to Newcastle. But that for which France,
far less meditative than Germany, is eminent, is the
prompt, ardent, and practical application of an idea,
when she seizes it, in all departments of human activity
which admit it. And that in which Germany most fails,
and by failing in which she appears so helpless and
impotent, is just this practical application of her innu-
merable ideas. "When Candide," says Heine himself,
"came to Eldorado," he saw in the streets a number of
boys who were playing with gold-nuggets instead of
marbles. This degree of luxury made him imagine that
they must be the king's children, and he was not a little
astonished when he found that in Eldorado gold-nuggets
are of no more value than marbles are with us, and that
the schoolboys play with them. A similar thing happened
to a friend of mine, a foreigner, when he came to
Germany and first read German books. He was perfectly astounded at the wealth of ideas which he found
in them ; but he soon remarked that ideas in Germany

are as plentiful as gold-nuggets in Eldorado, and that those writers whom he had taken for intellectual princes, were in reality only common school-boys."   Heine was, as he calls himself, a " Child of the French Revolution," an " Initiator," because he vigorously assured the Germans that ideas were not counters or marbles, to be played with for their own sake; because he exhibited in literature modern ideas applied with the utmost freedom, clearness, and originality.   And therefore he declared that the great task of his life had been the endeavour to establish a cordial relation between France and Germany. It is because he thus operates a junction between the French spirit, and German ideas and German culture, that he founds something new, opens a fresh period, and deserves the attention of criticism far more than the German poets his contemporaries, who merely continue an old period till it expires.   It may be predicted that in the literature of other countries, too, the French spirit is destined to make its influence felt,—as an element, in alliance with the native spirit, of novelty and movement,— as it has made its influence felt in German literature; fifty years hence a critic will be demonstrating to our grandchildren how this phenomenon has come to pass.

We in England, in our great burst of literature during the first thirty years of the present century, had no manifestation of the modern spirit, as this spirit manifests itself in Goethe's works or Heine's.   And the reason is not far to seek.   We had neither the German wealth of ideas, nor the French enthusiasm for applying ideas. There reigned in the mass of the nation that inveterate inaccessibility to ideas, that Philistinism,—to use the

German nickname,—which reacts even on the individual genius that is exempt from it.   In our greatest literary epoch, that of the Elizabethan age, English society at large was accessible to ideas, was permeated by them, was vivified by them, to a degree which has never been reached in England since.   Hence the unique greatness in English literature of Shakspeare and his contemporaries; they were powerfully upheld by the intellectual life of their nation ; they applied freely in literature the then modern ideas,—the ideas of the Renaissance and the Reformation.   A few years afterwards the great English middle class, the kernel of the nation, the class whose intelligent sympathy had upheld a Shakspeare, entered the prison of Puritanism, and had the key turned on its spirit there for two hundred years.   *He enlargeth a nation*, says Job, *and straiteneth it again.* In the literary movement of the beginning of the nineteenth century the signal attempt to apply freely the modern spirit was made in England by two members of the aristocratic class, Byron and Shelley. Aristocracies are, as such, naturally impenetrable by ideas ; but their individual members have a high courage and a turn for breaking bounds ; and a man of genius, who is the born child of the idea, happening to be born in the aristocratic ranks, chafes against the obstacles which prevent him from freely developing it.   But Byron and Shelley did not succeed in their attempt freely to apply the modern spirit in English literature ; they could not succeed in it ; the resistance to baffle them, the want of intelligent sympathy to guide and uphold them, were too great. Their literary creation, compared with the literary creation of Shakspeare and Spenser, compared with the literary creation of Goethe and Heine, is a failure. The best literary creation of that time in England proceeded from men who did not make the same bold attempt as Byron and Shelley. What, in fact, was the career of the chief English men of letters, their contemporaries? The greatest of them, Wordsworth, retired (in Middle-Age phrase) into a monastery. I mean, he plunged himself in the inward life, he voluntarily cut himself off from the modern spirit. Coleridge took to opium. Scott became the historiographer royal of feudalism. Keats passionately gave himself up to a sensuous genius, to his faculty for interpreting nature; and he died of consumption at twenty-five. Wordsworth, Scott, and Keats have left admirable works; far more solid and complete works than those which Byron and Shelley have left. But their works have this defect;—they do not belong to that which is the main current of the literature of modern epochs, they do not apply modern ideas to life; they constitute, therefore, *minor currents*, and all other literary work of our day, however popular, which has the same defect, also constitutes but a minor current. Byron and Shelley will be long remembered, long after the inadequacy of their actual work is clearly recognised, for their passionate, their Titanic effort to flow in the main stream of modern literature; their names will be greater than their writings; *stat magni nominis umbra.*

Heine's literary good fortune was greater than that of Byron and Shelley. His theatre of operations was Germany, whose Philistinism does not consist in her want of ideas, or in her inaccessibility to ideas, for she teems with them and loves them, but, as I have said, in her feeble and hesitating application of modern ideas to life. Heine's intense modernism, his absolute freedom, his utter rejection of stock classicism and stock romanticism, his bringing all things under the point of view of the nineteenth century, were understood and laid to heart by Germany, through virtue of her immense, tolerant intellectualism, much as there was in all Heine said to affront and wound Germany. The wit and ardent modern spirit of France Heine joined to the culture, the sentiment, the thought of Germany. This is what makes him so remarkable; his wonderful clearness, lightness, and freedom, united with such power of feeling and width of range. Is there anywhere keener wit than in his story of the French abbé who was his tutor, and who wanted to get from him that *la religion* is French for *der Glaube:* "Six times did he ask me the question : ' Henry, what is *der Glaube* in French ?' and six times, and each time with a greater burst of tears, did I answer him—' It is *le crédit.*' And at the seventh time, his face purple with rage, the infuriated questioner screamed out : ' It is *la religion;*' and a rain of cuffs descended upon me, and all the other boys burst out laughing. Since that day I have never been able to hear *la religion* mentioned, without feeling a tremor run through my back, and my cheeks grow red with shame." Or in that comment on the fate of Professor Saalfeld, who had been addicted to writing furious pamphlets against Napoleon, and who was a professor at Göttingen, a great seat, according to Heine, of pedantry and Philistinism : " It is curious," says Heine, " the three greatest adversaries of Napoleon have all of them ended miserably. Castlereagh cut his own throat; Louis the Eighteenth rotted upon his throne; and Professor Saalfeld is still a professor at Göttingen." It is impossible to go beyond that.

What wit, again, in that saying which every one has heard: "The Englishman loves liberty like his lawful wife, the Frenchman loves her like his mistress, the German loves her like his old grandmother." But the turn Heine gives to this incomparable saying is not so well known; and it is by that turn he shows himself the born poet he is,—full of delicacy and tenderness, of inexhaustible resource, infinitely new and striking :—

"And yet, after all, no one can ever tell how things may turn out. The grumpy Englishman, in an ill-temper with his wife, is capable of some day putting a rope round her neck, and taking her to be sold at Smithfield. The inconstant Frenchman may become unfaithful to his adored mistress, and be seen fluttering about the Palais Royal after another. *But the German will never quite abandon his old grandmother;* he will always keep for her a nook by the chimney-corner, where she can tell her fairy stories to the listening children."

Is it possible to touch more delicately and happily both the weakness and the strength of Germany ;—pedantic, simple, enslaved, free, ridiculous, admirable Germany ?

And Heine's verse,—his *Lieder* ? Oh, the comfort, after dealing with French people of genius, irresistibly impelled to try and express themselves in verse, launching out into a deep which destiny has sown with so many rocks for them,—the comfort of coming to a man of genius, who finds in verse his freest and most perfect

expression, whose voyage over the deep of poetry destiny
makes smooth !   After the rhythm, to us, at any rate, with
the German paste in our composition, so deeply unsatisfy-
ing, of—

> " Ah ! que me dites-vous, et que vous dit mon âme ?
>   Que dit le ciel à l'aube et la flamme à la flamme ! "

what a blessing to arrive at rhythms like—

> " Take, oh, take those lips away,
>   That so sweetly were forsworn— "

or—

> " Siehst sehr sterbeblässlich aus,
>   Doch getrost ! du bist zu Haus,"

in which one's soul can take pleasure !   The magic of
Heine's poetical form is incomparable ; he chiefly uses a
form of old German popular poetry, a ballad-form which
has more rapidity and grace than any ballad-form of ours ;
he employs this form with the most exquisite lightness
and ease, and yet it has at the same time the inborn
fulness, pathos, and old-world charm of all true forms of
popular poetry.   Thus in Heine's poetry, too, one perpetually blends the impression of French modernism and
clearness, with that of German sentiment and fulness ;
and to give this blended impression is, as I have said,
Heine's great characteristic.   To feel it, one must read
him ; he gives it in his form as well as in his contents,
and by translation I can only reproduce it so far as his
contents give it.   But even the contents of many of his
poems are capable of giving a certain sense of it.   Here,
for instance, is a poem in which he makes his profession
of faith to an innocent beautiful soul, a sort of Gretchen,

the child of some simple mining people having their hut among the pines at the foot of the Hartz Mountains, who reproaches him with not holding the old articles of the Christian creed :—

" Ah, my child, while I was yet a little boy, while I yet sate upon my mother's knee, I believed in God the Father, who rules up there in Heaven, good and great ;

" Who created the beautiful earth, and the beautiful men and women thereon ; who ordained for sun, moon, and stars their courses.

" When I got bigger, my child, I comprehended yet a great deal more than this, and comprehended, and grew intelligent ; and I believe on the Son also ;

" On the beloved Son, who loved us, and revealed love to us ; and for his reward, as always happens, was crucified by the people.

" Now, when I am grown up, have read much, have travelled much, my heart swells within me, and with my whole heart I believe on the Holy Ghost.

" The greatest miracles were of his working, and still greater miracles doth he even now work ; he burst in sunder the oppressor's stronghold, and he burst in sunder the bondsman's yoke.

" He heals old death-wounds, and renews the old right ; all mankind are one race of noble equals before him.

" He chases away the evil clouds and the dark cobwebs of the brain, which have spoilt love and joy for us, which day and night have loured on us.

" A thousand knights, well harnessed, has the Holy Ghost chosen out to fulfil his will, and he has put courage into their souls.

"Their good swords flash, their bright banners wave ;
what, thou wouldst give much, my child, to look upon
such gallant knights ?

"Well, on me, my child, look ! kiss me, and look
boldly upon me ! one of those knights of the Holy Ghost
am I."

One has only to turn over the pages of his *Romancero*,
—a collection of poems written in the first years of his
illness, with his whole power and charm still in them,
and not, like his latest poems of all, painfully touched
by the air of his *Matrazzen-gruft*, his " mattress-grave,"—
to see Heine's width of range ; the most varied figures
succeed one another,—Rhampsinitus, Edith with the Swan
Neck, Charles the First, Marie Antoinette, King David,
a heroine of *Mabille*, Melisanda of Tripoli, Richard Cœur
de Lion, Pedro the Cruel, Firdusi, Cortes, Dr. Döllinger ;
—but never does Heine attempt to be *hübsch objectiv*,
" beautifully objective," to become in spirit an old
Egyptian, or an old Hebrew, or a Middle-Age knight, or
a Spanish adventurer, or an English royalist ; he always
remains Heinrich Heine, a son of the nineteenth century.
To give a notion of his tone I will quote a few stanzas at
the end of the *Spanish Atridæ*, in which he describes, in
the character of a visitor at the court of Henry of Transtamare at Segovia, Henry's treatment of the children of
his brother, Pedro the Cruel.   Don Diego Albuquerque,
his neighbour, strolls after dinner through the castle
with him :—

" In the cloister-passage, which leads to the kennels
where are kept the king's hounds, that with their growling
and yelping let you know a long way off where they are,

"There I saw, built into the wall, and with a strong iron grating for its outer face, a cell like a cage.

"Two human figures sate therein, two young boys; chained by the leg, they crouched in the dirty straw.

"Hardly twelve years old seemed the one, the other not much older; their faces fair and noble, but pale and wan with sickness.

"They were all in rags, almost naked; and their lean bodies showed wounds, the marks of ill-usage; both of them shivered with fever.

"They looked up at me out of the depth of their misery; 'Who,' I cried in horror to Don Diego, 'are these pictures of wretchedness!'

"Don Diego seemed embarrassed; he looked round to see that no one was listening; then he gave a deep sigh; and at last, putting on the easy tone of a man of the world, he said:

"'These are a pair of king's sons, who were early left orphans; the name of their father was King Pedro, the name of their mother Maria de Padilla.

"'After the great battle of Navarette, when Henry of Transtamare had relieved his brother, King Pedro, of the troublesome burden of the crown,

"'And likewise of that still more troublesome burden, which is called life, then Don Henry's victorious magnanimity had to deal with his brother's children.

"'He has adopted them, as an uncle should; and he has given them free quarters in his own castle.

"'The room which he has assigned to them is certainly rather small, but then it is cool in summer, and not intolerably cold in winter.

N

" ' Their fare is rye bread, which tastes as sweet as if the goddess Ceres had baked it express for her beloved Proserpine.

" ' Not unfrequently, too, he sends a scullion to them with garbanzos, and then the young gentlemen know that it is Sunday in Spain.

" ' But it is not Sunday every day, and garbanzos do not come every day ; and the master of the hounds gives them the treat of his whip.

" ' For the master of the hounds, who has under his superintendence the kennels and the pack, and the nephews' cage also,

" ' Is the unfortunate husband of that lemon-faced woman with the white ruff, whom we remarked to-day at dinner.

" ' And she scolds so sharp, that often her husband snatches his whip, and rushes down here, and gives it to the dogs and to the poor little boys.

" ' But his majesty has expressed his disapproval of such proceedings, and has given orders that for the future his nephews are to be treated differently from the dogs.

" ' He has determined no longer to entrust the disciplining of his nephews to a mercenary stranger, but to carry it out with his own hands.'

" Don Diego stopped abruptly ; for the seneschal of the castle joined us, and politely expressed his hope that we had dined to our satisfaction."

Observe how the irony of the whole of that, finishing with the grim innuendo of the last stanza but one, is at once truly masterly and truly modern.

No account of Heine is complete which does not notice

the Jewish element in him. His race he treated with
the same freedom with which he treated everything else,
but he derived a great force from it, and no one knew
this better than he himself. He has excellently pointed
out how in the sixteenth century there was a double
renaissance,—a Hellenic renaissance and a Hebrew renaissance,—and how both have been great powers ever
since. He himself had in him both the spirit of Greece
and the spirit of Judæa; both these spirits reach the
infinite, which is the true goal of all poetry and all art,—
the Greek spirit by beauty, the Hebrew spirit by sub-
limity. By his perfection of literary form, by his love
of clearness, by his love of beauty, Heine is Greek; by
his intensity, by his untamableness, by his "longing which
cannot be uttered," he is Hebrew. Yet what Hebrew
ever treated the things of the Hebrews like this?—

"There lives at Hamburg, in a one-roomed lodging
in the Baker's Broad Walk, a man whose name is Moses
Lump; all the week he goes about in wind and rain,
with his pack on his back, to earn his few shillings; but
when on Friday evening he comes home, he finds the
candlestick with seven candles lighted, and the table
covered with a fair white cloth, and he puts away from
him his pack and his cares, and he sits down to table
with his squinting wife and yet more squinting daughter,
and eats fish with them, fish which has been dressed in
beautiful white garlic sauce, sings therewith the grandest
psalms of King David, rejoices with his whole heart over
the deliverance of the children of Israel out of Egypt,
rejoices, too, that all the wicked ones who have done
the children of Israel harm, have ended by taking them-

selves off; that King Pharaoh, Nebuchadnezzar, Haman, Antiochus, Titus, and all such people, are well dead, while he, Moses Lump, is yet alive, and eating fish with wife and daughter; and I can tell you, Doctor, the fish is delicate and the man is happy, he has no call to torment himself about culture, he sits contented in his religion and in his green bed-gown, like Diogenes in his tub, he contemplates with satisfaction his candles, which he on no account will snuff for himself; and I can tell you, if the candles burn a little dim, and the snuffers-woman, whose business it is to snuff them, is not at hand, and Rothschild the Great were at that moment to come in, with all his brokers, bill-discounters, agents, and chief clerks, with whom he conquers the world, and Rothschild were to say: 'Moses Lump, ask of me what favour you will, and it shall be granted you;'— Doctor, I am convinced, Moses Lump would quietly answer: 'Snuff me those candles!' and Rothschild the Great would exclaim with admiration: 'If I were not Rothschild, I would be Moses Lump.'"

There Heine shows us his own people by its comic side; in the poem of the *Princess Sabbath* he shows it to us by a more serious side. The Princess Sabbath, " the *tranquil Princess*, pearl and flower of all beauty, fair as the Queen of Sheba, Solomon's bosom friend, that blue-stocking from Ethiopia who wanted to shine by her *esprit*, and with her wise riddles made herself in the long run a bore" (with Heine the sarcastic turn is never far off), this princess has for her betrothed a prince whom sorcery has transformed into an animal of lower race, the Prince Israel.

" A dog with the desires of a dog, he wallows all the week long in the filth and refuse of life, amidst the jeers of the boys in the street.

"But every Friday evening, at the twilight hour, suddenly the magic passes off, and the dog becomes once more a human being.

"A man with the feelings of a man, with head and heart raised aloft, in festal garb, in almost clean garb, he enters the halls of his Father.

" Hail, beloved halls of my royal Father ! Ye tents of Jacob, I kiss with my lips your holy door-posts !"

Still more he shows us this serious side in his beautiful poem on Jehuda ben Halevy, a poet belonging to " the great golden age of the Arabian, Old-Spanish, Jewish school of poets," a contemporary of the troubadours :—

"He, too,—the hero whom we sing,—Jehuda ben Halevy, too, had his lady-love ; but she was of a special sort.

"She was no Laura, whose eyes, mortal stars, in the cathedral on Good Friday kindled that world-renowned flame.

"She was no châtelaine, who in the blooming glory of her youth presided at tourneys, and awarded the victor's crown.

"No casuistess in the Gay Science was she, no lady *doctrinaire*, who delivered her oracles in the judgment-chamber of a Court of Love.

"She, whom the Rabbi loved, was a wobegone poor darling, a mourning picture of desolation ; and her name was Jerusalem."

Jehuda ben Halevy, like the Crusaders, makes his pilgrimage to Jerusalem; and there, amid the ruins, sings a song of Sion which has become famous among his people :—

"That lay of pearled tears is the wide-famed Lament, which is sung in all the scattered tents of Jacob throughout the world,

"On the ninth day of the month which is called Ab, on the anniversary of Jerusalem's destruction by Titus Vespasianus.

"Yes, that is the song of Sion, which Jehuda ben Halevy sang with his dying breath amid the holy ruins of Jerusalem.

"Barefoot, and in penitential weeds, he sate there upon the fragment of a fallen column ; down to his breast fell,

"Like a grey forest, his hair ; and cast a weird shadow on the face which looked out through it,—his troubled pale face, with the spiritual eyes.

"So he sate and sang, like unto a seer out of the foretime to look upon : Jeremiah, the Ancient, seemed to have risen out of his grave.

"But a bold Saracen came riding that way, aloft on his barb, lolling in his saddle, and brandishing a naked javelin ;

"Into the breast of the poor singer he plunged his deadly shaft, and shot away like a winged shadow.

"Quietly flowed the Rabbi's life-blood, quietly he sang his song to an end ; and his last dying sigh was Jerusalem !"

But, most of all, he shows it us in a strange poem describing a public dispute before King Pedro and his court between a Jewish and a Christian champion, on the merits of their respective faiths. In the strain of the Jew all the fierceness of the old Hebrew genius, all its rigid defiant Monotheism, appear :—

"Our God has not died like a poor innocent lamb for mankind; he is no gushing philanthropist, no declaimer.

"Our God is not love; caressing is not his line; but he is a God of thunder, and he is a God of revenge.

"The lightnings of his wrath strike inexorably every sinner, and the sins of the fathers are often visited upon their remote posterity.

"Our God, he is alive, and in his hall of heaven he goes on existing away, throughout all the eternities.

"Our God, too, is a God in robust health, no myth, pale and thin as sacrificial wafers, or as shadows by Cocytus.

"Our God is strong. In his hand he upholds sun, moon, and stars; thrones break, nations reel to and fro, when he knits his forehead.

"Our God loves music, the voice of the harp and the song of feasting; but the sound of church-bells he hates, as he hates the grunting of pigs."

Nor must Heine's sweetest note be unheard,—his plaintive note, his note of melancholy. Here is a strain which came from him as he lay, in the winter night, on his "mattress-grave" at Paris, and let his thoughts wander home to Germany, "the great child, entertaining herself with her Christmas-tree." "Thou tookest,"—he cries to the German exile—

"Thou tookest thy flight towards sunshine and happiness; naked and poor returnest thou back. German truth, German shirts,—one gets them worn to tatters in foreign parts.

"Deadly pale are thy looks, but take comfort, thou art at home; one lies warm in German earth, warm as by the old pleasant fireside.

"Many a one, alas! became crippled, and could get home no more: longingly he stretches out his arms; God have mercy upon him!"

God have mercy upon him! for what remain of the days of the years of his life are few and evil. "Can it be that I still actually exist? My body is so shrunk that there is hardly anything of me left but my voice, and my bed makes me think of the melodious grave of the enchanter Merlin, which is in the forest of Broceliand in Brittany, under high oaks whose tops shine like green flames to heaven. Ah, I envy thee those trees, brother Merlin, and their fresh waving; for over my mattress-grave here in Paris no green leaves rustle; and early and late I hear nothing but the rattle of carriages, hammering, scolding, and the jingle of the piano. A grave without rest, death without the privileges of the departed, who have no longer any need to spend money, or to write letters, or to compose books. What a melancholy situation!"

He died, and has left a blemished name; with his crying faults,—his intemperate susceptibility, his unscrupulousness in passion, his inconceivable attacks on his enemies, his still more inconceivable attacks on his friends, his want of generosity, his sensuality, his incessant mocking,—how could it be otherwise? Not only was he not one of Mr. Carlyle's "respectable" people, he was profoundly *dis*respectable ; and not even the merit of not being a Philistine can make up for a man's being that. To his intellectual deliverance there was an addition of something else wanting, and that something else was something immense ; the old-fashioned, laborious, eternally needful moral deliverance. Goethe says that he was deficient in *love;* to me his weakness seems to be not so much a deficiency in love as a deficiency in self-respect, in true dignity of character. But on this negative side of one's criticism of a man of great genius, I for my part, when I have once clearly marked that this negative side is and must be there, have no pleasure in dwelling. I prefer to say of Heine something positive. He is not an adequate interpreter of the modern world. He is only a brilliant soldier in the war of liberation of humanity. But, such as he is, he is (and posterity too, I am quite sure, will say this), in the European literature of that quarter of a century which follows the death of Goethe, incomparably the most important figure.

What a spendthrift, one is tempted to cry, is Nature ! With what prodigality, in the march of generations, she employs human power, content to gather almost always little result from it, sometimes none ! Look at Byron, that Byron whom the present generation of Englishmen are forgetting ; Byron, the greatest natural force, the greatest elementary power, I cannot but think, which has appeared in our literature since Shakspeare. And what became of this wonderful production of nature ? He shattered himself, he inevitably shattered himself to pieces, against the huge, black, cloud-topped, interminable precipice of British Philistinism. But Byron, it may be

said, was eminent only by his genius, only by his inborn
force and fire ; he had not the intellectual equipment of
a supreme modern poet ; except for his genius he was an
ordinary nineteenth-century English gentleman, with little
culture and with no ideas. Well, then, look at Heine.
Heine had all the culture of Germany ; in his head fer-
mented all the ideas of modern Europe. And what have
we got from Heine ? A half-result, for want of moral
balance, and of nobleness of soul and character.   That
is what I say ; there is so much power, so many seem
able to run well, so many give promise of running well ;
so few reach the goal, so few are chosen. *Many are
called, few chosen.*

I READ the other day in the *Dublin Review:*—"We Catholics are apt to be cowed and scared by the lordly oppression of public opinion, and not to bear ourselves as men in the face of the anti-Catholic society of England. It is good to have an habitual consciousness that the public opinion of Catholic Europe looks upon Protestant England with a mixture of impatience and compassion, which more than balances the arrogance of the English people towards the Catholic Church in these countries."

The Holy Catholic Church, Apostolic and Roman, can take very good care of herself, and I am not going to defend her against the scorns of Exeter Hall. Catholicism is not a great visible force in this country, and the mass of mankind will always treat lightly even things the most venerable, if they do not present themselves as visible forces before its eyes. In Catholic countries, as the *Dublin Review* itself says with triumph, they make very little account of the greatness of Exeter Hall. The majority has eyes only for the things of the majority, and in England the immense majority is Protestant. And yet, in spite of all the shocks which the feeling of a good Catholic, like the writer in the *Dublin Review*, has in this Protestant country inevitably to undergo, in

spite of the contemptuous insensibility to the grandeur
of Rome which he finds so general and so hard to bear,
how much has he to console him, how many acts of
homage to the greatness of his religion may he see if he
has his eyes open ! I will tell him of one of them, Let
him go in London to that delightful spot, that Happy
Island in Bloomsbury, the reading-room of the British
Museum. Let him visit its sacred quarter, the region
where its theological books are placed. I am almost
afraid to say what he will find there, for fear Mr. Spurgeon, like a second Caliph Omar, should give the library
to the flames. He will find an immense Catholic work,
the collection of the Abbé Migne, lording it over that
whole region, reducing to insignificance the feeble Protestant forces which hang upon its skirts. Protestantism
is duly represented, indeed; Mr. Panizzi knows his
business too well to suffer it to be otherwise; all the
varieties of Protestantism are there ; there is the Library
of Anglo-Catholic Theology, learned, decorous, exem-
plary, but a little uninteresting ; there are the works of
Calvin, rigid, militant, menacing ; there are the works of
Dr. Chalmers, the Scotch thistle valiantly doing duty as
the rose of Sharon, but keeping something very Scotch
about it all the time ; there are the works of Dr. Channing, the last word of religious philosophy in a land
where every one has some culture and where superiorities
are discountenanced,—the flower of moral and intelligent
mediocrity. But how are all these divided against one
-another, and how, though they were all united, are they
dwarfed by the Catholic Leviathan, their neighbour !
Majestic in its blue and gold unity, this fills shelf after

shelf and compartment after compartment, its right mounting up into heaven among the white folios of the *Acta Sanctorum*, its left plunging down into hell among the yellow octavos of the *Law Digest*. Everything is there, in that immense *Patrologiæ Cursus Completus*, in that *Encyclopédie Théologique*, that *Nouvelle Encyclopédie Théologique*, that *Troisième Encyclopédie Théologique;* religion, philosophy, history, biography, arts, sciences, bibliography, gossip. The work embraces the whole range of human interests; like one of the great Middle-Age Cathedrals, it is in itself a study for a life. Like the net in Scripture, it drags everything to land, bad and good, lay and ecclesiastical, sacred and profane, so that it be but matter of human concern. Wide-embracing as the power whose product it is! a power, for history, at any rate, eminently *the Church;* not, I think, the Church of the future, but indisputably the Church of the past, and, in the past, the Church of the multitude.

This is why the man of imagination,—nay, and the philosopher too, in spite of her propensity to burn him,—will always have a weakness for the Catholic Church; because of the rich treasures of human life which have been stored within her pale. The mention of other religious bodies, or of their leaders, at once calls up in our mind the thought of men of a definite type as their adherents ; the mention of Catholicism suggests no such special following. Anglicanism suggests the English episcopate ; Calvin's name suggests Dr. Candlish; Chalmers', the Duke of Argyll; Channing's, Boston society ; but Catholicism suggests,—what shall I say?—all the pell-mell of the. men and women of Shakspeare's plays. This abundance the Abbé Migne's collection faithfully reflects. People talk of this or that work which they would choose, if they were to pass their life with only one ; for my part I think I would choose the Abbé Migne's collection. *Quicquid agunt homines,*—everything, as I have said, is there. Do not seek in it splendour of form, perfection of editing ; its paper is common, its type ugly, its editing indifferent, its printing careless. The greatest and most baffling crowd of misprints I ever met with in my life occurs in a very important page of the introduction to the *Dictionnaire des Apocryphes.* But this is just what you have in the world,—quantity rather than quality. Do not seek in it impartiality, the critical spirit ; in reading it you must do the criticism for yourself ; it loves criticism as little as the world loves it. Like the world, it chooses to have things all its own way, to abuse its adversary, to back its own notion through thick and thin, to put forward all the *pros* for its own notion, to suppress all the *contras ;* it does just all that the world does, and all that the critical spirit shrinks from. Open the *Dictionnaire des Erreurs Sociales :* "The religious persecutions of Henry the Eighth's and Edward the Sixth's time abated a little in the reign of Mary, to break out again with new fury in the reign of Elizabeth." There is a summary of the history of religious persecution under the Tudors ! But how unreasonable to reproach the Abbé Migne's work with wanting a criticism, which, by the very nature of things, it cannot have, and not rather to be grateful to it for its abundance, its variety, its infinite suggestiveness, its happy adoption, in many a delicate circumstance, of the urbane tone and temper of the man of the world, instead of the acrid tone and temper of the fanatic !

Still, in spite of their fascinations, the contents of this collection sometimes rouse the critical spirit within one. It happened that lately, after I had been thinking much of Marcus Aurelius and his times, I took down the *Dictionnaire des Origines du Christianisme,* to see what it had to say about paganism and pagans. I found much what I expected. I read the article, *Révélation Évangélique, sa Nécessité.* There I found what a sink of iniquity was the whole pagan world ; how one Roman fed his oysters on his slaves, how another put a slave to death that a curious friend might see what dying was like ; how Galen's mother tore and bit her waiting-women when she was in a passion with them. I found this account of the religion of paganism : " Paganism invented a mob of divinities with the most hateful character, and attributed to them the most monstrous and abominable crimes. It personified in them drunkenness, incest, kidnapping, adultery, sensuality, knavery, cruelty, and rage." And I found that from this religion there followed such practice as was to be expected ; " What must naturally have been the state of morals under the influence of such a religion, which penetrated with its own spirit the public life, the family life, and the individual life of antiquity !"

The colours in this picture are laid on very thick, and I for my part cannot believe that any human societies, with a religion and practice such as those just described, could ever have endured as the societies of Greece and Rome endured, still less have done what the societies of Greece and Rome did. We are not brought far by

descriptions of the vices of great cities, or even of individuals driven mad by unbounded means of self-indulgence. Feudal and aristocratic life in Christendom has
produced horrors of selfishness and cruelty not surpassed
by the noble of pagan Rome; and then, again, in
antiquity there is Marcus Aurelius's mother to set against
Galen's. Eminent examples of vice and virtue in individuals prove little as to the state of societies. What,
under the first emperors, was the condition of the
Roman poor upon the Aventine compared with that of
our poor in Spitalfields and Bethnal Green? What,
in comfort, morals, and happiness, were the rural population of the Sabine country under Augustus's rule, compared with the rural population of Hertfordshire and
Buckinghamshire under the rule of Queen Victoria?

But these great questions are not for me. Without
trying to answer them, I ask myself, when I read such
declamation as the foregoing, if I can find anything that
will give me a near, distinct sense of the real difference in
spirit and sentiment between paganism and Christianity,
and of the natural effect of this difference upon people
in general. I take a representative religious poem of
paganism,—of the paganism which all the world has in
its mind when its speaks of paganism. To be a representative poem, it must be one for popular use, one that
the multitude listens to. Such a religious poem may
be found at the end of one of the best and happiest
of Theocritus's idylls, the fifteenth. In order that the
reader may the better go along with me in the line of
thought I am following, I will translate it; and, that he
may see the medium in which religious poetry of this

sort is found existing, the society out of which it grows, the people who form it and are formed by it, I will translate the whole, or nearly the whole, of the idyll (it is not long) in which the poem occurs.

The idyll is dramatic. Somewhere about two hundred and eighty years before the Christian era, a couple of Syracusan women, staying at Alexandria, agreed on the occasion of a great religious solemnity,—the feast of Adonis,—to go together to the palace of King Ptolemy Philadelphus, to see the image of Adonis, which the queen Arsinoe, Ptolemy's wife, had had decorated with peculiar magnificence. A hymn, by a celebrated performer, was to be recited over the image. The names of the two women are Gorgo and Praxinoe; their maids, who are mentioned in the poem, are called Eunoe and Eutychis. Gorgo comes by appointment to Praxinoe's house to fetch her, and there the dialogue begins :—

Gorgo.—Is Praxinoe at home?

Praxinoe.—My dear Gorgo, at last! Yes, here I am. Eunoe, find a chair,—get a cushion for it.

Gorgo.—It will do beautifully as it is.

Praxinoe.—Do sit down.

Gorgo.—Oh, this gad-about spirit! I could hardly get to you, Praxinoe, through all the crowd and all the carriages. Nothing but heavy boots, nothing but men in uniform. And what a journey it is! My dear child, you really live *too* far off.

Praxinoe.—It is all that insane husband of mine. He has chosen to come out here to the end of the world, and take a hole of a place,—for a house it is not,—on purpose that you and I might not be neighbours. He is always just the same;—anything to quarrel with one! anything for spite!

Gorgo.—My dear, don't talk so of your husband before the little fellow. Just see how astonished he looks at you. Never mind, Zopyrio, my pet, she is not talking about papa.

Praxinoe.—Good heavens! the child does really understand.

Gorgo.—Pretty papa!

Praxinoe.—That pretty papa of his the other day (though I told him beforehand to mind what he was about), when I sent him to a shop to buy soap and rouge, brought me home salt instead;—stupid, great, big, interminable animal!

Gorgo.—Mine is just the fellow to him. . . . But never mind now, get on your things and let us be off to the palace to see the Adonis. I hear the queen's decorations are something splendid.

Praxinoe.—In grand people's houses everything is grand. What things you have seen in Alexandria! What a deal you will have to tell to anybody who has never been here!

Gorgo.—Come, we ought to be going.

Praxinoe.—Every day is holiday to people who have nothing to do. Eunoe, pick up your work; and take care, lazy girl, how you leave it lying about again; the cats find it just the bed they like. Come, stir yourself, fetch me some water, quick! I wanted the water first, and the girl brings me the soap. Never mind; give it me. Not all that, extravagant! Now pour out the water;—stupid! why don't you take care of my dress? That will do.

I have got my hands washed as it pleased God.   Where
is the key of the large wardrobe?   Bring it here;—
quick !

Gorgo.—Praxinoe, you can't think how well that dress,
made full, as you've got it, suits you.   Tell me, how
much did it cost?—the dress by itself, I mean.

Praxinoe.—Don't talk of it, Gorgo : more than eight
guineas of good hard money.   And about the work on
it I have almost worn my life out.

Gorgo.—Well, you couldn't have done better.

Praxinoe.—Thank you.   Bring me my shawl, and put
my hat properly on my head ;—properly.   No, child (*to
her little boy*), I am not going to take you; there's a bogy
on horseback, who bites.   Cry as much as you like ;
I'm not going to have you lamed for life.   Now we'll
start.   Nurse, take the little one and amuse him ; call
the dog in, and shut the street-door.   (*They go out.*)
Good heavens ! what a crowd of people !   How on earth
are we ever to get through all this?   They are like
ants : you can't count them.   My dearest Gorgo, what
will become of us ? here are the royal Horse Guards.
My good man, don't ride over me !   Look at that bay
horse rearing bolt upright ; what a vicious one !   Eunoe,
you mad girl, do take care !—that horse will certainly be
the death of the man on his back.   How glad I am
now, that I left the child safe at home !

Gorgo.—All right, Praxinoe, we are safe behind them ;
and they have gone on to where they are stationed.

Praxinoe.—Well, yes, I begin to revive again.   From
the time I was a little girl I have had more horror of
horses and snakes than of anything in the world.   Let

us get on; here's a great crowd coming this way upon us.

Gorgo (to an old woman).—Mother, are you from the palace?

Old Woman.—Yes, my dears.

Gorgo.—Has one a tolerable chance of getting there?

Old Woman.—My pretty young lady, the Greeks got to Troy by dint of trying hard; trying will do anything in this world.

Gorgo.—The old creature has delivered herself of an oracle and departed.

Praxinoe.—Women can tell you everything about everything, Jupiter's marriage with Juno not excepted.

Gorgo.—Look, Praxinoe, what a squeeze at the palace gates!

Praxinoe.—Tremendous! Take hold of me, Gorgo; and you, Eunoe, take hold of Eutychis!—tight hold, or you'll be lost. Here we go in all together. Hold tight to us, Eunoe! Oh, dear! oh, dear! Gorgo, there's my scarf torn right in two. For heaven's sake, my good man, as you hope to be saved, take care of my dress!

Stranger.—I'll do what I can, but it doesn't depend upon me.

Praxinoe.—What heaps of people! They push like a drove of pigs.

Stranger.—Don't be frightened, ma'am, we are all right.

Praxinoe.—May you be all right, my dear sir, to the last day you live, for the care you have taken of us! What a kind, considerate man! There is Eunoe jammed in a squeeze. Push, you goose, push. Capital! We

are all of us the right side of the door, as the bridegroom
said when he had locked himself in with the bride.

Gorgo.—Praxinoe, come this way. Do but look at
that work, how delicate it is !—how exquisite ! Why, they
might wear it in heaven.

Praxinoe.—Heavenly patroness of needlewomen, what
hands were hired to do that work ? Who designed
those beautiful patterns ? They seem to stand up and
move about, as if they were real ;—as if they were living
things, and not needlework. Well, man is a wonderful
creature ! And look, look, how charming he lies there
on his silver couch, with just a soft down on his cheeks,
that beloved Adonis,—Adonis, whom one loves, even
though he is dead !

Another Stranger.—You wretched women, do stop your
incessant chatter ! Like turtles, you go on for ever.
They are enough to kill one with their broad lingo,—
nothing but *a, a, a.*

Gorgo.—Lord, where does the man come from ? What
is it to you if we *are* chatterboxes ? Order about your
own servants ! Do you give orders to Syracusan women ?
If you want to know, we came originally from Corinth,
as Bellerophon did ; we speak Peloponnesian. I suppose Dorian women may be allowed to have a Dorian
accent.

Praxinoe.—Oh, honey-sweet Proserpine, let us have no
more masters than the one we've got ! We don't the
least care for *you ;* pray don't trouble yourself for
nothing.

Gorgo.—Be quiet, Praxinoe ! That first-rate singer,
the Argive woman's daughter, is going to sing the *Adonis*

hymn. She is the same who was chosen to sing the dirge last year. We are sure to have something first-rate from *her*. She is going through her airs and graces ready to begin.

So far the dialogue; and, as it stands in the original, it can hardly be praised too highly. It is a page torn fresh out of the book of human life. What freedom! What animation! What gaiety! What naturalness! It is said that Theocritus, in composing this poem, borrowed from a work of Sophron, a poet of an earlier and better time; but, even if this is so, the form is still Theocritus's own, and how excellent is that form, how masterly! And this in a Greek poem of the decadence; for Theocritus's poetry, after all, is poetry of the decadence. When such is Greek poetry of the decadence, what must be Greek poetry of the prime?

Then the singer begins her hymn :—

" Mistress, who lovest the haunts of Golgi, and Idalium, and high-peaked Eryx, Aphrodite that playest with gold! how have the delicate-footed Hours, after twelve months, brought thy Adonis back to thee from the ever-flowing Acheron! Tardiest of the immortals are the boon Hours, but all mankind wait their approach with longing, for they ever bring something with them. O Cypris, Dione's child! thou didst change,—so is the story among men,—Berenice from mortal to immortal, by dropping ambrosia into her fair bosom; and in gratitude to thee for this, O thou of many names and many temples! Berenice's daughter, Arsinoe, lovely Helen's living counterpart, makes much of Adonis with all manner of braveries.

"All fruits that the tree bears are laid before him, all treasures of the garden in silver baskets, and alabaster boxes, gold-inlaid, of Syrian unguent; and all confectionary that cunning women make on their kneading-tray, kneading up every sort of flowers with white meal, and all that they make of sweet honey and delicate oil, and all winged and creeping things are here set before him. And there are built for him green bowers with wealth of tender anise, and little boy-loves flutter about over them, like young nightingales trying their new wings on the tree, from bough to bough. Oh, the ebony, the gold, the eagle of white ivory that bears aloft his cup-bearer to Kronos-born Zeus! And up there, see! a second couch strewn for lovely Adonis, scarlet coverlets softer than sleep itself (so Miletus and the Samian wool-grower will say); Cypris has hers, and the rosy-armed Adonis has his, that eighteen or nineteen-year-old bridegroom. His kisses will not wound, the hair on his lip is yet light.

"Now, Cypris, good-night, we leave thee with thy bridegroom; but to-morrow morning, with the earliest dew, we will one and all bear him forth to where the waves splash upon the sea-strand, and letting loose our locks, and letting fall our robes, with bosoms bare, we will set up this, our melodious strain :

"'Beloved Adonis, alone of the demigods (so men say) thou art permitted to visit both us and Acheron! This lot had neither Agamemnon, nor the mighty moon-struck hero Ajax, nor Hector the first-born of Hecuba's twenty children, nor Patroclus, nor Pyrrhus who came home from Troy, nor those yet earlier Lapithæ and the sons of Deucalion, nor the Pelasgians, the root of Argos and of Pelops' isle. Be gracious to us now, loved Adonis, and be favourable to us for the year to come! Dear to us hast thou been at this coming, dear to us shalt thou be when thou comest again.' "

The poem concludes with a characteristic speech from Gorgo :—

"Praxinoe, certainly women are wonderful things. That lucky woman to know all that! and luckier still to have such a splendid voice! And now we must see about getting home. My husband has not had his dinner. That man is all vinegar, and nothing else; and if you keep him waiting for his dinner, he's dangerous to go near. Adieu, precious Adonis, and may you find us all well when you come next year!"

So, with the hymn still in her ears, says the incorrigible Gorgo.

But what a hymn that is! Of religious emotion, in our acceptation of the words, and of the comfort springing from religious emotion, not a particle. And yet many elements of religious emotion are contained in the beautiful story of Adonis. Symbolically treated, as the thoughtful man might treat it, as the Greek mysteries undoubtedly treated it, this story was capable of a noble and touching application, and could lead the soul to elevating and consoling thoughts. Adonis was the sun in his summer and in his winter course, in his time of triumph and his time of defeat; but in his time of triumph still moving towards his defeat, in his time of defeat still returning towards his triumph. Thus he became an emblem of the power of life and the bloom of beauty, the power of human life and the bloom of human beauty, hastening inevitably to diminution and decay, yet in that very decay finding

"Hope, and a renovation without end."

But nothing of this appears in the story as prepared for popular religious use, as presented to the multitude in a popular religious ceremony.   Its treatment is not devoid of a certain grace and beauty, but it has nothing whatever that is elevating, nothing that is consoling, nothing that is in our sense of the word religious.   The religious ceremonies of Christendom, even on occasion of the most joyful and mundane matters, present the multitude with strains of profoundly religious character, such as the *Kyrie eleison* and the *Te Deum*.   But this Greek hymn to Adonis adapts itself exactly to the tone and temper of a gay and pleasure-loving multitude,—of light-hearted people, like Gorgo and Praxinoe, whose moral nature is much of the same calibre as that of Phillina in Goethe's *Wilhelm Meister*, people who seem never made to be serious, never made to be sick or sorry. And, if they happen to be sick or sorry, what will they do then? But that we have no right to ask.   Phillina, within the enchanted bounds of Goethe's novel, Gorgo and Praxinoe, within the enchanted bounds of Theocritus's poem, never will be sick and sorry, never can be sick and sorry. The ideal, cheerful, sensuous, pagan life is not sick or sorry.   No; yet its natural end is in the sort of life which Pompeii and Herculaneum bring so vividly before us ; a life which by no means in itself suggests the thought of horror and misery, which even, in many ways, gratifies the senses and the understanding ; but by the very intensity and unremittingness of its appeal to the senses and the understanding, by its stimulating a single side of us too absolutely, ends by fatiguing and revolting us ; ends by leaving us with a sense of tightness, of oppression,—with a desire for an utter change, for clouds, storms, effusion and relief.

In the beginning of the thirteenth century, when the clouds and storms had come, when the gay sensuous pagan life was gone, when men were not living by the senses and understanding, when they were looking for the speedy coming of Antichrist, there appeared in Italy, to the north of Rome, in the beautiful Umbrian country at the foot of the Apennines, a figure of the most magical power and charm, St. Francis. His century is, I think, the most interesting in the history of Christianity after its primitive age; more interesting than even the century of the Reformation ; and one of the chief figures, perhaps the very chief, to which this interest attaches itself, is St. Francis. And why ? Because of the profound popular instinct which enabled him, more than any man since the primitive age, to fit religion for popular use. He brought religion to the people. He founded the most popular body of ministers of religion that has ever existed in the Church. He transformed monachism by uprooting the stationary monk, delivering him from the bondage of property, and sending him, as a mendicant friar, to be a stranger and sojourner, not in the wilderness, but in the most crowded haunts of men, to console them and to do them good. This popular instinct of his is at the bottom of his

famous marriage with poverty.   Poverty and suffering
are the condition of the people, the multitude, the
immense majority of mankind ; and it was towards this
people that his soul yearned.   " He listens," it was said
of him, " to those to whom God himself will not listen."

So in return, as no other man he was listened to.
When an Umbrian town or village heard of his approach,
the whole population went out in joyful procession to
meet him, with green boughs, flags, music, and songs of
gladness.   The master, who began with two disciples,
could in his own lifetime (and he died at forty-four)
collect to keep Whitsuntide with him, in presence of an
immense multitude, five thousand of his Minorites.   He
found fulfilment to his prophetic cry : " I hear in my
ears the sound of the tongues of all the nations who
shall come unto us ; Frenchmen, Spaniards, Germans,
Englishmen.   The Lord will make of us a great people,
even unto the ends of the earth."

Prose could not satisfy this ardent soul, and he made
poetry.   Latin was too learned for this simple, popular
nature, and he composed in his mother tongue, in
Italian.   The beginnings of the mundane poetry of
the Italians are in Sicily, at the court of kings ; the
beginnings of their religious poetry are in Umbria, with
St. Francis.   His are the humble upper waters of a
mighty stream: at the beginning of the thirteenth century it is St. Francis, at the end, Dante.   Now it happens
that St. Francis, too, like the Alexandrian songstress,
has his hymn for the sun, for Adonis ; *Canticle of the
Sun, Canticle of the Creatures*, the poem goes by both
names.   Like the Alexandrian hymn, it is designed for

popular use, but not for use by King Ptolemy's people ; artless in language, irregular in rhythm, it matches with the childlike genius that produced it, and the simple natures that loved and repeated it :—

"O most high, almighty, good Lord God, to thee belong praise, glory, honour, and all blessing !

" Praised be my Lord God with all his creatures ; and specially our brother the sun, who brings us the day, and who brings us the light ; fair is he, and shining with a very great splendour : O Lord, he signifies to us thee !

"Praised be my Lord for our sister the moon, and for the stars, the which he has set clear and lovely in heaven.

"Praised be my Lord for our brother the wind, and for air and cloud, calms and all weather, by the which thou upholdest in life all creatures.

"Praised be my Lord for our sister water, who is very serviceable unto us, and humble, and precious, and clean.

"Praised be my Lord for our brother fire, through whom thou givest us light in the darkness ; and he is bright, and pleasant, and very mighty, and strong.

" Praised be my Lord for our mother the earth, the which doth sustain us and keep us, and bringeth forth divers fruits, and flowers of many colours, and grass.

"Praised be my Lord for all those who pardon one another for his love's sake, and who endure weakness and tribulation ; blessed are they who peaceably shall endure ; for thou, O most Highest, shalt give them a crown !

" Praised be my Lord for our sister, the death of the

body, from whom no man escapeth.   Woe to him who dieth in mortal sin.   Blessed are they who are found walking by thy most holy will, for the second death shall have no power to do them harm.

"Praise ye, and bless ye the Lord, and give thanks unto him, and serve him with great humility."

It is natural that man should take pleasure in his senses.   It is natural, also, that he should take refuge in his heart and imagination from his misery.   When one thinks what human life is for the vast majority of mankind, how little of a feast for their senses it can possibly be, one understands the charm for them of a refuge offered in the heart and imagination.   Above all, when one thinks what human life was in the Middle Ages, one understands the charm of such a refuge.

Now, the poetry of Theocritus's hymn is poetry treating the world according to the demand of the senses; the poetry of St. Francis's hymn is poetry treating the world according to the demand of the heart and imagination.   The first takes the world by its outward, sensible side ; the second by its inward, symbolical side.   The first admits as much of the world as is pleasure-giving ; the second admits the whole world, rough and smooth, painful and pleasure-giving, all alike, but all transfigured by the power of a spiritual emotion, all brought under a law of supersensual love, having its seat in the soul.   It can thus even say : " Praised be my Lord for *our sister, the death of the body.*"

But these very words are an indication that we are touching upon an extreme.   When we see Pompeii, we can put our finger upon the pagan sentiment in its extreme. And when we read of Monte Alverno and the *stigmata*, when we read of the repulsive, because self-caused, sufferings of the end of St. Francis's life, when we find even him saying : " I have sinned against my brother the ass," meaning by these words that he had been too hard upon his own body, when we find him doubting "whether he who had destroyed himself by the severity of his penances could find mercy in eternity," we can put our finger on the mediæval Christian sentiment in its extreme. Human nature is neither all senses and understanding, nor all heart and imagination. Pompeii was a sign that for humanity at large the measure of sensualism had been over-passed ; St. Francis's doubt was a sign that for humanity at large the measure of spiritualism had been over-passed. Humanity, in its violent rebound from one extreme, had swung from Pompeii to Monte Alverno ; but it was sure not to stay there.

The Renaissance is, in part, a return towards the pagan spirit, in the special sense in which I have been using the word pagan ; a return towards the life of the senses and the understanding. The Reformation, on the other hand, is the very opposite to this ; in Luther there is nothing Greek or pagan ; vehemently as he attacked the adoration of St. Francis, Luther had himself something of St. Francis in him ; he was a thousand times more akin to St. Francis than to Theocritus or to Voltaire. The Reformation,—I do not mean the inferior piece given under that name, by Henry the Eighth and a second-rate company, in this island, but the real Reformation, the German Reformation, Luther's Reformation,—was a reaction of the moral and spiritual sense against the carnal and pagan sense ; it was a religious revival like St. Francis's, but this time against the Church of Rome, not within her ; for the carnal and pagan sense had now, in the government of the Church of Rome herself, its prime representative. The grand reaction against the rule of the heart and imagination, the strong return towards the rule of the senses and understanding, is in the eighteenth century. And this reaction has had no more brilliant champion than a man of the nineteenth, of whom I have already spoken ; a man who could feel not only the pleasureableness but the poetry of the life of the senses (and the life of the senses has its deep poetry) ; a man who, in his very last poem, divided the whole world into "barbarians and Greeks,"—Heinrich Heine. No man has reproached the Monte Alverno extreme in sentiment, the Christian extreme, the heart and imagination subjugating the senses and understanding, more bitterly than Heine ; no man has extolled the Pompeii extreme, the pagan extreme, more rapturously.

"All through the· Middle Age these sufferings, this fever, this over-tension lasted ; and we moderns still feel in all our limbs the pain and weakness from them. Even those of us who are cured have still to live with a hospital-atmosphere all around us, and find ourselves as wretched in it as a strong man among the sick. Some day or other, when humanity shall have got quite well again, when the body and soul shall have made their peace together, the factitious quarrel which Christianity has cooked up between them will appear something hardly comprehensible. The fairer and happier generations, offspring of unfettered unions, that will rise up and bloom in the atmosphere of a religion of pleasure, will smile sadly when they think of their poor ancestors, whose life was passed in melancholy abstinence from the joys of this beautiful earth, and who faded away into spectres, from the mortal compression which they put upon the warm and glowing emotions of sense. Yes, with assurance I say it, our descendants will be fairer and happier than we are; for I am a believer in progress, and I hold God to be a kind being who has intended man to be happy."

That is Heine's sentiment, in the prime of life, in the glow of activity, amid the brilliant whirl of Paris. I will no more blame it than I blamed the sentiment of the Greek hymn to Adonis. I wish to decide nothing as of my own authority; the great art of criticism is to get oneself out of the way and to let humanity decide. Well, the sentiment of the " religion of pleasure " has much that is natural in it; humanity will gladly accept it if it can live by it; to live by it one must never be sick or sorry, and the old, ideal, limited, pagan world never, I have said, *was* sick or sorry, never at least shows itself to us sick or sorry :—

> " What pipes and timbrels! what wild ecstasy ! "

For our imagination, Gorgo and Praxinoe cross the human stage chattering in their blithe Doric,—*like turtles,* as the cross stranger said,—and keep gaily chattering on till they disappear. But in the new, real, immense, post-pagan world,—in the barbarian world,—the shock of accident is unceasing, the serenity of existence is perpetually troubled, not even a Greek like Heine can get across the mortal stage without bitter calamity. How does the sentiment of the " religion of pleasure " serve then ? does it help, does it console ? Can a man live by it ? Heine again shall answer ; Heine just twenty years older, stricken with incurable disease, waiting for death :—

" The great pot stands smoking before me, but I have no spoon to help myself. What does it profit me that my health is drunk at banquets out of gold cups and in the most exquisite wines, if I myself, while these ovations are going on, lonely and cut off from the pleasures of the world, can only just wet my lips with barley-water ? What good does it do me that all the roses of Shiraz open their leaves and burn for me with passionate tenderness ? Alas ! Shiraz is some two thousand leagues from the Rue d'Amsterdam, where in the solitude of my sick chamber all the perfume I smell is that of hot towels. Alas ! the mockery of God is heavy upon me ! The great Author of the universe, the Aristophanes of Heaven, has determined to make the petty earthly author, the so-called Aristophanes of Germany, feel to his heart's core what pitiful needle-pricks his cleverest sarcasms have been, compared with the thunderbolts which his divine humour can launch against feeble mortals ! . . .

" In the year 1840," says the Chronicle of Limburg, "all over Germany everybody was strumming and humming certain songs more lovely and delightful than any which had ever yet been known in German countries ; and all people, old and young, the women particularly, were perfectly mad about them, so that from morning till night you heard nothing else. Only, the Chronicle adds, the author of these songs happened to be a young clerk afflicted with leprosy, and living apart from all the world in a desolate place. The excellent reader does not require to be told how horrible a complaint was leprosy in the Middle Ages, and how the poor wretches who had this incurable plague were banished from society, and had to keep at a distance from every human being. Like living corpses, in a grey gown reaching down to the feet, and with the hood brought over their face, they went about, carrying in their hands an 'enormous rattle, called Saint Lazarus's rattle. With this rattle they gave notice of their approach, that every one might have time to get out of their way. This poor clerk, then, whose poetical gift the Limburg Chronicle extols, was a leper, and he sate moping in the dismal deserts of his misery, whilst all Germany, gay and tuneful, was praising his songs.

"Sometimes, in my sombre visions of the night, I imagine that I see before me the poor leprosy-stricken clerk of the Limburg Chronicle, and from under his grey hood his distressed eyes look out upon me in a fixed and strange fashion; but the next instant he disappears, and I hear dying away in the distance, like the echo of a dream, the dull creak of Saint Lazarus's rattle."

We have come a long way from Theocritus there; the expression of that has nothing of the clear, positive, happy, pagan character; it has much more the character of one of the indeterminate grotesques of the suffering Middle Age. Profoundness and power it has, though at the same time it is not truly poetical; it is not natural enough for that, there is too much waywardness in it, too much bravado.   But as a condition of sentiment to be popular,—to be a comfort for the mass of mankind, under the pressure of calamity, to live by,—what a manifest failure is this last word of the religion of pleasure !   One man in many millions, a Heine, may console himself, and keep himself erect in suffering, by a colossal irony of this sort, by covering himself and the universe with the red fire of this sinister mockery ; but the many millions cannot,—cannot if they would.   That is where the sentiment of a religion of sorrow has such a vast advantage over the sentiment of a religion of pleasure ; in its power to be a general, popular, religious sentiment, a stay for the mass of mankind, whose lives are full of hardship. It really succeeds in conveying far more joy, far more of what the mass of mankind are so much without, than its rival.   I do not mean joy in prospect only, but joy in possession, actual enjoyment of the world.   Mediæval Christianity is reproached with its gloom and austerities ; it assigns the material world, says Heine, to the devil. But yet what a fulness of delight does St. Francis manage to draw from this material world itself, and from its commonest and most universally enjoyed elements,—sun, air, earth, water, plants !   His hymn expresses a far more cordial sense of happiness, even in the material world, than the hymn of Theocritus.   It is this which made the fortune of Christianity,—its gladness, not its sorrow ; not its assigning the spiritual world to Christ and the material world to the devil, but its drawing from the spiritual world a source of joy so abundant that it ran over upon the material world and transfigured it.

I have said a great deal of harm of paganism ; and, taking paganism to mean a state of things which it is commonly taken to mean, and which did really exist, no more harm than it well deserved. Yet I must not end without reminding the reader, that before this state of things appeared, there was an epoch in Greek life,—in pagan life,—of the highest possible beauty and value ; an epoch which alone goes far towards making Greece the Greece we mean when we speak of Greece,—a country hardly less important to mankind than Judæa. The poetry of later paganism lived by the senses and understanding ; the poetry of mediæval Christianity lived by the heart and imagination. But the main element of the modern spirit's life is neither the senses and understanding, nor the heart and imagination ; it is the imaginative reason. And there is a century in Greek life,—the century preceding the Peloponnesian war, from about the year 530 B.C. to about the year 430,—in which poetry made, it seems to me, the noblest, the most successful effort she has ever made as the priestess of the imaginative reason, of the element by which the modern spirit, if it would live right, has chiefly to live. Of this effort, of which the four great names are Simonides, Pindar, Æschylus, Sophocles, I must not now attempt more than the bare mention ; but it is right, it is necessary, after all I have said, to indicate it. No doubt that effort was imperfect. Perhaps everything, take it at what point in its existence you will, carries within itself the fatal law of its own ulterior development. Perhaps, even of the life of Pindar's time, Pompeii was the inevitable bourne. Perhaps the life of their beautiful Greece

could not afford to its poets all that fulness of varied
experience, all that power of emotion, which

> . . . the heavy and the weary weight
> Of all this unintelligible world

affords to the poet of after-times.   Perhaps in Sophocles
the thinking-power a little overbalances the religious
sense, as in Dante the religious sense overbalances the
thinking-power.   The present has to make its own poetry,
and not even Sophocles and his compeers, any more
than Dante and Shakspeare, are enough for it.   That I
will not dispute.   But no other poets so well show to the
poetry of the present the way it must take ; no other
poets have lived so much by the imaginative reason ; no
other poets have made their work so well balanced ; no
other poets, who have so well satisfied the thinking-
power, have so well satisfied the religious sense.

"Oh ! that my lot may lead me in the path of holy
innocence of word and deed, the path which august
laws ordain, laws that in the highest empyrean had their
birth, of which Heaven is the father alone, neither did
the race of mortal men beget them, nor shall oblivion
ever put them to sleep.   The power of God is mighty in
them, and groweth not old."

Let Theocritus or St. Francis beat that !

JOUBERT.

Why should we ever treat of any dead authors but the famous ones? Mainly for this reason: because, from these famous personages, home or foreign, whom we all know so well, and of whom so much has been said, the amount of stimulus which they contain for us has been in a great measure disengaged; people have formed their opinion about them, and do not readily change it. One may write of them afresh, combat received opinions about them, even interest one's readers in so doing; but the interest one's readers receive has to do, in general, rather with the treatment than with the subject; they are susceptible of a lively impression rather of the course of the discussion itself,—its turns, vivacity, and novelty, —than of the genius of the author who is the occasion of it. And yet what is really precious and inspiring, in all that we get from literature, except this sense of an immediate contact with genius itself, and the stimulus towards what is true and excellent which we derive from it? Now in literature, besides the eminent men of genius who have had their deserts in the way of fame, besides the eminent men of ability who have often had far more than their deserts in the way of fame, there are a certain number of personages who have been real men of genius,

—by which I mean, that they have had a genuine gift for what is true and excellent, and are therefore capable of emitting a life-giving stimulus,—but who, for some reason or other, in most cases for very valid reasons, have remained obscure, nay, beyond a narrow circle in their own country, unknown. It is salutary from time to time to come across a genius of this kind, and to extract his honey. Often he has more of it for us, as I have already said, than greater men; for, though it is by no means true that from what is new to us there is most to be learnt, it is yet indisputably true that from what is new to us we in general learn most.

Of a genius of this kind, Joseph Joubert, I am now going to speak. His name is, I believe, almost unknown in England; and even in France, his native country, it is not famous. M. Sainte-Beuve has given of him one of his incomparable portraits; but,—besides that even M. Sainte-Beuve's writings are far less known amongst us than they deserve to be,—every country has its own point of view from which a remarkable author may most profitably be seen and studied.

Joseph Joubert was born (and his date should be remarked) in 1754, at Montignac, a little town in Périgord. His father was a doctor with small means and a large family; and Joseph, the eldest, had his own way to make in the world. He was for eight years, as pupil first, and afterwards as an assistant-master, in the public school of Toulouse, then managed by the Jesuits, who seem to have left in him a most favourable opinion, not only of their tact and address, but of their really good qualities as teachers and directors. Compelled by the

weakness of his health to give up, at twenty-two, the
profession of teaching, he passed two important years of
his life in hard study, at home at Montignac ; and came
in 1778 to try his fortune in the literary world of Paris,
then perhaps the most tempting field which has ever yet
presented itself to a young man of letters. He knew
Diderot, D'Alembert, Marmontel, Laharpe ; he became
intimate with one of the celebrities of the next literary
generation, then, like himself, a young man,—Chateaubriand's friend, the future Grand Master of the University,
Fontanes. But, even then, it began to be remarked of
him, that M. Joubert *s'inquiétait de perfection bien plus
que de gloire*—" cared far more about perfecting himself
than about making himself a reputation." His severity
of morals may perhaps have been rendered easier to
him by the delicacy of his health; but the delicacy of
his health will not by itself account for his changeless
preference of being to seeming, knowing to showing,
studying to publishing ; for what terrible public per-
formers have some invalids been ! This preference he
retained all through his life, and it is by this that he is
characterised. " He has chosen," Chateaubriand (adopting Epicurus's famous words) said of him, "*to hide his
life.*" Of a life which its owner was bent on hiding
there can be but little to tell. Yet the only two public
incidents of Joubert's life, slight as they are, do all concerned in them so much credit that they deserve mention.
In 1790 the Constituent Assembly made the office of
justice of the peace elective throughout France. The
people of Montignac retained such an impression of the
character of their young townsman,—one of Plutarch's

men of virtue, as he had lived amongst them, simple, studious, severe,—that, though he had left them for years, they elected him in his absence without his knowing anything about it. The appointment little suited Joubert's wishes or tastes; but at such a moment he thought it wrong to decline it. He held it for two years, the legal term, discharging its duties with a firmness and integrity which were long remembered; and then, when he went out of office, his fellow-townsmen re-elected him. But Joubert thought that he had now accomplished his duty towards them, and he went back to the retirement which he loved. That seems to us a little episode of the great French Revolution worth remembering. The sage who was asked by the king, why sages were seen at the doors of kings, but not kings at the doors of sages, replied, that it was because sages knew what was good for them, and kings did not. But at Montignac the king,—for in 1790 the people in France was king with a vengeance,—knew what was good for him, and came to the door of the sage.

The other incident was this. When Napoleon, in 1809, reorganised the public instruction of France, founded the University, and made M. de Fontanes its Grand Master, Fontanes had to submit to the Emperor a list of persons to form the council or governing body of the new University. Third on his list, after two distinguished names, Fontanes placed the unknown name of Joubert. "This name," he said in his accompanying memorandum to the Emperor, "is not known as the two first are; and yet this is the nomination to which I attach most importance. I have known M. Joubert all my life. His

character and intelligence are of the very highest order.
I shall rejoice if your majesty will accept my guarantee
for him." Napoleon trusted his Grand Master, and
Joubert became a councillor of the University. It is
something that a man, elevated to the highest posts of
State, should not forget his obscure friends ; or that, if
he remembers and places them, he should regard in
placing them their merit rather than their obscurity. It
is more, in the eyes of those whom the necessities, real or
supposed, of a political system have long familiarised with
such cynical disregard of fitness in the distribution of office,
to see a minister and his master alike zealous, in giving
away places, to give them to the best men to be found.

Between 1792 and 1809 Joubert had married. His
life was passed between Villeneuve-sur-Yonne, where his
wife's family lived,—a pretty little Burgundian town, by
which the Lyons railroad now passes,—and Paris. Here,
in a house in the Rue St.-Honoré, in a room very high
up, and admitting plenty of the light which he so loved,
—a room from which he saw, in his own words, " a great
deal of sky and very little earth,"—among the treasures
of a library collected with infinite pains, taste, and skill,
from which every book he thought ill of was rigidly
excluded,—he never would possess either a complete
Voltaire or a complete Rousseau,—the happiest hours of
his life were passed. In the circle of one of those
women who leave a sort of perfume in literary history,
and who have the gift of inspiring successive generations
of readers with an indescribable regret not to have known
them,—Pauline de Montmorin, Madame de Beaumont,
—he had become intimate with nearly all which at that

time, in the Paris world of letters or of society, was most
attractive and promising. Amongst his acquaintances
one only misses the names of Madame de Staël and
Benjamin Constant; neither of them was to his taste,
and with Madame de Staël he always refused to become
acquainted; he thought she had more vehemence than
truth, and more heat than light. Years went on, and his
friends became conspicuous authors or statesmen; but
Joubert remained in the shade. His constitution was of
such fragility that how he lived so long, or accomplished
so much as he did, is a wonder; his soul had, for its
basis of operations, hardly any body at all; both from
his stomach and from his chest he seems to have had constant sufferings, though he lived by rule, and was as abste-
mious as a Hindoo. Often, after overwork in thinking,
reading, or talking, he remained for days together in a
state of utter prostration,—condemned to absolute silence
and inaction; too happy if the agitation of his mind
would become quiet also, and let him have the repose of
which he stood in so much need. With this weakness
of health, these repeated suspensions of energy he was
incapable of the prolonged contention of spirit necessary
for the creation of great works; but he read and thought
immensely; he was an unwearied note-taker, a charming
letter-writer, above all, an excellent and delightful talker.
The gaiety and amenity of his natural disposition were
inexhaustible; and his spirit, too, was of astonishing
elasticity; he seemed to hold on to life by a single thread
only, but that single thread was very tenacious. More
and more, as his soul and knowledge ripened more and
more, his friends pressed to his room in the Rue St.-

Honoré; often he received them in bed, for he seldom rose before three o'clock in the afternoon; and at his bedroom-door, on his bad days, Madame Joubert stood sentry, trying, not always with success, to keep back the thirsty comers from the fountain which was forbidden to flow. Fontanes did nothing in the University without consulting him, and Joubert's ideas and pen were always at his friend's service. When he was in the country, at Villeneuve, the young priests of his neighbourhood used to resort to him, in order to profit by his library and by his conversation. He, like our Coleridge, was particularly qualified to attract men of this kind and to benefit them: retaining perfect independence of mind, he was religious; he was a religious philosopher. As age came on, his infirmities became more and more overwhelming; some of his friends, too, died; others became so immersed in politics, that Joubert, who hated politics, saw them seldomer than of old; but the moroseness of age and infirmity never touched him, and he never quarrelled with a friend or lost one. From these miseries he was preserved by that quality in him of which we have already spoken; a quality which is best expressed by a word, not of common use in English,—alas, we have too little in our national character of the quality which this word expresses,—his inborn, his constant amenity. He lived till the year 1824. On the 4th of May in that year he died, at the age of seventy. A day or two after his death, M. de Chateaubriand inserted in the *Journal des Débats* a short notice of him, perfect for its feeling, grace, and propriety. *On ne vit dans la mémoire du monde*, he says, and says truly, *que par des travaux pour le monde*—"a man can live in the world's memory only by what he has done for the world." But Chateaubriand used the privilege which his great name gave him to assert, delicately but firmly, Joubert's real and rare merits, and to tell the world what manner of man had just left it.

Joubert's papers were accumulated in boxes and drawers. He had not meant them for publication; it was very difficult to sort them and to prepare them for it. Madame Joubert, his widow, had a scruple about giving them a publicity which her husband, she felt, would never have permitted. But, as her own end approached, the natural desire to leave of so remarkable a spirit some enduring memorial, some memorial to outlast the admiring recollection of the living who were so fast passing away, made her yield to the entreaties of his friends, and allow the printing, but for private circulation only, of a volume of his fragments. Chateaubriand edited it; it appeared in 1838, fourteen years after Joubert's death. The volume attracted the attention of those who were best fitted to appreciate it, and profoundly impressed them. M. Sainte-Beuve gave of it, in the *Revue des Deux Mondes*, the admirable notice of which I have already spoken; and so much curiosity was excited about Joubert, that the collection of his fragments, enlarged by many additions, was at last published for the benefit of the world in general. It has since been twice reprinted. The first or preliminary chapter has some fancifulness and affectation in it; the reader should begin with the second.

I have likened Joubert to Coleridge; and indeed the points of resemblance between the two men are numerous. Both of them great and celebrated talkers, Joubert attracting pilgrims to his upper chamber in the Rue St.-Honoré, as Coleridge attracted pilgrims to Mr. Gilman's at Highgate ; both of them desultory and incomplete writers,—here they had an outward likeness with one another. Both of them passionately devoted to reading in a class of books, and to thinking on a class of subjects, out of the beaten line of the reading and thought of their day ; both of them ardent students and critics of old literature, poetry, and the metaphysics of religion; both of them curious explorers of words, and of the latent significance hidden under the popular use of them ; both of them, in a certain sense, conservative in religion and politics, by antipathy to the narrow and shallow foolishness of vulgar modern liberalism;—here they had their inward and real likeness. But that in which the essence of their likeness consisted is this,— that they both had from nature an ardent impulse for seeking the genuine truth on all matters they thought about, and a gift for finding it and recognising it when it was found. To have the impulse for seeking it is much rarer than most people think; to have the gift for finding it is, I need not say, very rare indeed. By this they have a spiritual relationship of the closest kind with one another, and they become, each of them, a source of stimulus and progress for all of us.

Coleridge had less delicacy and penetration than Joubert, but more richness and power ; his production, though far inferior to what his nature at first seemed to promise, was abundant and varied. Yet in all his production how much is there to dissatisfy us ! How many reserves must be made in praising either his poetry, or his criticism, or his philosophy! How little either of his poetry, or of his criticism, or of his philosophy, can we expect permanently to stand! But that which will stand of Coleridge is this : the stimulus of his continual effort,—not a moral effort, for he had no morals,—but of his continual instinctive effort, crowned often with rich success, to get at and to lay bare the real truth of his matter in hand, whether that matter were literary, or philosophical, or political, or religious ; and this in a country where at that moment such an effort was almost unknown ; where the most powerful minds threw themselves upon poetry, which conveys truth, indeed, but conveys it indirectly ; and where ordinary minds were so habituated to do without thinking altogether, to regard considerations of established routine and practical convenience as paramount, that any attempt to introduce within the domain of these the disturbing element of thought, they were prompt to resent as an outrage. Coleridge's great action lay in his supplying in England, for many years and under critical circumstances, by the spectacle of this effort of his, a stimulus to all minds, in the generation which grew up round him, capable of profiting by it. His action will still be felt as long as the need for it continues ; when, with the cessation of the need, the action too has ceased, Coleridge's memory, in spite of the disesteem, nay, repugnance, which his character may and must inspire, will yet for ever remain invested with that interest and gratitude which invests the memory of founders.

M. de Rémusat, indeed, reproaches Coleridge with

his *jugements saugrenus;* the criticism of a gifted truth-
finder ought not to be *saugrenu;* so on this reproach we
must pause for a moment. *Saugrenu* is a rather vulgar
French word, but, like many other vulgar words, very
expressive ; used as an epithet for a judgment, it means
something like *impudently absurd.* The literary judgments of one nation about another are very apt to
be *saugrenus;* it is certainly true, as M. Sainte-Beuve
remarks in answer to Goethe's complaint against the
French that they have undervalued Du Bartas, that as to
the estimate of its own authors every nation is the best
judge ; the *positive* estimate of them, be it understood,
not, of course, the estimate of them in comparison with
the authors of other nations. Therefore a foreigner's
judgments about the intrinsic merit of a nation's authors
will generally, when at complete variance with that
nation's own, be wrong ; but there is a permissible
wrongness in these matters, and to that permissible
wrongness there is a limit. When that limit is ex-
ceeded, the wrong judgment becomes more than wrong,
it becomes *saugrenu,* or impudently absurd. For instance,
the high estimate which the French have of Racine is
probably in great measure deserved ; or, to take a yet
stronger case, even the high estimate which Joubert had
of the Abbé Delille is probably in great measure deserved ;
but the common disparaging judgment passed on Racine
by English readers is not *saugrenu,* still less is that passed
by them on the Abbé Delille *saugrenu,* because the beauty
of Racine and of Delille too, so far as Delille's beauty
goes, is eminently in their language, and this is a beauty
which a foreigner cannot perfectly seize;—this beauty of

diction, *apicibus verborum ligata*, as M. Sainte-Beuve, quoting Quintilian, says of Chateaubriand's. As to Chateaubriand himself, again, the common English judgment, which stamps him as a mere shallow rhetorician, all froth and vanity, is certainly wrong; one may even wonder that the English should judge Chateaubriand so wrongly, for his power goes far beyond beauty of diction; it is a power, as well, of passion and sentiment, and this sort of power the English can perfectly well appreciate. One production of Chateaubriand's, *René*, is akin to the most popular productions of Byron,—to the *Childe Harold* or *Manfred*,—in spirit, equal to them in power, superior to them in form. But this work, I hardly know why, is almost unread in England. And only consider this criticism of Chateaubriand's on the true pathetic! "It is a dangerous mistake, sanctioned, like so many other dangerous mistakes, by Voltaire, to suppose that the best works of imagination are those which draw most tears. One could name this or that melodrama, which no one would like to own having written, and which yet harrows the feelings far more than the Æneid. The true tears are those which are called forth by the *beauty* of poetry; there must be as much admiration in them as sorrow. They are the tears which come to our eyes when Priam says to Achilles, ἔτλην δ', οἷ' οὔπω . . .—'And I have endured,—the like whereof no soul upon the earth hath yet endured,—to carry to my lips the hand of him who slew my child;' or when Joseph cries out: 'I am Joseph your brother, whom ye sold into Egypt.'" Who does not feel that the man who wrote that was no shallow rhetorician, but a born man of genius, with the true instinct of genius for what is really admirable! Nay, take these words of Chateaubriand, an old man of eighty, dying amidst the noise and bustle of the ignoble revolution of February, 1848 : "Mon Dieu, mon Dieu, quand donc, quand donc serai-je délivré de tout ce monde, ce bruit ; quand donc, quand donc cela finira-t-il ?" Who, with any ear, does not feel that those are not the accents of a trumpery rhetorician, but of a rich and puissant nature,—the cry of the dying lion? I repeat it, Chateaubriand is most ignorantly underrated in England ; and we English are capable of rating him far more correctly if we knew him better. Still, Chateaubriand has such real and great faults, he falls so decidedly beneath the rank of the truly greatest authors, that the depreciatory judgment passed on him in England, though ignorant and wrong, can hardly be said to transgress the limits of permissible ignorance ; it is not a *jugement saugrenu*. But when a critic denies genius to a literature which has produced Bossuet and Molière, he passes the bounds ; and Coleridge's judgments on French literature and the French genius are undoubtedly, as M. de Rémusat calls them, *saugrenus*.

And yet, such is the impetuosity of our poor human nature, such its proneness to rush to a decision with imperfect knowledge, that his having delivered a *saugrenu* judgment or two in his life by no means proves a man not to have had, in comparison with his fellowmen in general, a remarkable gift for truth, or disqualifies him for being, by virtue of that gift, a source of vital stimulus for us. Joubert had far less smoke and turbid vehemence in him than Coleridge; he had also a far keener sense of what was absurd. But Joubert can write to M. Molé (the M. Molé who was afterwards Louis Philippe's well-known minister): "As to your Milton, whom the merit of the Abbé Delille" (the Abbé Delille translated *Paradise Lost*) "makes me admire, and with whom I have nevertheless still plenty of fault to find, why, I should like to know, are you scandalised that I have not enabled myself to read him? I don't understand the language in which he writes, and I don't much care to. If he is a poet one cannot put up with, even in the prose of the younger Racine, am I to blame for that? If by force you mean beauty manifesting itself with power, I maintain that the Abbé Delille has more force than Milton." That, to be sure, is a petulant outburst in a private letter; it is not, like Coleridge's, a deliberate proposition in a printed philosophical essay. But is it possible to imagine a more perfect specimen of a *saugrenu* judgment? It is even worse than Coleridge's, because it is *saugrenu* with reasons. That, however, does not prevent Joubert from having been really a man of extraordinary ardour in the search for truth, and of extraordinary fineness in the perception of it; and so was Coleridge.

Joubert had around him in France an atmosphere of literary, philosophical, and religious opinion as alien to him as that in England was to Coleridge. This is what makes Joubert, too, so remarkable, and it is on this account that I begged the reader to remark his date. He was born in 1754, he died in 1824. He was thus in the fulness of his powers at the beginning of the present century, at the epoch of Napoleon's consulate.

The French criticism of that day,—the criticism of Laharpe's successors, of Geoffroy and his colleagues in
the *Journal des Débats*,—had a dryness very unlike the
telling vivacity of the early Edinburgh reviewers, their
contemporaries, but a fundamental narrowness, a want
of genuine insight, much on a par with theirs. Joubert,
like Coleridge, has no respect for the dominant oracle ;
he treats his Geoffroy with about as little deference
as Coleridge treats his Jeffrey. " Geoffroy," he says
of an article in the *Journal des Débats* criticising Chateaubriand's *Génie du Christianisme*,—" Geoffroy in this
article begins by holding out his paw prettily enough ;
but he ends by a volley of kicks, which lets the whole
world see but too clearly the four iron shoes of the
four-footed animal." There is, however, in France a
sympathy with intellectual activity for its own sake,
and for the sake of its inherent pleasureableness and
beauty, keener than any which exists in England ; and
Joubert had more effect in Paris,—though his conversation was his only weapon, and Coleridge wielded besides
his conversation his pen,—than Coleridge had or could
have in London. I mean, a more immediate, appreciable
effect ; an effect not only upon the young and enthusi-
astic, to whom the future belongs, but upon formed and
important personages to whom the present belongs, and
who are actually moving society. He owed this partly
to his real advantages over Coleridge. If he had, as I
have already said, less power and richness than his
English parallel, he had more tact and penetration. He
was more *possible* than Coleridge ; his doctrine was more
intelligible than Coleridge's, more receivable. And yet,

with Joubert, the striving after a consummate and attractive clearness of expression came from no mere frivolous dislike of labour and inability for going deep, but was a part of his native love of truth and perfection. The delight of his life he found in truth, and in the satisfaction which the enjoying of truth gives to the spirit ; and he thought the truth was never really and worthily said, so long as the least cloud, clumsiness, and repulsiveness hung about the expression of it.

Some of his best passages are those in which he upholds this doctrine. Even metaphysics he would not allow to remain difficult and abstract ; so long as they spoke a professional jargon, the language of the schools, he maintained,—and who shall gainsay him ?—that metaphysics were imperfect ; or, at any rate, had not yet reached their ideal perfection.

"The true science of metaphysics," he says, "consists not in rendering abstract that which is sensible, but in rendering sensible that which is abstract ; apparent that which is hidden ; imaginable, if so it may be, that which is only intelligible ; and intelligible, finally, that which an ordinary attention fails to seize."

And therefore :—

"Distrust, in books on metaphysics, words which have not been able to get currency in the world, and are only calculated to form a special language."

Nor would he suffer common words to be employed in a special sense by the schools :—

"Which is the best, if one wants to be useful and to be really understood, to get one's words in the world, or to get them in the schools ? I maintain that the good

plan is to employ words in their popular sense rather
than in their philosophical sense ; and the better plan
still, to employ them in their natural sense rather than in
their popular sense.   By their natural sense, I mean the
popular and universal acceptation of them brought to that
which in this is essential and invariable.   To prove a
thing by definition proves nothing, if the definition is
purely philosophical ; for such definitions only bind him
who makes them.   To prove a thing by definition, when
the definition expresses the necessary, inevitable, and
clear idea which the world at large attaches to the object,
is, on the contrary, all in all ; because then what one does
is simply to show people what they do really think, in
spite of themselves and without knowing it.   The rule
that one is free to give to words what sense one will, and
that the only thing needful is to be agreed upon the sense
one gives them, is very well for the mere purposes of
argumentation, and may be allowed in the schools where
this sort of fencing is to be practised ; but in the sphere
of the true-born and noble science of metaphysics, and
in the genuine world of literature, it is good for nothing.
One must never quit sight of realities, and one must
employ one's expressions simply as media,—as glasses,
through which one's thoughts can be best made evident.
I know, by my own experience, how hard this rule is to
follow ; but I judge of its importance by the failure of
every system of metaphysics.   Not one of them has succeeded ; for the simple reason, that in every one ciphers
have been constantly used instead of values, artificial
ideas instead of native ideas, jargon instead of idiom."

I do not know whether the metaphysician will ever

adopt Joubert's rules; but I am sure that the man of
letters, whenever he has to speak of metaphysics, will do
well to adopt them. He, at any rate, must remember :—

"It is by means of familiar words that style takes hold
of the reader and gets possession of him. It is by means
of these that great thoughts get currency and pass for
true metal, like gold and silver which have had a recognised stamp put upon them. They beget confidence in
the man who, in order to make his thoughts more clearly
perceived, uses them; for people feel that such an employment of the language of common human life betokens
a man who knows that life and its concerns, and who
keeps himself in contact with them. Besides, these words
make a style frank and easy. They show that an author
has long made the thought or the feeling expressed his
mental food; that he has so assimilated them and familiarised them, that the most common expressions suffice
him in order to express ideas which have become every-
day ideas to him by the length of time they have been in
his mind. And lastly, what one says in such words looks
more true; for, of all the words in use, none are so clear
as those which we call common words; and clearness is
so eminently one of the characteristics of truth, that often
it even passes for truth itself."

These are not, in Joubert, mere counsels of rhetoric;
they come from his accurate sense of perfection, from his
having clearly seized the fine and just idea that beauty
and light are properties of truth, and that truth is in-
completely exhibited if it is exhibited without beauty
and light :—

"Be profound with clear terms and not with obscure

terms.   What is difficult will at last become easy; but
as one goes deep into things, one must still keep a
charm, and one must carry into these dark depths of
thought, into which speculation has only recently penetrated, the pure and antique clearness of centuries less
learned than ours, but with more light in them."

And elsewhere he speaks of those " spirits, lovers
of light, who, when they have an idea to put forth,
brood long over it first, and wait patiently till it *shines*,
as Buffon enjoined, when he defined genius to be the
aptitude for patience; spirits who know by experience
that the driest matter and the dullest words hide within
them the germ and spark of some brightness, like those
fairy nuts in which were found diamonds if one broke
the shell and was the right person ; spirits who maintain
that, to see and exhibit things in beauty, is to see and
show things as in their essence they really are, and not
as they exist for the eye of the careless, who do not look
beyond the outside ; spirits hard to satisfy, because of a
keen-sightedness in them, which makes them discern but
too clearly both the models to be followed and those to
be shunned ; spirits active though meditative, who cannot
rest except in solid truths, and whom only beauty can
make happy; spirits far less concerned for glory than for
perfection, who, because their art is long and life is
short, often die without leaving a monument, having had
their own inward sense of life and fruitfulness for their
best reward."

No doubt there is something a little too ethereal in all
this, something which reminds one of Joubert's physical
want of body and substance ; no doubt, if a man wishes

to be a great author, it is "to consider too curiously, to consider" as Joubert did ; it is a mistake to spend so much of one's time in setting up one's ideal standard of perfection, and in contemplating it. Joubert himself knew this very well : "I cannot build a house for my ideas," said he ; "I have tried to do without words, and words take their revenge on me by their difficulty." "If there is a man upon earth tormented by the cursed desire to get a whole book into a page, a whole page into a phrase, and this phrase into one word,—that man is my-self." "I can sow, but I cannot build." Joubert, how-ever, makes no claim to be a great author ; by renouncing all ambition to be this, by not trying to fit his ideas into a house, by making no compromise with words in spite of their difficulty, by being quite single-minded in his pursuit of perfection, perhaps he is enabled to get closer to the truth of the objects of his study, and to be of more service to us by setting ideals, than if he had composed a celebrated work. I doubt whether, in an elaborate work on the philosophy of religion, he would have got his ideas about religion to *shine*, to use his own expression, as they shine when he utters them in perfect freedom. Penetration in these matters is valueless without soul, and soul is valueless without penetration ; both of these are delicate qualities, and, even in those who have them, easily lost ; the charm of Joubert is, that he has and keeps both :—

"One should be fearful of being wrong in poetry when one thinks differently from the poets, and in religion when one thinks differently from the saints.

"There is a great difference between taking for idols

Mahomet and Luther, and bowing down before Rousseau
and Voltaire. People at any rate imagined they were
obeying God when they followed Mahomet, and the
Scriptures when they hearkened to Luther. And perhaps
one ought not too much to disparage that inclination
which leads mankind to put into the hands of those
whom it thinks the friends of God the direction and
government of its heart and mind. It is the subjection
to irreligious spirits which alone is fatal, and, in the fullest
sense of the word, depraving.

" May I say it? It is not hard to know God, provided
one will not force oneself to define him.

" Do not bring into the domain of reasoning that which
belongs to our innermost feeling. State truths of sentiment, and do not try to prove them. There is a danger
in such proofs; for in arguing it is necessary to treat that
which is in question as something problematic; now that
which we accustom ourselves to treat as problematic ends
by appearing to us as really doubtful. In things that
are visible and palpable, never prove what is believed
already; in things that are certain and mysterious,—
mysterious by their greatness and by their nature,—make
people believe them, and do not prove them; in things
that are matters of practice and duty, command, and do
not explain. 'Fear God,' has made many men pious;
the proofs of the existence of God have made many men
atheists. From the defiance springs the attack; the
advocate begets in his hearer a wish to pick holes; and
men are almost always led on, from the desire to contradict the doctor, to the desire to contradict the doctrine.
Make truth lovely, and do not try to arm her: man-

kind will then be far less inclined to contend with her.

"Why is even a bad preacher almost always heard by the pious with pleasure? *Because he talks to them about what they love.* But you who have to expound religion to the children of this world, you who have to speak to them of that which they once loved perhaps, or which they would be glad to love,—remember that they do not love it yet, and, to make them love it, take heed to speak with power.

"You may do what you like, mankind will believe no one but God; and he only can persuade mankind who believes that God has spoken to him. No one can give faith unless he has faith; the persuaded persuade, as the indulgent disarm.

"The only happy people in the world are the good man, the sage, and the saint; but the saint is happier than either of the others, so much is man by his nature formed for sanctity."

The same delicacy and penetration which he here shows in speaking of the inward essence of religion, Joubert shows also in speaking of its outward form, and of its manifestation in the world :—

"Piety is not a religion, though it is the soul of all religions. A man has not a religion simply by having pious inclinations, any more than he has a country simply by having philanthropy. A man has not a country until he is a citizen in a state, until he undertakes to follow and uphold certain laws, to obey certain magistrates, and to adopt certain ways of living and acting.

"Religion is neither a theology nor a theosophy; it is

more than all this ; it is a discipline, a law, a yoke, an indissoluble engagement."

Who, again, has ever shown with more truth and beauty the good and imposing side of the wealth and splendour of the Catholic Church, than Joubert in the following passage :—

" The pomps and magnificence with which the Church is reproached are in truth the result and the proof of her incomparable excellence. From whence, let me ask, have come this power of hers and these excessive riches, except from the enchantment into which she threw all the world ? Ravished with her beauty, millions of men from age to age kept loading her with gifts, bequests, cessions. She had the talent of making herself loved, and the talent of making men happy. It is that which wrought prodigies for her; it is from thence that she drew her power."

" She had the talent of making herself *feared*,"—one should add that too, in order to be perfectly just ; but Joubert, because he is a true child of light, can see that the wonderful success of the Catholic Church must have been due really to her good rather than to her bad qualities ; to her making herself loved rather than to her making herself feared.

How striking and suggestive, again, is this remark on the Old and New Testaments :—

" The Old Testament teaches the knowledge of good and evil ; the Gospel, on the other hand, seems written for the predestinated ; it is the book of innocence. The one is made for earth, the other seems made for heaven. According as the one or the other of these books takes hold of a nation, what may be called the *religious humours* of nations differ."

So the British and North-American Puritans are the children of the Old Testament, as Joachim of Flora and St. Francis are the children of the New. And does not the following maxim exactly fit the Church of England, of which Joubert certainly never thought when he was writing it? "The austere sects excite the most enthusiasm at first; but the temperate sects have always been the most durable."

And these remarks on the Jansenists and Jesuits, interesting in themselves, are still more interesting because they touch matters we cannot well know at first hand, and which Joubert, an impartial observer, had had the means of studying closely. We are apt to think of the Jansenists as having failed by reason of their merits; Joubert shows us how far their failure was due to their defects :—

"We ought to lay stress upon what is clear in Scripture, and to pass quickly over what is obscure; to light up what in Scripture is troubled, by what is serene in it; what puzzles and checks the reason, by what satisfies the reason. The Jansenists have done just the reverse. They lay stress upon what is uncertain, obscure, afflicting, and they pass lightly over all the rest; they eclipse the luminous and consoling truths of Scripture, by putting between us and them its opaque and dismal truths. For example, 'Many are called;' there is a clear truth: 'Few are chosen;' there is an obscure truth. 'We are children of wrath;' there is a sombre, cloudy, terrifying truth : 'We are all the children of God;' 'I came not to

call the righteous, but sinners to repentance ;' there are
truths which are full of clearness, mildness, serenity,
light. The Jansenists trouble our cheerfulness, and
shed no cheering ray on our trouble. They are not,
however, to be condemned for what they say, because
what they say is true ; but they are to be condemned
for what they fail to say, for that is true too,—truer, even,
than the other ; that is, its truth is easier for us to seize,
fuller, rounder, and more complete. Theology, as the
Jansenists exhibit her, has but the half of her disk."

Again :—

"The Jansenists erect 'grace' into a kind of fourth
person of the Trinity. They are, without thinking or
intending it, Quaternitarians. St. Paul and St. Augustine, too exclusively studied, have done the whole
mischief. Instead of 'grace,' say help, succour, a
divine influence, a dew of heaven ; then one can come
to a right understanding. The word 'grace' is a sort
of talisman, all the baneful spell of which can be broken
by translating it. The trick of personifying words is a
fatal source of mischief in theology."

Once more :—

"The Jansenists tell men to love God ; the Jesuits
make men love him. The doctrine of these last is full
of loosenesses, or, if you will, of errors ; still,—singular
as it may seem, it is undeniable,—they are the better
directors of souls.

"The Jansenists have carried into religion more
thought than the Jesuits, and they go deeper ; they are
faster bound with its sacred bonds. They have in their
way of thinking an austerity which incessantly constrains

the will to keep the path of duty; all the habits of their understanding, in short, are more Christian. But they seem to love God without affection, and solely from reason, from duty, from justice. The Jesuits, on the other hand, seem to love him from pure inclination; out of admiration, gratitude, tenderness; for the pleasure of loving him, in short. In their books of devotion you find joy, because with the Jesuits nature and religion go hand in hand. In the books of the Jansenists there is a sadness and a moral constraint, because with the Jansenists religion is for ever trying to put nature in bonds."

The Jesuits have suffered, and deservedly suffered, plenty of discredit from what Joubert gently calls their " loosenesses;" let them have the merit of their amiability.

The most characteristic thoughts one can quote from any writer are always his thoughts on matters like these; but the maxims of Joubert on purely literary subjects also, have the same purged and subtle delicacy; they show the same sedulousness in him to preserve perfectly true the balance of his soul. Let me begin with this, which contains a truth too many people fail to perceive : " Ignorance, which in matters of morals extenuates the crime, is itself, in matters of literature, a crime of the first order."

And here is another sentence, worthy of Goethe, to clear the air at one's entrance into the region of literature :—

" With the fever of the senses, the delirium of the passions, the weakness of the spirit; with the storms of

the passing time and with the great scourges of human
life,—hunger, thirst, dishonour, diseases, and death,—
authors may as long as they like go on making novels
which shall harrow our hearts; but the soul says all the
while, 'You hurt me.' "

And again :—

" Fiction has no business to exist unless it is more
beautiful than reality. Certainly the monstrosities of
fiction may be found in the booksellers' shops; you buy
them there for a certain number of francs, and you talk
of them for a certain number of days ; but they have no
place in literature, because in literature the one aim of
art is the beautiful. Once lose sight of that, and you
have the mere frightful reality."

That is just the right criticism to pass on these "monstrosities ;" *they have no place in literature*, and those
who produce them are not really men of letters. One
would think that this was enough to deter from such
production any man of genuine ambition. But most of
us, alas ! are what we must be, not what we ought to be,
—not even what we know we ought to be.

The following, of which the first part reminds one of
Wordsworth's sonnet, " If thou indeed derive thy light
from heaven," excellently defines the true salutary function
of literature, and the limits of this function :—

" Whether one is an eagle or an ant, in the intellectual
world, seems to me not to matter much ; the essential
thing is to have one's place marked there, one's station
assigned, and to belong decidedly to a regular and wholesome order. A small talent, if it keeps within its limits
and rightly fulfils its task, may reach the goal just as well

as a greater one. To accustom mankind to pleasures
which depend neither upon the bodily appetites nor upon
money, by giving them a taste for the things of the
mind, seems to me, in fact, the one proper fruit which
nature has meant our literary productions to have. When
they have other fruits, it is by accident, and, in general,
not for good. Books which absorb our attention to such
a degree that they rob us of all fancy for other books,
are absolutely pernicious. In this way they only bring
fresh crotchets and sects into the world; they multiply
the great variety of weights, rules, and measures already
existing; they are morally and politically a nuisance."

Who can read these words and not think of the limiting
effect exercised by certain works in certain spheres
and for certain periods; exercised even by the works
of men of genius or virtue,—by the works of Rousseau,
the works of Wesley, the works of Swedenborg? And what
is it which makes the Bible so admirable a book, to be
the one book of those who can have only one, but the
miscellaneous character of the contents of the Bible?

Joubert was all his life a passionate lover of Plato; I
hope other lovers of Plato will forgive me for saying that
their adored object has never been more truly described
than he is here :—

" Plato shows us nothing, but he brings brightness with
him; he puts light into our eyes, and fills us with a clearness by which all objects afterwards become illuminated.
He teaches us nothing; but he prepares us, fashions us,
and makes us ready to know all. Somehow or other, the
habit of reading him augments in us the capacity for
discerning and entertaining whatever fine truths may

afterwards present themselves. Like mountain-air, it sharpens our organs, and gives us an appetite for wholesome food."

"Plato loses himself in the void" (he says again); "but one sees the play of his wings, one hears their rustle." And the conclusion is: "It is good to breathe his air, but not to live upon him."

As a pendant to the criticism on Plato, this on the French moralist Nicole is excellent :—

"Nicole is a Pascal without style. It is not what he says which is sublime, but what he thinks ; he rises, not by the natural elevation of his own spirit, but by that of his doctrines. One must not look to the form in him, but to the matter, which is exquisite. He ought to be read with a direct view of practice."

English people have hardly ears to hear the praises of Bossuet, and the Bossuet of Joubert is Bossuet at his very best ; but this is a far truer Bossuet than the "declaimer" Bossuet of Lord Macaulay, himself a born rhetorician, if ever there was one :—

"Bossuet employs all our idioms, as Homer employed all the dialects. The language of kings, of statesmen, and of warriors; the language of the people and of the student, of the country and of the schools, of the sanctuary and of the courts of law ; the old and the new, the trivial and the stately, the quiet and the resounding,—he turns all to his use; and out of all this he makes a style, simple, grave, majestic. His ideas are, like his words, varied,—common and sublime together. Times and doctrines in all their multitude were ever before his spirit, as things and words in all their multitude were ever before it. He is not so much a man as a human nature, with the temperance of a saint, the justice of a bishop, the prudence of a doctor, and the might of a great spirit."

After this on Bossuet, I must quote a criticism on Racine, to show that Joubert did not indiscriminately worship all the French gods of the grand century :—

"Those who find Racine enough for them are poor souls and poor wits ; they are souls and wits which have never got beyond the callow and boarding-school stage. Admirable, as no doubt he is, for his skill in having made poetical the most humdrum sentiments and the most middling sort of passions, he can yet stand us in stead of nobody but himself. He is a superior writer': and, in literature, that at once puts a man on a pinnacle. But he is not an inimitable writer."

And again : " The talent of Racine is in his works. but Racine himself is not there. That is why he himself became disgusted with them." " Of Racine, as of his ancients, the genius lay in taste. His elegance is perfect, but it is not supreme, like that of Virgil." And, indeed, there is something *supreme* in an elegance which exercises such a fascination as Virgil's does ; which makes one return to his poems again and again, long after one thinks one has done with them ; which makes them one of those books that, to use Joubert's words, "lure the reader back to them, as the proverb says good wine lures back the wine-bibber." And the highest praise Joubert can at last find for Racine is this, that he is the Virgil of the ignorant ;—" Racine est le Virgile des ignorants."

Of Boileau, too, Joubert says : " Boileau is a powerful

poet, but only in the world of half poetry." How true is that of Pope also! And he adds: "Neither Boileau's poetry nor Racine's flows from the fountain-head." No Englishman, controverting the exaggerated French estimate of these poets, could desire to use fitter words.

I will end with some remarks on Voltaire and Rousseau, remarks in which Joubert eminently shows his prime merit as a critic,—the soundness and completeness of his judgments. I mean that he has the faculty of judging with all the powers of his mind and soul at work together in due combination; and how rare is this faculty! how seldom is it exercised towards writers who so powerfully as Voltaire and Rousseau stimulate and call into activity a single side in us!

"Voltaire's wits came to their maturity twenty years sooner than the wits of other men, and remained in full vigour thirty years longer. The charm which our style in general gets from our ideas, his ideas get from his style. Voltaire is sometimes afflicted, sometimes strongly moved; but serious he never is. His very graces have an effrontery about them. He had correctness of judgment, liveliness of imagination, nimble wits, quick taste, and a moral sense in ruins. He is the most debauched of spirits, and the worst of him is that one gets debauched along with him. If he had been a wise man, and had had the self-discipline of wisdom, beyond a doubt half his wit would have been gone; it needed an atmosphere of *license* in order to play freely. Those people who read him every day, create for themselves, by an invincible law, the necessity of liking him. But those people who, having given up reading him, gaze steadily down upon the influences which his spirit has shed abroad, find themselves in simple justice and duty compelled to detest him. It is impossible to be satisfied with him, and impossible not to be fascinated by him."

The literary sense in us is apt to rebel against so severe a judgment on such a charmer of the literary sense as Voltaire, and perhaps we English are not very liable to catch Voltaire's vices, while of some of his merits we have signal need; still, as the real definitive judgment on Voltaire, Joubert's is undoubtedly the true one. It is nearly identical with that of Goethe. Joubert's sentence on Rousseau is in some respects more favourable :—

"That weight in the speaker (*auctoritas*) which the ancients talk of, is to be found in Bossuet more than in any other French author; Pascal, too, has it, and La Bruyère; even Rousseau has something of it, but Voltaire not a particle. I can understand how a Rousseau,—I mean a Rousseau cured of his faults,—might at the present day do much good, and may even come to be greatly wanted ; but under no circumstances can a Voltaire be of any use."

The peculiar power of Rousseau's style has never been better hit off than in the following passage :—

"Rousseau imparted, if I may so speak, *bowels of feeling* to the words he used (*donna des entrailles à tous les mots*), and poured into them such a charm, sweetness so penetrating, energy so puissant, that his writings have an effect upon the soul something like that of those illicit pleasures which steal away our taste and intoxicate our reason."

The final judgment, however, is severe, and justly severe :—

"Life without actions; life entirely resolved into affections and half-sensual thoughts; do-nothingness setting up for a virtue; cowardliness with voluptuousness; fierce pride with nullity underneath it; the strutting phrase of the most sensual of vagabonds, who has made his system of philosophy and can give it eloquently forth : there is Rousseau! A piety in which there is no religion; a severity which brings corruption with it; a dogmatism which serves to ruin all authority: there is Rousseau's philosophy! To all tender, ardent, and elevated natures, I say: Only Rousseau can detach you from religion, and only true religion can cure you of Rousseau."

I must yet find room, before I end, for one at least of Joubert's sayings on political matters; here, too, the whole man shows himself; and here, too, the affinity with Coleridge is very remarkable. How true, how true in France especially, is this remark on the contrasting direction taken by the aspirations of the community in ancient and in modern states :—

"The ancients were attached to their country by three things,—their temples, their tombs, and their forefathers. The two great bonds which united them to their government were the bonds of habit and antiquity. With the moderns, hope and the love of novelty have produced a total change. The ancients said *our forefathers*, we say *posterity*; we do not, like them, love our *patria*, that is to say, the country and the laws of our fathers, rather we love the laws and the country of our children ; the charm we are most sensible to is the charm of the future, and not the charm of the past."

And how keen and true is this criticism on the changed sense of the word " liberty :"—

" A great many words have changed their meaning. The word *liberty*, for example, had at bottom among the ancients the same meaning as the word *dominium*. *I would be free* meant, in the mouth of the ancient, *I would take part in governing or administering the State;* in the mouth of a modern it means, *I would be independent.* The word *liberty* has with us a moral sense; with them its sense was purely political."

Joubert had lived through the French Revolution, and to the modern cry for liberty he was prone to answer :—

" Let your cry be for free souls rather even than for free men. Moral liberty is the one vitally important liberty, the one liberty which is indispensable ; the other liberty is good and salutary only so far as it favours this. Subordination is in itself a better thing than independence. The one implies order and arrangement ; the other implies only self-sufficiency with isolation. The one means harmony, the other a single tone ; the one is the whole, the other is but the part."

" Liberty ! liberty !" he cries again ; " in all things let us have *justice*, and then we shall have enough liberty."

Let us have justice, *and then we shall have enough liberty.* The wise man will never refuse to echo those words; but then, such is the imperfection of human governments, that almost always, in order to get justice, one has first to secure liberty.

I do not hold up Joubert as a very astonishing and

powerful genius, but rather as a delightful and edifying genius. I have not cared to exhibit him as a sayer of brilliant epigrammatic things, such things as, "Notre vie est du vent tissu . . . les dettes abrégent la vie . . . celui qui a de l'imagination sans érudition a des ailes et n'a pas de pieds" (*Our life is woven wind . . . debts take from life . . . the man of imagination without learning has wings and no feet*), though for such sayings he is famous. In the first place, the French language is in itself so favourable a vehicle for such sayings, that the making them in it has the less merit; at least half the merit ought to go, not to the maker of the saying, but to the French language. In the second place, the peculiar beauty of Joubert is not there; it is not in what is exclusively intellectual,—it is in the union of *soul* with intellect, and in the delightful, satisfying result which this union produces. "Vivre, c'est penser et sentir son âme . . . le bon heur est de sentir son âme bonne . . . toute vérité nue et crue n'a pas assez passé par l'âme . . . les hommes ne sont justes qu'envers ceux qu'ils aiment" (*The essence of life lies in thinking and being conscious of one's soul . . . happiness is the sense of one's soul's being good . . . if a truth is nude and crude, that is a proof it has not been steeped long enough in the soul; . . . man cannot even be just to his neighbour, unless he loves him*); it is much rather in sayings like these that Joubert's best and innermost nature manifests itself. He is the most prepossessing and convincing of witnesses to the good of loving light. Because he sincerely loved light, and did not prefer to it any little private darkness of his own, he found light; his eye was single, and therefore his whole body was full of light. And because he was full of light, he was also full of happiness. In spite of his infirmities, in spite of his sufferings, in spite of his obscurity, he was the happiest man alive ; his life was as charming as his thoughts. For certainly it is natural that the love of light, which is already, in some measure, the possession of light, should irradiate and beatify the whole life of him who has it. There is something unnatural and shocking where, as in the case of Coleridge, it does not. Joubert pains us by no such contradiction ; "the same penetration of spirit which made him such delightful company to his friends, served also to make him perfect in his own personal life, by enabling him always to perceive and do what was right;" he loved and sought light till he became so habituated to it, so accustomed to the joyful testimony of a good conscience, that, to use his own words, "he could no longer exist without this, and was obliged to live without reproach if he would live without misery."

Joubert was not famous while he lived, and he will not be famous now that he is dead. But, before we pity him for this, let us be sure what we mean, in literature, by *famous*. There are the famous men of genius in literature,—the Homers, Dantes, Shakspeares : of them we need not speak ; their praise is for ever and ever. Then there are the famous men of ability in literature : their praise is in their own generation. And what makes this difference? The work of the two orders of men is at the bottom the same,—*a criticism of life*. The end and aim of all literature, if one considers it attentively, is, in truth, nothing but that. But the criticism which the men

of genius pass upon human life is permanently acceptable
to mankind ; the criticism which the men of ability pass
upon human life is transitorily acceptable.   Between
Shakspeare's criticism of human life and Scribe's the difference is there ;—the one is permanently acceptable, the
other transitorily.   Whence then, I repeat, this difference?
It is that the acceptableness of Shakspeare's criticism
depends upon its inherent truth : the acceptableness of
Scribe's upon its suiting itself, by its subject-matter, ideas,
mode of treatment, to the taste of the generation that
hears it.   But the taste and ideas of one generation are
not those of the next.   This next generation in its turn
arrives ;—first its sharp-shooters, its quick-witted, auda-
cious light troops ; then the elephantine main body.
The imposing array of its predecessor it confidently
assails, riddles it with bullets, passes over its body.   It
goes hard then with many once popular reputations, with
many authorities once oracular.   Only two kinds of
authors are safe in the general havoc.   The first kind
are the great abounding fountains of truth, whose criticism of life is a source of illumination and joy to the
whole human race for ever,—the Homers, the Shakspeares.   These are the sacred personages, whom all civilised warfare respects.   The second are those whom the
out-skirmishers of the new generation, its forerunners,—
quick-witted soldiers, as I have said, the select of the
army,—recognise, though the bulk of their comrades
behind might not, as of the same family and character
with the sacred personages, exercising like them an immortal function, and like them inspiring a permanent
interest.   They snatch them up, and set them in a place

of shelter, where the on-coming multitude may not over-
whelm them.   These are the Jouberts.   They will never,
like the Shakspeares, command the homage of the multitude ; but they are safe ; the multitude will not trample
them down.   Except these two kinds, no author is safe.
Let us consider, for example, Joubert's famous contemporary, Lord Jeffrey.   All his vivacity and accomplishment
avail him nothing; of the true critic he had in an eminent
degree no quality, except one,—curiosity.   Curiosity he
had, but he had no organ for truth ; he cannot illuminate
and rejoice us ; no intelligent out-post of the new generation cares about him, cares to put him in safety ; at
this moment we are all passing over his body.   Let us
consider a greater than Jeffrey, a critic whose reputation
still stands firm,—will stand, many people think, for ever,
—the great apostle of the Philistines, Lord Macaulay.
Lord Macaulay was, as I have already said, a born rhetorician ; a splendid rhetorician doubtless, and, beyond that,
an *English* rhetorician also, an *honest* rhetorician ; still,
beyond the apparent rhetorical truth of things he never
could penetrate ; for their vital truth, for what the French
call the *vraie vérité*, he had absolutely no organ ; therefore his reputation, brilliant as it is, is not secure.   Rhetoric so good as his excites and gives pleasure ; but by
pleasure alone you cannot permanently bind men's spirits
to you.   Truth illuminates and gives joy, and it is by the
bond of joy, not of pleasure, that men's spirits are indis-
solubly held.   As Lord Macaulay's own generation dies
out, as a new generation arrives, without those ideas and
tendencies of its predecessor which Lord Macaulay so
deeply shared and so happily satisfied, will he give the

same pleasure ? and, if he ceases to give this, has he
enough of light in him to make him safe ? Pleasure the
new generation will get from its own novel ideas and
tendencies ; but light is another and a rarer thing, and
must be treasured wherever it can be found. Will
Macaulay be saved, in the sweep and pressure of time,
for his light's sake, as Johnson has already been saved by
two generations, Joubert by one ? I think it very doubtful.
But for a spirit of any delicacy and dignity, what a fate,
if he could foresee it ! to be an oracle for one generation, and then of little or no account for ever. How
far better, to pass with scant notice through one's own
generation, but to be singled out and preserved by the
very iconoclasts of the next, then in their turn by those
of the next, and so, like the lamp of life itself, to be
handed on from one generation to another in safety !
This is Joubert's lot, and it is a very enviable one.   The
new men of the new generations, while they let the dust
deepen on a thousand Laharpes, will say of him : " He
lived in the Philistines' day, in a place and time when
almost every idea current in literature had the mark of
Dagon upon it, and not the mark of the children of light.
Nay, the children of light were as yet hardly so much
as heard of : the Canaanite was then in the land.
Still, there were even then a few, who, nourished on
some secret tradition, or illumined, perhaps, by a divine
inspiration, kept aloof from the reigning superstitions,
never bowed the knee to the gods of Canaan ; and one
of these few was called *Joubert*."

SPINOZA.

" By the sentence of the angels, by the decree of the saints, we anthematise, cut off, curse, and execrate Baruch Spinoza, in the presence of these sacred books with the six hundred and thirteen precepts which are written therein, with the anathema wherewith Joshua anathematised Jericho ; with the cursing wherewith Elisha cursed the children ; and with all the cursings which are written in the Book of the Law : cursed be he by day, and cursed by night ; cursed when he lieth down, and cursed when he riseth up ; cursed when he goeth out, and cursed when he cometh in ; the Lord pardon him never ; the wrath and fury of the Lord burn upon this man, and bring upon him all the curses which are written in the Book of the Law. The Lord blot out his name under heaven. The Lord set him apart for destruction from all the tribes of Israel, with all the curses of the firmament which are written in the Book of this Law. . . . There shall no man speak to him, no man write to him, no man show him any kindness, no man stay under the same roof with him, no man come nigh him."

With these amenities, the current compliments of theological parting, the Jews of the Portuguese synagogue at Amsterdam took in 1656 (and not in 1660 as has till now been commonly supposed) their leave of their erring brother, Baruch or Benedict Spinoza. They remained children of Israel, and he became a child of modern Europe.

That was in 1656, and Spinoza died in 1677, at the early age of forty-four. Glory had not found him out. His short life,—a life of unbroken diligence, kindliness, and purity,—was past in seclusion. But in spite of that seclusion, in spite of the shortness of his career, in spite of the hostility of the dispensers of renown in the 18th century,—of Voltaire's disparagement and Bayle's detraction,—in spite of the repellent form which he has given to his principal work, in spite of the exterior semblance of a rigid dogmatism alien to the most essential tendencies of modern philosophy, in spite, finally, of the immense weight of disfavour cast upon him by the long-repeated charge of atheism, Spinoza's name has silently risen in importance, the man and his work have attracted a steadily increasing notice, and bid fair to become soon what they deserve to become,—in the history of modern philosophy, the central point of interest. An avowed translation of one of his works,—his *Tractacus Thelogico-Politicus*,—at last makes its appearance in English. It is the principal work which Spinoza published in his lifetime; his book on ethics, the work on which his fame rests, is posthumous.

The English translator has not done his task well. Of the character of his version there can, I am afraid, be no doubt; one such passage as the following is decisive :—

"I confess that, *while with them* (the theologians) *I have never been able sufficiently to admire the unfathomed*

*mysteries of Scripture I have still found them giving utter-
ance to nothing but Aristotelian and Platonic speculations,*
artfully dressed up and cunningly accommodated to Holy
Writ, lest the speakers should show themselves too plainly
to belong to the sect of the Grecian heathens. *Nor was
it enough for these men to discourse with the Greeks; they
have further taken to raving with the Hebrew prophets."*

This professes to be a translation of these words of
Spinoza : " Fateor, eos nunquam satis mirari potuisse
Scripturæ profundissima mysteria ; attamen præter Aris-
totelicorum vel Platonicorum speculationes nihil docuisse
video, atque his, ne gentiles sectari viderentur, Scripturam
accommodaverunt. Non satis his fuit cum Græcis in-
sanire, sed prophetas cum iisdem deliravisse voluerunt."
After one such specimen of a translator's force, the ex-
perienced reader has a sort of instinct that he may as
well close the book at once, with a smile or a sigh,
according as he happens to be a follower of the weeping
or of the laughing philosopher. If, in spite of this instinct, he persists in going on with the English version of
the *Tractatus Theologico-Politicus*, he will find many more
such specimens. It is not, however, my intention to
fill my space with these, or with strictures upon their
author. I prefer to remark, that he renders a service to
literary history by pointing out, in his preface, how " to
Bayle may be traced the disfavour in which the name of
Spinoza was so long held ;" that, in his observations on
the system of the Church of England, he shows a laudable
freedom from the prejudices of ordinary English Liberals
of that advanced school to which he clearly belongs ;
and lastly, that, though he manifests little familiarity with

Latin, he seems to have considerable familiarity with philosophy, and to be well able to follow and comprehend speculative reasoning. Let me advise him to unite his forces with those of some one who has that accurate knowledge of Latin which he himself has not, and then, perhaps, of that union a really good translation of Spinoza will be the result. And, having given him this advice, let me again turn, for a little, to the *Tractatus Theologico-Politicus* itself.

This work, as I have already said, is a work on the interpretation of Scripture,—it treats of the Bible. What was it exactly which Spinoza thought about the Bible and its inspiration? That will be, at the present moment, the central point of interest for the English readers of his Treatise. Now, it is to be observed, that just on this very point the Treatise, interesting and remarkable as it is, will fail to satisfy the reader. It is important to seize this notion quite firmly, and not to quit hold of it while one is reading Spinoza's work. The scope of that work is this :—Spinoza sees that the life and practice of Christian nations, professing the religion of the Bible, are not the due fruits of the religion of the Bible ; he sees only hatred, bitterness, and strife, where he might have expected to see love, joy, and peace in believing ; and he asks himself the reason of this. The reason is, he says, that these people misunderstand their Bible. Well, then, is his conclusion, I will write a *Tractatus Theologico-Politicus*. I will show these people, that, taking the Bible for granted, taking it to be all which it asserts itself to be, taking it to have all the authority which it claims, it is not what they imagine it to be, it does not say what they imagine it to say. I will show them what it really does say, and I will show them that they will do well to accept this real teaching of the Bible, instead of the phantom with which they have so long been cheated. I will show their Governments that they will do well to remodel the National Churches, to make of them institutions informed with the spirit of the true Bible, instead of institutions informed with the spirit of this false phantom.

Such is really the scope of Spinoza's work. He pursues a great object, and pursues it with signal ability ; but it is important to observe that he does not give us his own opinion about the Bible's fundamental character. He takes the Bible as it stands, as he might take the phenomena of nature, and he discusses it as he finds it. Revelation differs from natural knowledge, he says, not by being more divine or more certain than natural knowledge, but by being conveyed in a different way ; it differs from it because it is a knowledge "of which the laws of human nature considered in themselves alone cannot be the cause." What is really its cause, he says, we need not here inquire (*verum nec nobis jam opus est propheticæ cognitionis causam scire*), for we take Scripture, which contains this revelation, as it stands, and do not ask how it arose (*documentorum causas nihil curamus*).

Proceeding on this principle, Spinoza leaves the attentive reader somewhat baffled and disappointed, clear as is his way of treating his subject, and remarkable as are the conclusions with which he presents us. He starts, we feel, from what is to him a hypothesis, and we want to know what he really thinks about this hypothesis.

His greatest novelties are all within limits fixed for him by this hypothesis. He says that the voice which called Samuel was an imaginary voice ; he says that the waters of the Red Sea retreated before a strong wind ; he says that the Shunammite's son was revived by the natural heat of Elisha's body ; he says that the rainbow which was made a sign to Noah appeared in the ordinary course of nature. Scripture itself, rightly interpreted, says, he affirms, all this. But he asserts that the Voice which uttered the Commandments on Mount Sinai was a real voice, a *vera vox.* He says, indeed, that this voice could not really give to the Israelites that proof which they imagined it gave to them of the existence of God, and that God on Sinai was dealing with the Israelites only according to their imperfect knowledge. Still he asserts the voice to have been a real one ; and for this reason, that we do violence to Scripture if we do not admit it to have been a real one (*nisi Scriptura vim inferre velimus, omnino concedendum est, Israëlitas veram vocem audivisse).* The attentive reader wants to know what Spinoza himself thought about this *vera vox* and its possibility ; he is much more interested in knowing this, than in knowing what Spinoza considered Scripture to affirm about the matter.

The feeling of perplexity thus caused is not diminished by the language of the chapter on miracles. In this chapter Spinoza broadly affirms a miracle to be an impossibility. But he himself contrasts the method of demonstration *à priori,* by which he claims to have established this proposition, with the method which he has pursued in treating of prophetic revelation.

"This revelation," he says, "is a matter out of human reach, and therefore I was bound to take it as I found it." *Monere volo, me aliâ prorsus methodo circa miracula processisse, quam circa prophetiam . . . quod etiam consulto feci quia de prophetia, quandoquidem ipsa captum humanum superat et quæstio mere theologica est, nihil affirmare, neque etiam scire poteram in quo ipsa potissimum constiterit, nisi ex fundamentis revelatis.* The reader feels that Spinoza, proceeding on a hypothesis, has presented him with the assertion of a miracle, and afterwards, proceeding *à priori*, has presented him with the assertion that a miracle is impossible. He feels that Spinoza does not adequately reconcile these two assertions by declaring that any event really miraculous, if found recorded in Scripture, must be "a spurious addition made to Scripture by sacrilegious men." Is, then, he asks, the *vera vox* of Mount Sinai in Spinoza's opinion a spurious addition made to Scripture by sacrilegious men ; or, if not, how is it not miraculous ?

Spinoza, in his own mind, regarded the Bible as a vast collection of miscellaneous documents, many of them quite disparate and not at all to be harmonised with others ; documents of unequal value and of varying applicability, some of them conveying ideas salutary for one time, others for another. But in the *Tractatus Theologico-Politicus* he by no means always deals in this free spirit with the Bible. Sometimes he chooses to deal with it in the spirit of the veriest worshipper of the letter ; sometimes he chooses to treat the Bible as if all its parts were (so to speak) equipollent ; to snatch an isolated text which suits his purpose, without caring whether it is annulled by the context, by the general drift of Scripture, or by other passages of more weight and authority. The great critic thus voluntarily becomes as uncritical as Exeter Hall. The epicurean Solomon, whose *Ecclesiastes* the Hebrew doctors, even after they had received it into the canon, forbade the young and weak-minded among their community to read, Spinoza quotes as of the same authority with the severe Moses; he uses promiscuously, as documents of identical force, without discriminating between their essentially different character, the softened cosmopolitan teaching of the prophets of the captivity, and the rigid national teaching of the instructors of Israel's youth. He is capable of extracting, from a chance expression of Jeremiah, the assertion of a speculative idea which Jeremiah certainly never entertained, and from which he would have recoiled in dismay,—the idea, namely, that miracles are impossible; just as the ordinary Englishman can extract from God's words to Noah, *Be fruitful and multiply*, an exhortation to himself to have a large family. Spinoza, I repeat, knew perfectly well what this verbal mode of dealing with the Bible was worth; but he sometimes uses it because of the hypothesis from which he set out; because of his having agreed "to take Scripture as it stands, and not to ask how it arose."

No doubt the sagacity of Spinoza's rules for biblical interpretation, the power of his analysis of the contents of the Bible, the interest of his reflections on Jewish history, are, in spite of this, very great, and have an absolute worth of their own, independent of the silence or ambiguity of their author upon a point of cardinal importance.

Few candid people will read his rules of interpretation without exclaiming that they are the very dictates of good sense, that they have always believed in them; and without adding, after a moment's reflection, that they have passed their lives in violating them. And what can be more interesting, than to find that perhaps the main cause of the decay of the Jewish polity was one of which from our English Bible, which entirely mistranslates the 26th verse of the 20th chapter of Ezekiel, we hear nothing,— the perpetual reproach of impurity and rejection cast upon the mass of the Hebrew nation by the exclusive priesthood of the tribe of Levi? What can be more suggestive, after Mr. Mill and Dr. Stanley have been telling us how great an element of strength to the Hebrew nation was the institution of prophets, than to hear from the ablest of Hebrews how this institution seems to him to have been to his nation one of her main elements of weakness? No intelligent man can read the *Tractatus Theologico-Politicus* without being profoundly instructed by it; but neither can he read it without feeling that, as a speculative work, it is, to use a French military expression, *in the air;* that, in a certain sense, it is in want of a base and in want of supports; that this base and these supports are, at any rate, not to be found in the work itself, and, if they exist, must be sought for in other works of the author.

The genuine speculative opinions of Spinoza, which the *Tractatus Theologico-Politicus* but imperfectly reveals, may in his Ethics and in his Letters be found set forth clearly. It is, however, the business of criticism to deal with every independent work as with an independent whole, and,—instead of establishing between the *Tractatus Theologico-Politicus* and the Ethics of Spinoza a relation which Spinoza himself has not established,—to seize, in dealing with the *Tractatus Theologico-Politicus*, the important fact that this work has its source, not in the axioms and definitions of the Ethics, but in a hypothesis. The Ethics are not yet translated into English, and I have not here to speak of them. Then will be the right time for criticism to try and seize the special character and tendencies of that remarkable work, when it is dealing with it directly. The criticism of the Ethics is far too serious a task to be undertaken incidentally, and merely as a supplement to the criticism of the *Tractatus Theologico-Politicus.* Nevertheless, on certain governing ideas of Spinoza, which receive their systematic expression, indeed, in the Ethics, and on which the *Tractatus Theologico-Politicus* is not formally based, but which are yet never absent from Spinoza's mind in the composition of any work, which breathe through all his works, and fill them with a peculiar effect and power, I have a word or two to say.

A philosopher's real power over mankind resides not in his metaphysical formulas, but in the spirit and tendencies which have led him to adopt those formulas. Spinoza's critic, therefore, has rather to bring to light that spirit and those tendencies of his author, than to exhibit his metaphysical formulas. Propositions about substance pass by mankind at large like the idle wind, which mankind at large regards not; it will not even listen to a word about these propositions, unless it first learns what their author was driving at with them, and finds that this object of his is one with which it sympathises, one, at any rate, which commands its attention. And mankind is so far right that this object of the author is really, as has been said, that which is most important, that which sets all his work in motion, that which is the secret of his attraction for other minds, which, by different ways, pursue the same object.

Mr. Maurice, seeking for the cause of Goethe's great admiration for Spinoza, thinks that he finds it in Spinoza's Hebrew genius. " He spoke of God," says Mr. Maurice, "as an actual being, to those who had fancied Him a name in a book. The child of the circumcision had a message for Lessing and Goethe which the pagan schools of philosophy could not bring." This seems to me, I confess, fanciful. An intensity and impressiveness, which came to him from his Hebrew nature, Spinoza no doubt has ; but the two things which are most remarkable about him, and by which, as I think, he chiefly impressed Goethe, seem to me not to come to him from his Hebrew nature at all,—I mean his denial of final causes, and his stoicism, a stoicism not passive, but active. For a mind like Goethe's,—a mind profoundly impartial and passionately aspiring after the science, not of men only, but of universal nature,—the popular philosophy which explains all things by reference to man, and regards universal nature as existing for the sake of man, and even of certain classes of men, was utterly repulsive. Unchecked, this philosophy would gladly maintain that the donkey exists in order that the invalid Christian may have donkey's milk before breakfast; and such views of nature as this were exactly what Goethe's whole soul abhorred.

Creation, he thought, should be made of sterner stuff; he desired to rest the donkey's existence on larger grounds. More than any philosopher who has ever lived, Spinoza satisfied him here. The full exposition of the counter-doctrine to the popular doctrine of final causes is to be found in the Ethics; but this denial of final causes was so essential an element of all Spinoza's thinking that we shall, as has been said already, find it in the work with which we are here concerned, the *Tractatus Theologico-Politicus*, and, indeed, permeating that work and all his works. From the *Tractatus Theologico-Politicus* one may take as good a general statement of this denial as any which is to be found in the Ethics :—

"Deus naturam dirigit, prout ejus leges universales, non autem prout humanæ naturæ particulares leges exigunt, adeoque Deus non solius humani generis, sed totius naturæ rationem habet." (*God directs nature, according as the universal laws of nature, but not according as the particular laws of human nature require; and so God has regard, not of the human race only, but of entire nature.*)

And, as a pendant to this denial by Spinoza of final causes, comes his stoicism :—

"Non studemus, ut natura nobis, sed contra ut nos naturæ pareamus." (*Our desire is not that nature may obey us, but, on the contrary, that we may obey nature.*)

Here is the second source of his attractiveness for Goethe; and Goethe is but the eminent representative of a whole order of minds whose admiration has made Spinoza's fame. Spinoza first impresses Goethe and any man like Goethe, and then he composes him ; first he fills and satisfies his imagination by the width and grandeur of his view of nature, and then he fortifies and stills his mobile, straining, passionate, poetic temperament by the moral lesson he draws from his view of nature. And a moral lesson not of mere resigned acquiescence, not of melancholy quietism, but of joyful activity within the limits of man's true sphere :—

"Ipsa hominis essentia est conatus quo unusquisque suum esse conservare conatur. . . . Virtus hominis est ipsa hominis essentia, quatenus a solo conatu suum esse conservandi definitur. . . . Felicitas in eo consistit quod homo suum esse conservare potest. . . . Lætitia est hominis transitio ad majorem perfectionem. . . . Tristitia est hominis transitio ad minorem perfectionem." (*Man's very essence is the effort wherewith each man strives to maintain his own being. . . . Man's virtue is this very essence, so far as it is defined by this single effort to maintain man's being. . . . Happiness consists in a man's being able to maintain his own being. . . . Joy is man's passage to a greater perfection. . . . Sorrow is man's passage to a lesser perfection.*)

It seems to me that by neither of these, his grand characteristic doctrines, is Spinoza truly Hebrew or truly Christian. His denial of final causes is essentially alien to the spirit of the Old Testament, and his cheerful and self-sufficing stoicism is essentially alien to the spirit of the New. The doctrine that "God directs nature, not according as the particular laws of human nature, but according as the universal laws of nature require," is at utter variance with that Hebrew mode of representing

God's dealings, which makes the locusts visit Egypt to punish Pharaoh's hardness of heart, and the falling dew avert itself from the fleece of Gideon. The doctrine that "all sorrow is a passage to a lesser perfection" is at utter variance with the Christian recognition of the blessedness of sorrow, working "repentance to salvation not to be repented of;" of sorrow, which, in Dante's words, "remarries us to God." Spinoza's repeated and earnest assertions that the love of God is man's *summum bonum* do not remove the fundamental diversity between his doctrine and the Hebrew and Christian doctrines. By the love of God he does not mean the same thing which the Hebrew and Christian religions mean by the love of God. He makes the love of God to consist in the knowledge of God ; and, as we know God only through his manifestation of himself in the laws of nature, it is by knowing these laws that we love God, and the more we know them the more we love him. This may be true, but this is not what the Christian means by the love of God. Spinoza's ideal is the intellectual life; the Christian's ideal is the religious life. Between the two conditions there is all the difference which there is between the being in love, and the following, with delighted comprehension, a demonstration of Euclid. For Spinoza, undoubtedly, the crown of the intellectual life is a transport, as for the saint the crown of the religious life is a transport ; but the two transports are not the same.

This is true ; yet it is true, also, that by thus crowning the intellectual life with a sacred transport, by thus retaining in philosophy, amid the discontented murmurs of all the army of atheism, the name of God, Spinoza maintains a profound affinity with that which is truest in religion, and inspires an indestructible interest. "It is true," one may say to the wise and devout Christian, "Spinoza's conception of beatitude is not yours, and cannot satisfy you ; but whose conception of beatitude would you accept as satisfying ? Not even that of the devoutest of your fellow-Christians. Fra Angelico, the sweetest and most inspired of devout souls, has given us, in his great picture of the Last Judgment, his conception of beatitude. The elect are going round in a ring on long grass under laden fruit-trees ; two of them, more restless than the others, are flying up a battlemented street,—a street blank with all the ennui of the Middle Ages. Across a gulf is visible, for the delectation of the saints, a blazing caldron in which Beelzebub is sousing the damned. This is hardly more your conception of beatitude than Spinoza's is. But 'in my Father's house are many mansions ;' only, to reach any one of these mansions, are needed the wings of a genuine sacred transport, of an 'immortal longing.'" These wings Spinoza had ; and, because he had them, he horrifies a certain school of his admirers by talking of "God" where they talk of "forces," and by talking of "the love of God" where they talk of "a rational curiosity."

One of these admirers, M. Van Vloten, has recently published at Amsterdam a supplementary volume to Spinoza's works, containing the interesting document of Spinoza's sentence of excommunication, from which I have already quoted, and containing, besides, several lately found works alleged to be Spinoza's, which seem to me to be of doubtful authenticity, and, even if authentic, of no great importance. M. Van Vloten (who, let me be permitted to say in passing, writes a Latin which would make one think that the art of writing Latin must be now a lost art in the country of Lipsius) is very anxious that Spinoza's unscientific retention of the name of God should not afflict his reader with any doubts as to his perfect scientific orthodoxy :—

" It is a great mistake," he cries, " to disparage Spinoza as merely one of the dogmatists before Kant. By keeping the name of God, while he did away with his person and character, he has done himself injustice. Those who look to the bottom of things will see, that, long ago as he lived, he had even then reached the point to which the post-Hegelian philosophy and the study of natural science has only just brought our own times. Leibnitz expressed his apprehension lest those who did away with final causes should do away with God at the same time. But it is in his having done away with final causes, *and with God along with them*, that Spinoza's true merit consists."

Now it must be remarked that to use Spinoza's denial of final causes in order to identify him with the Coryphæi of atheism, is to make a false use of Spinoza's denial of final causes, just as to use his assertion of the all-importance of loving God to identify him with the saints, would be to make a false use of his assertion of the all-importance of loving God. He is no more to be identified with the post-Hegelian philosophers than he is to be identified with St. Augustine. Nay, when M. Van Vloten violently presses the parallel with the post-Hegelians, one feels that the parallel with St. Augustine is the far truer one. Compared with the soldier of irreligion M. Van Vloten would have him to be, Spinoza is religious. His own language about himself, about his aspirations and his course, are true : his foot is in the *vera vita*, his eye on the beatific vision.

MARCUS AURELIUS.

MR. MILL says, in his book on Liberty, that " Christian morality is in great part merely a protest against paganism ; its ideal is negative rather than positive, passive rather than active." He says, that, in certain most important respects, " it falls far below the best morality of the ancients." Now the object of systems of morality is to take possession of human life, to save it from being abandoned to passion or allowed to drift at hazard, to give it happiness by establishing it in the practice of virtue ; and this object they seek to attain by prescribing to human life fixed principles of action, fixed rules of conduct. In its uninspired as well as in its inspired moments, in its days of languor and gloom as well as in its days of sunshine and energy, human life has thus always a clue to follow, and may always be making way towards its goal. Christian morality has not failed to supply to human life aids of this sort. It has supplied them far more abundantly than many of its critics imagine. The most exquisite document, after those of the New Testament, of all that the Christian spirit has ever inspired,— the *Imitation*,—by no means contains the whole of Christian morality ; nay, the disparagers of this morality would think themselves sure of triumphing if one agreed

to look for it in the *Imitation* only. But even the
Imitation is full of passages like these : " Vita sine pro-
posito languida et vaga est ;"—" Omni die renovare
debemus propositum nostrum, dicentes : nunc hodie
perfecte incipiamus, quia nihil est quod hactenus feci-
mus ;" — " Secundum propositum nostrum est cursus
profectûs nostri ;"—" Raro etiam unum vitium perfecte
vincimus, et ad *quotidianum* profectum non accendimur ;"
—" Semper aliquid certi proponendum est ;"—" Tibi ipsi
violentiam frequenter fac ;" (*A life without a purpose is
a languid, drifting thing;—Every day we ought to renew
our purpose, saying to ourselves : " this day let us make a
sound beginning, for what we have hitherto done is nought;"
—Our improvement is in proportion to our purpose ;—
We hardly ever manage to get completely rid even of one
fault, and do not set our hearts on daily improvement ;—
Always place a definite purpose before thee;—Get the
habit of mastering thine inclination.*) These are moral
precepts, and moral precepts of the best kind. As rules
to hold possession of our conduct, and to keep us in the
right course through outward troubles and inward perplexity, they are equal to the best ever furnished by the
great masters of morals,—Epictetus or Marcus Aurelius.

But moral rules, apprehended as ideas first, and then
rigorously followed as laws, are, and must be, for the sage
only. The mass of mankind have neither force of intellect enough to apprehend them clearly as ideas, nor
force of character enough to follow them strictly as laws.
The mass of mankind can be carried along a course full
of hardship for the natural man, can be borne over the
thousand impediments of the narrow way, only by the

tide of a joyful and bounding emotion. It is impossible
to rise from reading Epictetus or Marcus Aurelius without
a sense of constraint and melancholy, without feeling
that the burden laid upon man is well-nigh greater than
he can bear. Honour to the sages who have felt this, and
yet have borne it! Yet, even for the sage, this sense of
labour and sorrow in his march towards the goal constitutes a relative inferiority; the noblest souls of whatever
creed, the pagan Empedocles as well as the Christian
Paul, have insisted on the necessity of an inspiration, a
living emotion, to make moral action perfect; an obscure
indication of this necessity is the one drop of truth in
the ocean of verbiage with which the controversy on
justification by faith has flooded the world. But, for the
ordinary man, this sense of labour and sorrow constitutes
an absolute disqualification; it paralyses him; under the
weight of it, he cannot make way towards the goal at all.
The paramount virtue of religion is, that it has *lighted up*
morality; that it has supplied the emotion and inspiration needful for carrying the sage along the narrow way
perfectly, for carrying the ordinary man along it at all.
Even the religions with most dross in them have had
something of this virtue; but the Christian religion
manifests it with unexampled splendour. "Lead me,
Zeus and Destiny," says the prayer of Epictetus, "whither-
soever I am appointed to go; I will follow without
wavering; even though I turn coward and shrink, I shall
have to follow all the same." The fortitude of that is for
the strong, for the few; even for them, the spiritual atmosphere with which it surrounds them is bleak and grey.
But, "Let thy loving spirit lead me forth into the land

of righteousness;"—"The Lord shall be unto thee an everlasting light, and thy God thy glory;"—"Unto you that fear my name shall the sun of righteousness arise with healing in his wings," says the Old Testament; "Born, not of blood, nor of the will of the flesh, nor of the will of man, but of God;"—"Except a man be born again, he cannot see the kingdom of God;"—"Whatsoever is born of God, overcometh the world," says the New. The ray of sunshine is there, the glow of a divine warmth;—the austerity of the sage melts away under it, the paralysis of the weak is healed; he who is vivified by it renews his strength; "all things are possible to him;" "he is a new creature."

Epictetus says: "Every matter has two handles, one of which will bear taking hold of, the other not. If thy brother sin against thee, lay not hold of the matter by this, that he sins against thee; for by this handle the matter will not bear taking hold of. But rather lay hold of it by this, that he is thy brother, thy born mate; and thou wilt take hold of it by what will bear handling." Jesus, asked whether a man is bound to forgive his brother as often as seven times, answers: "I say not unto thee, until seven times, but until seventy times seven." Epictetus here suggests to the reason grounds for forgiveness of injuries which Jesus does not; but it is vain to say that Epictetus is on that account a better moralist than Jesus, if the warmth, the emotion, of Jesus's answer fires his hearer to the practice of forgiveness of injuries, while the thought in Epictetus's leaves him cold. So with Christian morality in general; its distinction is not that it propounds the maxim, "Thou shalt love God

and thy neighbour," with more development, closer reasoning, truer sincerity, than other moral systems; it is
that it propounds this maxim with an inspiration which
wonderfully catches the hearer and makes him act upon
it. It is because Mr. Mill has attained to the perception
of truths of this nature, that he is,—instead of being, like
the school from which he proceeds, doomed to sterility,
—a writer of distinguished mark and influence, a writer
deserving all attention and respect; it is (I must be pardoned for saying) because he is not sufficiently leavened
with them, that he falls just short of being a great
writer.

That which gives to the moral writings of the Emperor
Marcus Aurelius their peculiar character and charm, is
their being suffused and softened by something of this
very sentiment whence Christian morality draws its best
power. Mr. Long has recently published in a convenient
form a translation of these writings, and has thus enabled
English readers to judge Marcus Aurelius for themselves;
he has rendered his countrymen a real service by so
doing. Mr. Long's reputation as a scholar is a sufficient
guarantee of the general fidelity and accuracy of his
translation; on these matters, besides, I am hardly en-
titled to speak, and my praise is of no value. But that
for which I and the rest of the unlearned may venture to
praise Mr. Long is this; that he treats Marcus Aurelius's
writings, as he treats all the other remains of Greek and
Roman antiquity which he touches, not as a dead and
dry matter of learning, but as documents with a side of
modern applicability and living interest, and valuable
mainly so far as this side in them can be made clear;

that as in his notes on Plutarch's Roman Lives he deals with the modern epoch of Cæsar and Cicero, not as food for schoolboys, but as food for men, and men engaged in the current of contemporary life and action, so in his remarks and essays on Marcus Aurelius, he treats this truly modern striver and thinker not as a Classical Dictionary hero, but as a present source from which to draw "example of life, and instruction of manners." Why may not a son of Dr. Arnold say, what might naturally here be said by any other critic, that in this lively and fruitful way of considering the men and affairs of ancient Gréece and Rome, Mr. Long resembles Dr. Arnold?

One or two little complaints, however, I have against Mr. Long, and I will get them off my mind at once. In the first place, why could he not have found gentler and juster terms to describe the translation of his best known predecessor, Jeremy Collier, — the redoutable enemy of stage plays,—than these : " a most coarse and vulgar copy of the original?" As a matter of taste, a translator should deal leniently with his predecessor ; but, putting that out of the question, Mr. Long's language is a great deal too hard. Most English people who knew Marcus Aurelius before Mr. Long appeared as his intro-ducer, knew him through Jeremy Collier. And the acquaintance of a man like Marcus Aurelius is such an imperishable benefit, that one can never lose a peculiar sense of obligation towards the man who confers it. Apart from this claim upon one's tenderness, however, Jeremy Collier's version deserves respect for its genuine spirit and vigour, the spirit and vigour of the age of

Dryden. Jeremy Collier too, like Mr. Long, regarded in Marcus Aurelius the living moralist, and not the dead classic; and his warmth of feeling gave to his style an impetuosity and rhythm which from Mr. Long's style (I do not blame it on that account) are absent. Let us place the two side by side. The impressive opening of Marcus Aurelius's fifth book, Mr. Long translates thus :—

"In the morning when thou risest unwillingly, let this thought be present: I am rising to the work of a human being. Why then am I dissatisfied if I am going to do the things for which I exist and for which I was brought into the world ? Or have I been made for this, to lie in the bed-clothes and keep myself warm ?—But this is more pleasant.—Dost thou exist then to take thy pleasure, and not at all for action or exertion ?"

Jeremy Collier has :—

"When you find an unwillingness to rise early in the morning, make this short speech to yourself: 'I am getting up now to do the business of a man; and am I out of humour for going about that which I was made for, and for the sake of which I was sent into the world ? Was I then designed for nothing but to doze and batten beneath the counterpane ? I thought action had been the end of your being.' "

In another striking passage, again, Mr. Long has :—

"No longer wander at hazard; for neither wilt thou read thy own memoirs, nor the acts of the ancient Romans and Hellenes, and the selections from books which thou wast reserving for thy old age. Hasten then to the end which thou hast before thee, and, throwing away idle hopes, come to thine own aid, if thou carest at all for thyself, while it is in thy power."

Here his despised predecessor has :—

" Don't go too far in your books and overgrasp yourself. Alas, you have no time left to peruse your diary, to read over the Greek and Roman history : come, don't flatter and deceive yourself; look to the main chance, to the end and design of reading, and mind life more than notion : I say, if you have a kindness for your person, drive at the practice and help yourself, for that is in your own power."

It seems to me that here for style and force Jeremy Collier can (to say the least) perfectly stand comparison with Mr. Long. Jeremy Collier's real defect as a translator is not his coarseness and vulgarity, but his imperfect acquaintance with Greek ; this is a serious defect, a fatal one ; it renders a translation like Mr. Long's necessary. Jeremy Collier's work will now be forgotten, and Mr. Long stands master of the field ; but he may be content, at any rate, to leave his predecessor's grave unharmed, even if he will not throw upon it, in passing, a handful of kindly earth.

Another complaint I have against Mr. Long is, that he is not quite idiomatic and simple enough. It is a little formal, at least, if not pedantic, to say *Ethic* and *Dialectic*, instead of *Ethics* and *Dialectics*, and to say " *Hellenes* and Romans" instead of " *Greeks* and Romans." And why, too,—the name of Antoninus being preoccupied by Antoninus Pius,—will Mr. Long call his author Marcus *Antoninus* instead of Marcus *Aurelius ?* Small as these matters appear, they are important when one has to

deal with the general public, and not with a small circle
of scholars ; and it is the general public that the translator of a short masterpiece on morals, such as is the
book of Marcus Aurelius, should have in view ; his aim
should be to make Marcus Aurelius's work as popular as
the *Imitation*, and Marcus Aurelius's name as familiar
as Socrates's.   In rendering or naming him, therefore,
punctilious accuracy of phrase is not so much to be
sought as accessibility and currency ; everything which
may best enable the Emperor and his precepts *volitare
per ora virum*.   It is essential to render him in language
perfectly plain and unprofessional, and to call him by the
name by which he is best and most distinctly known.
The translators of the Bible talk of *pence* and not *denarii*,
and the admirers of Voltaire do not celebrate him under
the name of Arouet.

But, after these trifling complaints are made, one must
end, as one began, in unfeigned gratitude to Mr. Long for
his excellent and substantial reproduction in English of an
invaluable work.   In general the substantiality, soundness,
and precision of his rendering are (I will venture, after all,
to give my opinion about them) as conspicuous as the
living spirit with which he treats antiquity ; and these
qualities are particularly desirable in the translator of a
work like Marcus Aurelius's, of which the language is
often corrupt, almost always hard and obscure.   Any one
who wants to appreciate Mr. Long's merits as a translator
may read, in the original and in Mr. Long's translation,
the seventh chapter of the tenth book ; he will see how,
through all the dubiousness and involved manner of the
Greek, Mr. Long has firmly seized upon the clear thought

which is certainly at the bottom of that troubled wording, and, in distinctly rendering this thought, has at the same time thrown round its expression a characteristic shade of painfulness and difficulty which just suits it. And Marcus Aurelius's book is one which, when it is rendered so accurately as Mr. Long renders it, even those who know Greek tolerably well may choose to read rather in the translation than in the original. For not only are the contents here incomparably more valuable than the external form, but this form, this Greek of a Roman, is not one of those styles which have a physiognomy, which are an essential part of their author, which stamp an indelible impression of him on the reader's mind. An old Lyons commentator finds, indeed, in Marcus Aurelius's Greek, something characteristic, something specially firm and imperial; but I think an ordinary mortal will hardly find this ; he will find crabbed Greek, without any charm of distinct physiognomy. The Greek of Thucydides and Plato has this charm, and he who reads them in a translation, however accurate, loses it, and loses much in losing it ; but the Greek of Marcus Aurelius, like the Greek of the New Testament, and even more than the Greek of the New Testament, is wanting in it. If one could be assured that the English Testament were made perfectly accurate, one might be perfectly content never to open a Greek Testament again ; and, Mr. Long's version of Marcus Aurelius being what it is, an Englishman who reads to live, and does not live to read, may henceforth let the Greek original repose upon its shelf.

The man whose thoughts Mr. Long has thus faithfully reproduced, is perhaps the most beautiful figure in history.

He is one of those consoling and hope-inspiring marks,
which stand for ever to remind our weak and easily
discouraged race how high human goodness and perse-
verance have once been carried, and may be carried
again.   The interest of mankind is peculiarly attracted
by examples of signal goodness in high places ; for that
testimony to the worth of goodness is the most striking
which is borne by those to whom all the means of pleasure and self-indulgence lay open, by those who had at
their command the kingdoms of the world and the glory
of them.   Marcus Aurelius was the ruler of the grandest
of empires ; and he was one of the best of men.   Besides
him, history presents one or two other sovereigns eminent
for their goodness, such as Saint Louis or Alfred.   But
Marcus Aurelius has, for us moderns, this great superiority
in interest over Saint Louis or Alfred, that he lived and
acted in a state of society modern by its essential characteristics, in an epoch akin to our own, in a brilliant
centre of civilisation.   Trajan talks of " our enlightened
age " just as glibly as the *Times* talks of it.   Marcus
Aurelius thus becomes for us a man like ourselves, a man
in all things tempted as we are.   Saint Louis inhabits an
atmosphere of mediæval Catholicism, which the man of
the nineteenth century may admire, indeed, may even
passionately wish to inhabit, but which, strive as he will,
he cannot really inhabit ; Alfred belongs to a state of
society (I say it with all deference to the *Saturday
Review* critic who keeps such jealous watch over the
honour of our Saxon ancestors) half barbarous.   Neither
Alfred nor Saint Louis can be morally and intellectually
as near to us as Marcus Aurelius.

The record of the outward life of this admirable man has in it little of striking incident. He was born at Rome on the 26th of April, in the year 121 of the Christian era. He was nephew and son-in-law to his predecessor on the throne, Antoninus Pius. When Antoninus died, he was forty years old, but from the time of his earliest manhood he had assisted in administering public affairs. Then, after his uncle's death in 161, for nineteen years he reigned as emperor. The barbarians were pressing on the Roman frontier, and a great part of Marcus Aurelius's nineteen years of reign was passed in campaigning. His absences from Rome were numerous and long; we hear of him in Asia Minor, Syria, Egypt, Greece; but, above all, in the countries on the Danube, where the war with the barbarians was going on,—in Austria, Moravia, Hungary. In these countries much of his Journal seems to have been written; parts of it are dated from them; and there, a few weeks before his fifty-ninth birthday, he fell sick and died.* The record of him on which his fame chiefly rests is the record of his inward life,—his *Journal*, or *Commentaries*, or *Meditations*, or *Thoughts*, for by all these names has the work been called. Perhaps the most interesting of the records of his outward life is that which the first book of this work supplies, where he gives an account of his education, recites the names of those to whom he is indebted for it, and enumerates his obligations to each of them. It is a refreshing and consoling picture, a priceless treasure for those, who, sick of the " wild and dreamlike trade of blood and guile," which seems to be nearly the

* He died on the 17th of March, 180.

whole of what history has to offer to our view, seek eagerly for that substratum of right thinking and well-doing which in all ages must surely have somewhere existed, for without it the continued life of humanity would have been impossible. "From my mother I learnt piety and beneficence, and abstinence not only from evil deeds but even from evil thoughts; and further, simplicity in my way of living, far removed from the habits of the rich." Let us remember that, the next time we are reading the sixth satire of Juvenal. "From my tutor I learnt" (hear it, ye tutors of princes!) "endurance of labour, and to want little, and to work with my own hands, and not to meddle with other people's affairs, and not to be ready to listen to slander." The vices and foibles of the Greek sophist or rhetorician,—the *Græculus esuriens*,—are in everybody's mind; but he who reads Marcus Aurelius's account of his Greek teachers and masters, will understand how it is that, in spite of the vices and foibles of individual *Græculi*, the education of the human race owes to Greece a debt which can never be overrated. The vague and colourless praise of history leaves on the mind hardly any impression of Antoninus Pius; it is only from the private memoranda of his nephew that we learn what a disciplined, hard-working, gentle, wise, virtuous man he was; a man who, perhaps, interests mankind less than his immortal nephew only because he has left in writing no record of his inner life,—*caret quia vate sacro.* Of the outward life and circumstances of Marcus Aurelius, beyond these notices which he has himself supplied, there are few of much interest and importance. There is the fine anecdote of his speech when he heard of the assassination of the revolted Avidius Cassius, against whom he was marching ; *he was sorry*, he said, *to be deprived of the pleasure of pardoning him.* And there are one or two more anecdotes of him which show the same spirit. But the great record for the outward life of a man who has left such a record of his lofty inward aspirations as that which Marcus Aurelius has left, is the clear consenting voice of all his contemporaries,—high and low, friend and enemy, pagan and Christian,—in praise of his sincerity, justice, and goodness. The world's charity does not err on the side of excess, and here was a man occupying the most conspicuous station in the world, and professing the highest possible standard of conduct ;—yet the world was obliged to declare that he walked worthily of his profession. Long after his death, his bust was to be seen in the houses of private men through the wide Roman empire ; it may be the vulgar part of human nature which busies itself with the semblance and doings of living sovereigns, it is its nobler part which busies itself with those of the dead ; these busts of Marcus Aurelius, in the homes of Gaul, Britain, and Italy, bore witness, not to the inmates' frivolous curiosity about princes and palaces, but to their reverential memory of the passage of a great man upon the earth.

Two things, however, before one turns from the outward to the inward life of Marcus Aurelius, force themselves upon one's notice, and demand a word of comment; he persecuted the Christians, and he had for his son the vicious and brutal Commodus. The persecution at Lyons, in which Attalus and Pothinus suffered, the persecution at Smyrna, in which Polycarp suffered, took place in his reign. Of his humanity, of his tolerance, of his horror of cruelty and violence, of his wish to refrain from severe measures against the Christians, of his anxiety to temper the severity of these measures when they appeared to him indispensable, there is no doubt; but, on the one hand, it is certain that the letter, attributed to him, directing that no Christian should be punished for being a Christian, is spurious; it is almost certain that his alleged answer to the authorities of Lyons, in which he directs that Christians persisting in their profession shall be dealt with according to law, is genuine. Mr. Long seems inclined to try and throw doubt over the persecution at Lyons, by pointing out that the letter of the Lyons Christians relating it, alleges it to have been attended by miraculous and incredible incidents. "A man," he says, "can only act consistently by accepting all this letter or rejecting it all, and we cannot blame him for either." But it is contrary to all experience to say that because a fact is related with incorrect additions and embellishments, therefore it probably never happened at all; or that it is not, in general, easy for an impartial mind to distinguish between the fact and the embellishments. I cannot doubt that the Lyons persecution took place, and that the punishment of Christians for being Christians was sanctioned by Marcus Aurelius. But then I must add that nine modern readers out of ten, when they read this, will, I believe, have a perfectly false notion of what the moral action of Marcus Aurelius, in sanctioning that punishment, really was. They imagine Trajan, or Antoninus Pius, or Marcus Aurelius, fresh

from the perusal of the Gospel, fully aware of the spirit
and holiness of the Christian saints, ordering their exter-
mination because they loved darkness rather than light.
Far from this, the Christianity which these emperors
aimed at repressing was, in their conception of it, something philosophically contemptible, politically subversive,
and morally abominable. As men, they sincerely regarded it much as well-conditioned people, with us,
regard Mormonism ; as rulers, they regarded it much as
Liberal statesmen, with us, regard the Jesuits. A kind
of Mormonism, constituted as a vast secret society, with
obscure aims of political and social subversion, was what
Antoninus Pius and Marcus Aurelius believed themselves
to be repressing when they punished Christians. The
early Christian apologists again and again declare to us
under what odious imputations the Christians lay, how
general was the belief that these imputations were well-
grounded, how sincere was the horror which the belief
inspired. The multitude, convinced that the Christians
were atheists who ate human flesh and thought incest no
crime, displayed against them a fury so passionate as to
embarrass and alarm their rulers. The severe expressions
of Tacitus, *exitiabilis superstitio—odio humani generis con-
victi*, show how deeply the prejudices of the multitude
imbued the educated class also. One asks oneself with
astonishment how a doctrine so benign as that of Christ
can have incurred misrepresentation so monstrous. The
inner and moving cause of the misrepresentation lay, no
doubt, in this,—that Christianity was a new spirit in the
Roman world, destined to act in that world as its dissolvent ; and it was inevitable that Christianity in the

Roman world, like democracy in the modern world, like
every new spirit with a similar mission assigned to it,
should at its first appearance occasion an instinctive
shrinking and repugnance in the world which it was to
dissolve.   The outer and palpable causes of the misrepresentation were, for the Roman public at large, the
confounding of the Christians with the Jews, that isolated,
fierce, and stubborn race, whose stubbornness, fierceness,
and isolation, real as they were, the fancy of a civilised
Roman yet further exaggerated ; the atmosphere of
mystery and novelty which surrounded the Christian
rites ; the very simplicity of Christian theism : for the
Roman statesman, the character of secret assemblages
which the meetings of the Christian community wore,
under a State-system as jealous of unauthorised associations as the State-system of modern France.

A Roman of Marcus Aurelius's time and position could
not well see the Christians except through the mist of
these prejudices.   Seen through such a mist, the Christians appeared with a thousand faults not their own ; but
it has not been sufficiently remarked that faults, really
their own, many of them assuredly appeared with besides,
faults especially likely to strike such an observer as
Marcus Aurelius, and to confirm him in the prejudices
of his race, station, and rearing.   We look back upon
Christianity after it has proved what a future it bore
within it, and for us the sole representatives of its early
struggles are the pure and devoted spirits through whom
it proved this ; Marcus Aurelius saw it with its future
yet unshown, and with the tares among its professed
progeny not less conspicuous than the wheat.   Who can

doubt that among the professing Christians of the second century, as among the professing Christians of the nineteenth, there was plenty of folly, plenty of rabid nonsense, plenty of gross fanaticism ; who will even venture to affirm that, separated in great measure from the intellect and civilisation of the world for one or two centuries, Christianity, wonderful as have been its fruits, had the development perfectly worthy of its inestimable germ ? Who will venture to affirm that, by the alliance of Christianity with the virtue and intelligence of men like the Antonines,—of the best product of Greek and Roman civilisation, while Greek and Roman civilisation had yet life and power,—Christianity and the world, as well as the Antonines themselves, would not have been gainers ? That alliance was not to be ;—the Antonines lived and died with an utter misconception of Christianity ; Christianity grew up in the Catacombs, not on the Palatine. Marcus Aurelius incurs no moral reproach by having authorised the punishment of the Christians; he does not thereby become in the least what we mean by a *persecutor*. One may concede that it was impossible for him to see Christianity as it really was ;—as impossible as for even the moderate and sensible Fleury to see the Antonines as they really were ;—one may concede that the point of view from which Christianity appeared something anti-civil and anti-social, which the State had the faculty to judge and the duty to suppress, was inevitably his. Still, however, it remains true, that this sage, who made perfection his aim and reason his law, did Christianity an immense injustice, and rested in an idea of State-attributes which was illusive. And this is, in truth, characteristic of Marcus Aurelius, that he is blameless, yet, in a certain sense, unfortunate ; in his character, beautiful as it is, there is something melancholy, circumscribed, and ineffectual.

For of his having such a son as Commodus, too, one must say that he is not to be blamed on that account, but that he is unfortunate. Disposition and temperament are inexplicable things ; there are natures on which the best education and example are thrown away ; excellent fathers may have, without any fault of theirs, incurably vicious sons. It is to be remembered, also, that Commodus was left, at the perilous age of nineteen, master of the world ; while his father, at that age, was but beginning a twenty years' apprenticeship to wisdom, labour, and self-command, under the sheltering teachership of his uncle Antoninus. Commodus was a prince apt to be led by favourites ; and if the story is true which says that he left, all through his reign, the Christians untroubled, and ascribes this lenity to the influence of his mistress Marcia, it shows that he could be led to good as well as to evil ;—for such a nature to be left at a critical age with absolute power, and wholly without good counsel and direction, was the more fatal. Still one cannot help wishing that the example of Marcus Aurelius could have availed more with his own only son ; one cannot but think that with such virtue as his there should go, too, the ardour which removes mountains, and that the ardour which removes mountains might have even won Commodus ; the word *ineffectual* again rises to one's mind ; Marcus Aurelius saved his own soul by his righteousness, and he could do no more. Happy they, who can do this! but still happier, who can do more!

Yet, when one passes from his outward to his inward life, when one turns over the pages of his *Meditations*,—entries jotted down from day to day, amid the business of the city or the fatigues of the camp, for his own guidance and support, meant for no eye but his own, without the slightest attempt at style, with no care, even, for correct writing, not to be surpassed for naturalness and sincerity,—all disposition to carp and cavil dies away, and one is overpowered by the charm of a character of such purity, delicacy, and virtue. He fails neither in small things nor in great; he keeps watch over himself both that the great springs of action may be right in him, and that the minute details of action may be right also; how admirable in a hard-tasked ruler, and a ruler, too, with a passion for thinking and reading, is such a memorandum as the following :—

"Not frequently nor without necessity to say to any one, or to write in a letter, that I have no leisure; nor continually to excuse the neglect of duties required by our relation to those with whom we live, by alleging urgent occupation."

And, when that ruler is a Roman emperor, what an "idea" is this to be written down and meditated by him :—

"The idea of a polity in which there is the same law for all, a polity administered with regard to equal rights and equal freedom of speech, and the idea of a kingly government which respects most of all the freedom of the governed."

And, for all men who "drive at practice," what prac-

tical rules may not one accumulate out of these *Meditations :—*

"The greatest part of what we say or do being unnecessary, if a man takes this away, he will have more
leisure and less uneasiness. Accordingly, on every
occasion a man should ask himself: 'Is this one of the
unnecessary things?' Now a man should take away not
only unnecessary acts, but also unnecessary thoughts,
for thus superfluous acts will not follow after."

And again :—

"We ought to check in the series of our thoughts
everything that is without a purpose and useless, but
most of all the over-curious feeling and the malignant ;
and a man should use himself to think of those things
only about which if one should suddenly ask, 'What
hast thou now in thy thoughts?' with perfect openness
thou mightest immediately answer, 'This or That ;' so
that from thy words it should be plain that everything in
thee is simple and benevolent, and such as befits a social
animal, and one that cares not for thoughts about sensual
enjoyments, or any rivalry or envy and suspicion, or
anything else for which thou wouldst blush if thou
shouldst say thou hadst it in thy mind."

So, with a stringent practicalness worthy of Franklin,
he discourses on his favourite text, *Let nothing be done
without a purpose.* But it is when he enters the region
where Franklin cannot follow him, when he utters his
thoughts on the ground-motives of human action, that
he is most interesting ;—that he becomes the unique, the
incomparable Marcus Aurelius. Christianity uses language very liable to be misunderstood when it seems

to tell men to do good, not, certainly, from the vulgar motives of worldly interest, or vanity, or love of human praise, but that "their Father which seeth in secret may reward them openly." The motives of reward and punishment have come, from the misconception of language of this kind, to be strangely over-pressed by many Christian moralists, to the deterioration and disfigurement of Christianity. Marcus Aurelius says, truly and nobly :—

"One man, when he has done a service to another, is ready to set it down to his account as a favour conferred. Another is not ready to do this, but still in his own mind he thinks of the man as his debtor, and he knows what he has done. A third in a manner does not even know what he has done, *but he is like a vine which has produced grapes, and seeks for nothing more after it has once produced its proper fruit.* As a horse when he has run, a dog when he has caught the game, a bee when it has made its honey, so a man when he has done a good act, does not call out for others to come and see, but he goes on to another act, as a vine goes on to produce again the grapes in season. Must a man, then, be one of these, who in a manner acts thus without observing it? Yes."

And again :—

"What more dost thou want when thou hast done a man a service? Art thou not content that thou hast done something conformable to thy nature, and dost thou seek to be paid for it, *just as if the eye demanded a recompense for seeing, or the feet for walking !*"

Christianity, in order to match morality of this strain,

has to correct its apparent offers of external reward, and to say : *The kingdom of God is within you.*

I have said that it is by its accent of emotion that the morality of Marcus Aurelius acquires a special character, and reminds one of Christian morality. The sentences of Seneca are stimulating to the intellect ; the sentences of Epictetus are fortifying to the character ; the sentences of Marcus Aurelius find their way to the soul. I have said that religious emotion has the power to *light up* morality ; the emotion of Marcus Aurelius does not quite light up his morality, but it suffuses it ; it has not power to melt the clouds of effort and austerity quite away, but it shines through them and glorifies them ; it is a spirit, not so much of gladness and elation, as of gentleness and sweetness ; a delicate and tender sentiment, which is less than joy and more than resignation. He says that in his youth he learned from Maximus, one of his teachers, "cheerfulness in all circumstances as well as in illness ; *and a just admixture in the moral character of sweetness and dignity*;" and it is this very admixture of sweetness with his dignity which makes him so beautiful a moralist. It enables him to carry even into his observation of nature a delicate penetration, a sympathetic tenderness, worthy of Wordsworth ; the spirit of such a remark as the following has hardly a parallel, so far as my knowledge goes, in the whole range of Greek and Roman literature :—

" Figs, when they are quite ripe, gape open ; and in the ripe olives the very circumstance of their being near to rottenness adds a peculiar beauty to the fruit. And the ears of corn bending down, and the lion's eyebrows, and the foam which flows from the mouth of wild boars, and many other things,—though they are far from being beautiful, in a certain sense,—still, because they come in the course of nature, have a beauty in them, and they please the mind ; so that if a man should have a feeling and a deeper insight with respect to the things which are produced in the universe, there is hardly anything which comes in the course of nature which will not seem to him to be in a manner disposed so as to give pleasure."

But it is when his strain passes to directly moral subjects that his delicacy and sweetness lend to it the greatest charm. Let those who can feel the beauty of spiritual refinement read this, the reflection of an emperor who prized mental superiority highly :—

"Thou sayest, 'Men cannot admire the sharpness of thy wits.' Be it so ; but there are many other things of which thou canst not say, 'I am not formed for them by nature.' Show those qualities, then, which are altogether in thy power,—sincerity, gravity, endurance of labour, aversion to pleasure, contentment with thy portion and with few things, benevolence, frankness, no love of superfluity, freedom from trifling, magnanimity. Dost thou not see how many qualities thou art at once able to exhibit, as to which there is no excuse of natural incapacity and unfitness, and yet thou still remainest voluntarily below the mark ? Or art thou compelled, through being defectively furnished by nature, to murmur, and to be mean, and to flatter, and to find fault with thy poor body, and to try to please men, and to make great display, and to be so restless in thy mind ? No, indeed ;

but thou mightest have been delivered from these things long ago. Only, if in truth thou canst be charged with being rather slow and dull of comprehension, thou must exert thyself about this also, not neglecting nor yet taking pleasure in thy dulness."

The same sweetness enables him to fix his mind, when he sees the isolation and moral death caused by sin, not on the cheerless thought of the misery of this condition, but on the inspiriting thought that man is blest with the power to escape from it :—

"Suppose that thou hast detached thyself from the natural unity,—for thou wast made by nature a part, but now thou hast cut thyself off,—yet here is this beautiful provision, that it is in thy power again to unite thyself. God has allowed this to no other part,—after it has been separated and cut asunder, to come together again. But consider the goodness with which he has privileged man ; for he has put it in his power, when he has been separated, to return and to be united and to resume his place."

It enables him to control even the passion for retreat and solitude, so strong in a soul like his, to which the world could offer no abiding city :—

"Men seek retreat for themselves, houses in the country, sea-shores, and mountains ; and thou, too, art wont to desire such things very much. But this is altogether a mark of the most common sort of men, for it is in thy power whenever thou shalt choose to retire into thyself. For nowhere either with more quiet or more freedom from trouble does a man retire than into his own soul, particularly when he has within him such thoughts that by looking into them he is immediately in perfect tranquillity. Constantly, then, give to thyself this retreat, and renew thyself; and let thy principles be brief and fundamental, which, as soon as thou shalt recur to them, will be sufficient to cleanse the soul completely, and to send thee back free from all discontent with the things to which thou returnest."

Against this feeling of discontent and weariness, so natural to the great for whom there seems nothing left to desire or to strive after, but so enfeebling to them, so deteriorating, Marcus Aurelius never ceased to struggle. With resolute thankfulness he kept in remembrance the blessings of his lot; the true blessings of it, not the false:—

"I have to thank Heaven that I was subjected to a ruler and a father (Antoninus Pius) who was able to take away all pride from me, and to bring me to the knowledge that it is possible for a man to live in a palace without either guards, or embroidered dresses, or any show of this kind; but that it is in such a man's power to bring himself very near to the fashion of a private person, without being for this reason either meaner in thought or more remiss in action with respect to the things which must be done for public interest. . . . I have to be thankful that my children have not been stupid nor deformed in body; that I did not make more proficiency in rhetoric, poetry, and the other studies, by which I should perhaps have been completely engrossed, if I had seen that I was making great progress in them; . . . that I knew Apollonius, Rusticus, Maximus; . . . that I received clear and frequent impressions about living according to nature, and what kind of a life that

is, so that, so far as depended on Heaven, and its gifts,
help, and inspiration, nothing hindered me from forthwith
living according to nature, though I still fall short of it
through my own fault, and through not observing the
admonitions of Heaven, and, I may almost say, its direct
instructions ; that my body has held out so long in such
a kind of life as mine ; that though it was my mother's
lot to die young, she spent the last years of her life with
me ; that whenever I wished to help any man in his need,
I was never told that I had not the means of doing it ;
that, when I had an inclination to philosophy, I did not
fall into the hands of a sophist."

And, as he dwelt with gratitude on these helps and
blessings vouchsafed to him, his mind (so, at least, it
seems to me) would sometimes revert with awe to the
perils and temptations of the lonely height where he
stood, to the lives of Tiberius, Caligula, Nero, Domitian,
in their hideous blackness and ruin ; and then he wrote
down for himself such a warning entry as this, significant
and terrible in its abruptness :—

" A black character, a womanish character, a stubborn
character, bestial, childish, animal, stupid, counterfeit,
scurrilous, fraudulent, tyrannical ! "

Or this :—

" About what am I now employing my soul ? On every
occasion I must ask myself this question, and enquire,
What have I now in this part of me which they call the
ruling principle, and whose soul have I now ?—that of a
child, or of a young man, or of a weak woman, or of a
tyrant, or of one of the lower animals in the service of
man, or of a wild beast ?"

The character he wished to attain he knew well, and beautifully he has marked it, and marked, too, his sense of shortcoming :—

"When thou hast assumed these names,—good, modest, true, rational, equal-minded, magnanimous,—take care that thou dost not change these names ; and, if thou shouldst lose them, quickly return to them. If thou maintainest thyself in possession of these names without desiring that others should call thee by them, thou wilt be another being, and wilt enter on another life. For to continue to be such as thou hast hitherto been, and to be torn in pieces and defiled in such a life, is the character of a very stupid man, and one overfond of his life, and like those half-devoured fighters with wild beasts, who though covered with wounds and gore still entreat to be kept to the following day, though they will be exposed in the same state to the same claws and bites. Therefore fix thyself in the possession of these few names : and if thou art able to abide in them, abide as if thou wast removed to the Happy Islands."

For all his sweetness and serenity, however, man's point of life " between two infinities " (of that expression Marcus Aurelius is the real owner) was to him anything but a Happy Island, and the performances on it he saw through no veils of illusion. Nothing is in general more gloomy and monotonous than declamations on the hollowness and transitoriness of human life and grandeur : but here, too, the great charm of Marcus Aurelius, his emotion, comes in to relieve the monotony and to break through the gloom ; and even on this eternally used topic, he is imaginative, fresh, and striking :—

" Consider, for example, the times of Vespasian. Thou wilt see all these things, people marrying, bringing up children, sick, dying, warring, feasting, trafficking, cultivating the ground, flattering, obstinately arrogant, suspecting, plotting, wishing for somebody to die, grumbling about the present, loving, heaping up treasure, desiring to be consuls or kings. Well then, that life of these people no longer exists at all. Again, go to the times of Trajan. All is again the same. Their life too is gone. But chiefly thou shouldst think of those whom thou hast thyself known distracting themselves about idle things, neglecting to do what was in accordance with their proper constitution, and to hold firmly to this and to be content with it."

Again :—

" The things which are much valued in life are empty, and rotten, and trifling ; and people are like little dogs biting one another, and little children quarrelling, crying, and then straightway laughing. But fidelity, and modesty, and justice, and truth, are fled

'Up to Olympus from the wide-spread earth.'

What then is there which still detains thee here ? "

And once more :—

" Look down from above on the countless herds of men, and their countless solemnities, and the infinitely varied voyagings in storms and calms, and the differences among those who are born, who live together, and die. And consider too the life lived by others in olden time, and the life now lived among barbarous nations, and how many know not even thy name, and how many will soon forget it, and how they who perhaps now are praising thee will very soon blame thee, and that neither a posthumous name is of any value, nor reputation, nor anything else."

He recognised, indeed, that (to use his own words) "the prime principle in man's constitution is the social," and he laboured sincerely to make not only his acts towards his fellow-men, but his thoughts also, suitable to this conviction :—

" When thou wishest to delight thyself, think of the virtues of those who live with thee ; for instance, the activity of one, and the modesty of another, and the liberality of a third, and some other good quality of a fourth."

Still, it is hard for a pure and thoughtful man to live in a state of rapture at the spectacle afforded to him by his fellow-creatures ; above all is it hard, when such a man is placed as Marcus Aurelius was placed, and has had the meanness and perversity of his fellow-creatures thrust, in no common measure, upon his notice,—has had, time after time, to experience how "within ten days thou wilt seem a god to those to whom thou art now a beast and an ape." His true strain of thought as to his relations with his fellow-men is rather the following. He has been enumerating the higher consolations which may support a man at the approach of death, and he goes on :—

" But if thou requirest also a vulgar kind of comfort which shall reach thy heart, thou wilt be made best reconciled to death by observing the objects from which thou art going to be removed, and the morals of those with whom thy soul will no longer be mingled. For it is no way right to be offended with men, but it is thy duty to care for them and to bear with them gently; and yet to remember that thy departure will not be from men who have the same principles as thyself. For this is the only thing, if there be any, which could draw us the contrary way and attach us to life, to be permitted to live with those who have the same principles as ourselves. But now thou seest how great is the distress caused by the difference of those who live together, so that thou mayest say : 'Come quick, O death, lest perchance I too should forget myself.' "

O faithless and perverse generation ! how long shall I be with you ? how long shall I suffer you ? Sometimes this strain rises even to passion :—

"Short is the little which remains to thee of life. Live as on a mountain. Let men see, let them know, a real man, who lives as he was meant to live. If they cannot endure him, let them kill him. For that is better than to live as men do."

It is remarkable how little of a merely local and temporary character, how little of those *scoriæ* which a reader has to clear away before he gets to the precious ore, how little that even admits of doubt or question, the morality of Marcus Aurelius exhibits. In general, the action he prescribes is action which every sound nature must recognise as right, and the motives he assigns are motives which every clear reason must recognise as valid.*

* Perhaps there is one exception. He is fond of urging as a motive for man's cheerful acquiescence in whatever befalls him, that " whatever happens to every man *is for the interest of the universal ;*

And so he remains the especial friend and comforter of all scrupulous and difficult, yet pure and upward-striving souls, in those ages most especially that walk by sight not by faith, that have no open vision; he cannot give such souls, perhaps, all they yearn for, but he gives them much; and what he gives them, they can receive.

that the whole contains nothing *which is not for its advantage;* that everything which happens to a man is to be accepted, "even if it seems disagreeable, *because it leads to the health of the universe.*" And the whole course of the universe, he adds, has a providential reference to man's welfare: "all other things have been made for the sake of rational beings." Religion has in all ages freely used this language, and it is not religion which will object to Marcus Aurelius's use of it; but science can hardly accept as severely accurate this employment of the terms *interest* and *advantage;* even to a sound nature and a clear reason the proposition that things happen "for the interest of the universal," as men conceive of interest, may seem to have no meaning at all, and the proposition that "all things have been made for the sake of rational beings" may seem to be false. Yet even to this language, not irresistibly cogent when it is thus absolutely used, Marcus Aurelius gives a turn which makes it true and useful, when he says: "The ruling part of man can make a material for itself out of that which opposes it, as fire lays hold of what falls into it, and rises higher by means of this very material; "— when he says: "What else are all things except exercises for the reason? Persevere then until thou shalt have made all things thine own, as the stomach which is strengthened makes all things its own, as the blazing fire makes flame and brightness out of everything that is thrown into it; "—when he says: "Thou wilt not cease to be miserable till thy mind is in such a condition, that, what luxury is to those who enjoy pleasure, such shall be to thee, in every matter which presents itself, the doing of the things which are conformable to man's constitution; for a man ought to consider as an enjoyment everything which it is in his power to do according to his own nature,—and it is in his power everywhere." In this sense it is most true that "all things have been made for the sake of rational beings;" that "all things work together for good."

Yet no, it is not on this account that such souls love
him most; it is rather because of the emotion which
gives to his voice so touching an accent, it is because he,
too, yearns as they do for something unattained by him.
What an affinity for Christianity had this persecutor of
the Christians! the effusion of Christianity, its relieving
tears, its happy self-sacrifice, were the very element, one
feels, for which his soul longed : they were near him, he
touched them, he passed them by.   One feels, too, that
the Marcus Aurelius one knows must still have remained,
even had they presented themselves to him, in a great
measure himself; he would have been no Justin : but
how would they have affected him? in what measure
would they have changed him?   Granted that he might
have found, like the Alogi in ancient and modern times,
in the most beautiful of the Gospels, the Gospel which
has leavened Christendom most powerfully, the Gospel
of St. John, too much Greek metaphysics, too much
gnosis; granted that this Gospel might have looked too
like what he knew already to be a total surprise to him :
what, then, would he have said to the Sermon on the
Mount, to the twenty-sixth chapter of St. Matthew? what
would have become of his notions of the *exitiabilis superstitio,* of the "obstinacy of the Christians!"   Vain
question ! yet the greatest charm of Marcus Aurelius is
that he makes us ask it.   We see him wise, just, self-
governed, tender, thankful, blameless; yet, with all this,
agitated, stretching out his arms for something beyond;—
tendentemque manus ripæ ulterioris amore.